PRAISE FOR HÅKAN NESSER

THE INSPECTOR AND SILENCE

'The atmosphere of the small town, the mysterious
fringes of the forest full of aspens and blueberries, are
evocatively drawn . . . The clarity of Nesser's vision, the
inner problems of good and evil with which Van Veeteren
struggles, recall the films of Bergman'
Independent

'Satisfying novel from a rising Swedish star . . .
Van Veeteren [the detective], disengaged, thinking
of retirement and wonderfully enigmatic, makes an
enjoyable change from all those fictional policemen who
persist in taking their work home with disastrous
consequences . . . an intense read'
Guardian Review

'Nesser works the slow pace skilfully and Van Veeteren
is an appealing companion'
Metro **Crime Books of the Year**

WOMAN WITH A BIRTHMARK

'Håkan Nesser is in the front rank of Swedish crime
writers . . . A novel with superior plot and characters'
The Times

'It's set to become Nesser's breakthrough novel in this
country, and he is being favourably compared with
Henning Mankell and Stieg Larsson'
Sunday Times

'Nesser is one of the best of the Swedish
crime writers . . . a literate writing style, a brooding
atmosphere and a plot that never wallows in the purely
salacious . . . what might have been a routine serial-killer
novel becomes a tense and subtle morality tale'
Mail on Sunday

THE MIND'S EYE

'Van Veeteren is a terrific character, and the courtroom
scenes that begin this novel are cracking'
Daily Telegraph

'Håkan Nesser's Chief Inspector Van Veeteren has
earned his place among the great Swedish detectives
with a series of intriguing investigations . . . This is
Van Veeteren at his quirkiest and most engaging'
Seven magazine, *Sunday Telegraph*

'A psychological thriller in a class of its own . . .
This stunning novel by one of Sweden's foremost
crime writers might have been written as a
script for Alfred Hitchcock'
Sunday Times

THE RETURN

'Nesser made a strong impression with *Borkmann's Point*,
the first of his novels published into English.
The Return is just as tense and clever'
Marcel Berlins, *The Times*

'Nesser's insight into his main characters and gently
humorous narrative raise his otherwise conventional
police procedural to a higher level'
Sunday Telegraph

'This is splendid stuff: Scandinavian crime writing that
is so rivetingly written it makes most contemporary
crime fare – Nordic or otherwise – seem
rather thin gruel'
Barry Forshaw, *Waterstone's Books Quarterly*

BORKMANN'S POINT

'An absorbing tale with an unexpected ending'
Sunday Telegraph

'The novel's prime asset is the mordant clarity of
Nesser's voice. Its understatement is a pleasure in itself,
as investigations pause for Van Veeteren to
finish his beer'
Times Literary Supplement

'Van Veeteren is destined for a place amongst
the great European detectives'
Colin Dexter

WOMAN WITH A BIRTHMARK

Håkan Nesser is one of Sweden's most popular crime writers, receiving numerous awards for his novels featuring Inspector Van Veeteren, including the European Crime Fiction Star Award (Ripper Award) 2010/11, the Swedish Crime Writers' Academy Prize (three times) and Scandinavia's Glass Key Award. The Van Veeteren series is published in over 25 countries and has sold over 5 million copies worldwide. Håkan Nesser lives in Uppsala with his wife and two sons, and spends part of each year in the UK.

Also by Håkan Nesser

HÅKAN NESSER

WOMAN WITH A BIRTHMARK

AN INSPECTOR VAN VEETEREN MYSTERY

Translated from the Swedish by
Laurie Thompson

PAN BOOKS

First published in Sweden 1996 as *Kvinna med födelsemärke*
by Albert Bonniers Forlag, Stockholm

First published in English 2009 by Pantheon books,
a division of Random House, Inc., New York

First published in Great Britain 2009 by Macmillan

This paperback edition published 2011 by Pan Books
an imprint of Pan Macmillan, a division of Macmillan Publishers Limited
Pan Macmillan, 20 New Wharf Road, London N1 9RR
Basingstoke and Oxford
Associated companies throughout the world
www.panmacmillan.com

ISBN 978-0-330-49279-9

7 9 8 6

A CIP catalogue record for this book is available from
the British Library.

Typeset by Intype Libra Ltd
Printed in the UK by CPI Group (UK), Croydon, CR0 4YY

Visit www.panmacmillan.com to read more about all our books
and to buy them. You will also find features, author interviews and
news of any author events, and you can sign up for e-newsletters
so that you're always first to hear about our new releases.

To Sanna and Johannes

And then, of course, there is a certain type of action
that we can never leave behind us,
nor buy ourselves free from.
Perhaps we can't even beg forgiveness for such deeds.

W. Klimke, therapist

ONE

23 DECEMBER TO 14 JANUARY

1

She felt cold.

The day had started with a promising light snowfall, but as lunchtime approached, the strong wind blowing off the sea had transformed the precipitation into diagonal, driving rain of the very worst kind. It chilled you to the bone, forced the stall owners down by the harbour to shut up shop hours earlier than usual, and in Zimmermann's bar they were serving about three times as many hot toddies as on a normal December day.

To make matters worse, the cemetery was facing southwest. On a gently sloping, treeless hillside, totally exposed to every kind of weather and wind, and when the little group finally reached the newly dug, muddy grave, one of those thoughts struck her.

At least it was sheltered from the wind down there. There was no need to take the wind and this damned rain with you into the grave. Every cloud has its silver lining.

The clergyman snuffled, and his accomplice – or

whatever you should call him – struggled with the umbrella. Tried to make it cover both the man in black and himself, but the gusts were capricious and the correct angle shifted from second to second. The bearers dug their heels into the soaking wet soil and started to lower the coffin. Her bouquet on the lid already looked a mess. Like a dollop of vegetables that had boiled for too long. One of the bearers slipped but managed to regain his balance. The clergyman blew his nose and started to read the liturgy. His accomplice fumbled with the spade. The rain grew even worse.

It was typical. She couldn't help acknowledging that as she clenched her fists in her overcoat pockets and stamped on the ground in an attempt to warm up her feet.

Absolutely bloody typical. A ceremony just as shambolic and undignified as the rest of the dead woman's life had been. So she couldn't even be granted a decent burial. The day before Christmas Eve. A patch of blue sky, or the light snowfall lasting into the afternoon – would that have been too much to ask? Would that have been too much trouble?

Of course it would. Her mother's life had been littered with defeats and messy failures; to be honest, all this was both fitting and expected, and she felt herself having to bite her lip so as not to burst out crying.

A totally consistent and logical conclusion, then. In the

same key all the way through. And no crying. Not yet, in any case.

For some confounded, inscrutable reason her mother had urged just that. Don't cry! Whatever you do, don't stand there blubbing at my funeral. Tears have never been any use in any circumstances, believe you me. I've sobbed bucketfuls in my lifetime. No, do something, my girl! Take action! Do something magnificent that I can applaud up there in my heaven!

She had squeezed her daughter's hand with both her own chafed and weak hands as she said that. Fixed her with her dying eyes, and it had become clear that for once this was serious. For once, her mother had begged her to do something; it was a bit late and the wording was hardly crystal clear, but there could be no doubt about what she meant. Or could there?

Half an hour later she was dead.

Do something, my girl. Take action!

The clergyman fell silent. Looked at her from under the dripping umbrella, and she realized that he was expecting her to do something as well. What? It wasn't easy to tell. It was only the second time in her life that she had attended a funeral; the first time, she had been eight or nine years old, and she was there for her mother's sake on that occasion as well. She took several cautious steps forward. Stopped a safe distance short of the grave to avoid the farce of slipping and joining her mother down below. Bowed her head and closed her eyes. Clasped her hands in front of her.

I expect the bastards think I'm standing here praying, she thought. Or at least, they're pretending to. Goodbye, Mum! You can rely on me. I know what I have to do. You'll be able to warm the palms of your hands up there with the angels.

And so it was all over. The clergyman and his accomplice each held out a cold, damp hand to shake hers, and ten minutes later she was standing under the leaking roof of a bus shelter, longing for a hot bath and a glass of red wine.

Or a brandy. Or both.

One mourner, she thought. At my mother's interment there was only a single mourner. Me. So that was that.

But I sincerely hope that several more will be mourning soon.

That was quite nicely put, and as she stood there fighting against the cold and the damp and her desire to cry, it was as if those words had lit a small flame inside her. Set fire to something combustible at last, something that slowly began to heat up all the old frozen and stiff lumber lying around in her soul.

A conflagration, no less, that soon enough would begin to spread and cause others to burn and perish in its flames . . . cause many others to fear this sea of anger that in due course would surround and destroy them all!

She smiled at that thought as well. Something she had read, presumably; or perhaps it really was true what one of her very first lovers had maintained. That she had a gift. A sort of aptitude for poetry and putting things into words.

For the truth, and passion. Or suffering, perhaps. Yes, that seemed to be more correct, without doubt. She had suffered all right. Not as much as her mother, of course, but she had endured her due share of suffering. And more.

I'm freezing cold, she thought. Come on, you fucking bus!

But there was no sign of the bus. No sign of anything, and it dawned on her as she stood stamping her feet in the gathering dusk in the leaky shelter that this was exactly what her whole life had been like. This was the ideal image for what it was all about, at bottom.

Standing waiting for something that never came. A bus. A good man. A proper job.

A chance. Just one bloody chance to make something sensible of her life.

Standing waiting in the darkness and wind and rain. And now it was too late.

She was twenty-nine years of age, and it was too late already.

My mother and I, she thought. One mourning at the

side of the grave. The other lying in it. We might just as well have changed places. Or lain down beside each other. Nobody would have had any objections. If it weren't for . . .

And she felt the flame set fire to her resolve once more, and everything inside her welled up and filled her with warmth. A strong, almost tangible warmth, which caused her to smile in the midst of her grief, and to clench her fists even harder deep down in her overcoat pockets.

She took one final look at the long bend but there was no trace of a headlight. So she turned her back on it all and started walking towards the town.

2

Christmas came and went.

New Year came and went. Rain shower followed rain shower, and the blue-grey days passed in a state of monotonous indifference. Her doctor's certificate ran out, and she had to sign on for unemployment benefit. There was no noticeable difference. Off work from what? Unemployed from what?

Her telephone had been cut off. When she received the warning in the autumn, she had purposely failed to pay the bill, and now the company had taken action. The wheels had turned.

It was pleasant. Not only did she not have to meet people, she avoided having to listen to them as well. Not that there would have been all that many for her to put up with. There was no denying that her circle of acquaintances had shrunk recently. During the first fourteen days after the funeral she spoke to a grand total of two people. Heinzi and Gergils; she had met both of them by accident in the square, and within thirty seconds they had both tried to cadge something off her. Heroin or a bit of hash, or a bottle of wine, at least – for fuck's sake, surely she had something to give to an old mate? A shower, then, and a quick screw, perhaps?

Only Gergils had gone so far as to suggest that, and for a few seconds she had toyed with the idea of letting him have her for half an hour. Just for the pleasure of possibly infecting him as well.

But of course it couldn't be guaranteed that he would get it. On the contrary. The chances were small. It wasn't easy to catch it, despite all the stories you heard, even the doctors had stressed that; but on this occasion she had managed to hold herself in check. Besides, there were quite a few people who had survived whose behaviour entailed a much higher risk factor than hers.

Risk factor? What a stupid expression. Hadn't she spent the whole of her life taking one bloody risk after another? But it was no doubt true what Lennie used to tell her many years ago: if you were born on the edge of a barrel of shit, you had to accept the likelihood of falling into it now and again. That was only to be expected. The trick was clambering out again.

And of course eventually you didn't. Didn't clamber out. You just lay down in the shit, and then, naturally, it was only a matter of time.

But that was old hat now. Thought about and fretted about and left behind. November had changed a lot of things. And her mother's death, of course.

Or rather, her mother's story. The words that came tumbling out of her like a thirty-year-old miscarriage not long before her time was up. Yes, if the news she had been given in November was what made her want to be alone, her mother's story did the rest. Gave her strength and determination. Something had suddenly become easier. Clearer and more definite for the first time in her troubled life. Her willpower and drive had grown, and her drug addiction had ebbed away and died without her needing to exert herself in the least. No more of the heavy stuff. A bit of hash and a bottle of wine now and again, no more, but most important of all – no more of that accursed and desperate contact with all the rest of them perched on the edge of the shit barrel. It had been easier to shake them off than she could ever have suspected, just as easy as the drugs, in fact, and of course each of those developments had assisted the other. Maybe what all the quacks and counsellors had been droning on about all those years was actually true: it was all down to your own inner strength. That alone, nothing else.

Courage and resolve, in other words.

And the mission, she added.

*

The mission? She certainly hadn't been clear about that from the start, it sneaked its way in later on. Difficult to pin it down precisely, and just as difficult to say where it came from. Was it her mother's decision or her own? Not that it mattered all that much, but it could be interesting to think about.

About cause and responsibility and things like that. About revenge, and the importance of putting things right. The fact that her mother had ten thousand guilders hidden away came as a surprise and also a helping hand, of course. It was a nice round figure, and no doubt would come in very useful.

Had done already, in fact. On 12 January she had spent two thousand of it; but it wasn't wasted money. In a drawer of her bedside table she had a list of names and addresses and a fair amount of other information. She had a gun, and she had a furnished room waiting for her in Maardam. What more could she ask for?

Even more courage? Resolve? A pinch of good luck?

The night before she set off she prayed to a very much unspecified god, asking him to stand by her and grant her those precise things; and when she turned off the bedside light she had a strong feeling that there wasn't very much in this world capable of placing obstacles in her way.

Nothing at all, most probably. That night she slept in a

foetal position, warm and with a smile on her face, and in the knowledge that she had never felt less vulnerable in all her life.

3

Finding a room was one of the things that hadn't needed much effort. She had simply answered an advert in *Neuwe Blatt* – but when she saw the result, she realized that she could hardly have done better.

Mrs Klausner had been widowed early – at the dawn of the 1980s when she was in her middle-aged prime – but instead of selling the much loved and charming old two-storey house in the Deijkstraa district, she had it adapted and refurbished to suit her new circumstances after the major's sudden and unexpected heart attack. She retained possession of the ground floor together with the garden, two cats and four thousand books. The upper floor, comprising the old children's rooms and guest bedrooms, had been transformed into bedsits: four rooms in all, each with running water and limited cooking facilities. Plus shared bathroom and shower room in the hall. The staircase was supplied with its own entrance in a gable wall, at a safe distance from Mrs Klausner's bedroom; and even if she had the occasional butterfly in her stomach when she launched her new enterprise, she soon found she could congratulate herself on an excellent set-up. She let rooms only to single women, and never for more than six months at a time. Most of them were students in the latter stages of their courses in the Faculties of Law and Medicine who needed peace and quiet for their studies. Or nurses on short supplementary courses at the nearby Gemejnte hospital. Two or more of the rooms were often vacant during the summer, but she earned enough during the rest of the year to satisfy her needs. Major Klausner would have had nothing against the reorganization, she knew that; and sometimes when she was queueing at the bank to pay in the rents she had received, she thought she could see him nodding approvingly up there, on the final battlefield.

As agreed, the new tenant moved in on Sunday, 14 January, the evening before she was due to begin a three-month course for finance managers at the Elizabeth Institute. She paid for six weeks in advance, and after receiving the necessary instructions (explained in a most friendly manner and lasting less than a minute), she took possession of the red room. Mrs Klausner knew the importance of respecting her tenants' privacy: as long as she was not disturbed in her reading or during the night, and they didn't fly at each other's throats, she found no reason to interfere in whatever they got up to. Everything was based on unspoken mutual respect, and so far – after thirteen years in the business – she had never experienced any serious disappointments or setbacks.

People are good, she used to tell herself. Others treat us as we treat them.

There was a mirror hanging over the little sink in the kitchen alcove, and when she had finished unpacking her bags she stood in front of it for a couple of minutes and contemplated her new face.

She had not changed much, but the effect was astounding. With her hair cut short and dyed brown, with no make-up and wearing round, metal-framed spectacles, she suddenly looked like a librarian or a bored handicrafts teacher. Nobody would have recognized her, and just for a moment – as she stood there pulling faces and trying out angles – she had the distinct feeling that she was somebody else.

New features and a new name. A new town and a mission that only six months ago would have seemed to her like the ravings of a lunatic, or a bad joke.

But here she was. She tried one more time – the last one? – to see if she could find any trace of doubt or uncertainty, but no matter how deep the soundings she made into her soul, all she came up against was solid rock. Solid and unyielding ground, and it was clear to her that it was time for her to begin.

Begin in earnest. Her list was complete in every respect, and even though three months can be quite a long period, there was no reason to mark time in the early stages. On the contrary: every name required its own meticulous planning, its own specific treatment, and it was better to make full use of the early days and avoid being under stress towards the end. Once she had started on her mission, and people had caught on to what was happening, she would naturally need to be on the alert for problems. Everybody would be on the lookout – the general public, the police, her opponents.

That was the way it had to be. It was all dictated by the circumstances.

But she was already convinced that she would not have any worries. No insurmountable ones, at least, and as she lay on her bed that first night and examined her gun, she could feel that the scale of the challenge would doubtless make the allure that little bit stronger.

That little bit more exciting and more enjoyable.

I'm crazy, she thought. Completely and utterly mad.

But it was a daring and irresistible madness. And who could blame her, after all?

She looked at the list of names again. Studied them one

by one. She had already decided who would be first, but, even so, pretended to reconsider it one more time.

Then she breathed a sigh of satisfaction and drew two thick red lines round his name. Lit a cigarette and started to think through how she would go about it.

TWO

18–19 JANUARY

TWO

16–19 JANUARY

4

It was hardly a part of Ryszard Malik's normal routine to drink two large whiskies before dinner, but he had good cause to do so today.

Two reasons, in fact. The contract he was negotiating with Winklers had finally collapsed, despite two hours of intensive telephone discussions during the afternoon; and when he finally left the office he discovered that a sudden cold snap had transformed the streets, soaking wet after all the rain, into an ice rink. If it had been exclusively up to him, of course, that wouldn't have been a problem – not for nothing did he have thirty years of blameless driving behind him, and he had often driven on slippery roads – but he wasn't the only one on the road. The rush-hour traffic from the centre of town to the residential districts and garden suburbs was still very much in evidence, and it happened just before the roundabout in Hagmaar Allé. A white, Swiss-registered Mercedes travelling far too fast slid into the back of his Renault. He swore under his breath, unfastened his seat belt and got out of the car to establish the damage done and argue about what to do next. Right rear light smashed, rather a large dent in the wing and two deep scratches in the paintwork. Various unlikely excuses, some forced politeness, an exchange of business cards and insurance company details – it all took a considerable time, and it was over forty minutes later when he was able to continue his journey home.

Malik didn't like coming home late. True enough, his wife rarely had the evening meal ready before seven; but an hour, preferably an hour and a half, with the newspaper and a whisky and water in his study was something he was reluctant to miss.

Over the years it had become a habit, and a necessary one at that. A sort of buffer between work and a wife growing increasingly conscious of her importance.

Today there was only time for a quarter of an hour. And it was to go some way towards compensating for the loss – of both the precious minutes and his rear light – that he skipped the newspaper and instead devoted all his attention to the whisky.

Well, not quite all. There was that telephone call as well. What the devil was it all about? 'The Rise and Fall of Flingel Bunt'. What the hell was the point of phoning somebody and then playing an old sixties hit? Over and over again.

Or once a day at any rate. Ilse had answered twice, and

he had taken one of the calls. It had started the day before yesterday. He hadn't mentioned to her that whoever it was had called again yesterday evening . . . No need to worry her unnecessarily. No need to tell her that he recognized the tune either.

Quite early in the sixties, if he remembered rightly. The Shadows. 'Sixty-four or 'sixty-five, presumably. Irrelevant anyway: the question was what the hell it signified, if it signified anything at all. And who was behind it. Perhaps it was just a loony. Some out-of-work screwball who had nothing better to do than to phone decent citizens and stir up a bit of trouble.

It was probably no more than that. Obviously, one could consider bringing in the police if it continued, but so far at least it was no more than a minor irritation. Which was bad enough on a day like today.

A pain in the arse, as Wolff would have put it. A scratch in the paintwork or a shattered rear light.

There came the call. The food was on the table, it seemed. He sighed. Downed the rest of the whisky and left his study.

'It's nothing to get worked up about.'

'I'm not getting worked up.'

'Glad to hear it.'

'You always think I'm getting worked up. That's typical of the way you regard women.'

'All right. Let's talk about something else. This sauce is not bad at all. What have you put in it?'

'A drop of Madeira. You've had it fifty times before. I listened for longer today.'

'Really?'

'A minute, at least. There was nothing else.'

'What else did you expect there to be?'

'What else did I expect there to be? A voice, of course. Most people who make a phone call have something to say.'

'I expect there's a natural explanation.'

'Oh yes? What, for example? Why ring somebody and just play a piece of music?'

Malik took a large sip of wine and thought that one over.

'Well,' he said, 'a new radio station, or something of the sort.'

'That's the silliest thing I've ever heard.'

He sighed.

'Are you sure it was the same song both times?'

She hesitated. Stroked her brow with her index finger, the way she did when a migraine attack was in the offing.

'I think so. The first time, I put the phone down after only a few seconds. Like I said.'

'Don't worry about it. It's bound to be just a mistake.'

'A mistake? How could that be a mistake?'

Hold your tongue, he thought. Stop nagging, or I'll throw this glass of wine in your face!

'I don't know,' he said. 'Let's drop the subject. I had a little accident today.'

'An accident?'

'Nothing serious. Somebody skidded into me from behind.'

'Good Lord! Why didn't you say something?'

'It was a minor thing. Nothing to speak of.'

'Nothing to speak of? You always say that. What shall we speak about then? You tell me. We receive some mysterious telephone calls, but we should just ignore them. You have a car accident, and you don't think it's even worth mentioning to your wife. That's so typical. What you mean, of course, is that we should just sit here every evening without saying a word. That's the way you want it. Quiet and peaceful. I'm not even worth talking to any more.'

'Rubbish. Don't be silly.'

'Maybe there's a connection.'

'Connection? What the hell do you mean?'

'The telephone calls and the car crash, of course. I hope you took his number?'

Oh my God, Malik thought, and gulped down the rest

of the wine. There's something the matter with her. Pure paranoia. No wonder the hotel wanted to sack her.

'Have you heard anything from Jacob?' He tried to change the subject, but realized his error the moment the words left his mouth.

'Not for two weeks. He's too much like you, it would never occur to him to phone us. Unless he needed some money, of course.'

The hell he would, Malik thought, and hoped that his grim inner smile wouldn't shine through to the outside. He had spoken to their son a couple of times in the last few days, without having to shell out a single guilder. And although he would never admit it, he regarded his son's passive distancing himself from his mother as a healthy development, and a perfectly natural one.

'Ah well,' he said, wiping his lips with a napkin, 'that's the way young people are nowadays. Is there anything worth watching on the box tonight?'

When the fourth call came, he was lucky enough to be able to answer it himself. Ilse was still watching the Hungarian feature film on Channel 4, and when he answered it on the bedroom extension he was able to tell the anonymous disturber of the peace to go to hell in no uncertain terms, without a risk of her hearing him and guessing what it was about. First he established that it really was 'The Rise and Fall of Flingel Bunt'; then he listened to it for half a minute before delivering a series of threats that could hardly be misunderstood and replacing the receiver.

However, he had no way of knowing if there really was somebody listening at the other end.

Maybe there was somebody there. Maybe there wasn't.

But that tune, he thought. Was there something? . . . But it was just a faint shadow of a suspicion, and no clear memories at all cropped up in his somewhat over-excited brain.

'Who was that?' asked his wife as he settled down again on the sofa in the television room.

'Jacob,' he lied. 'He sends you his greetings, and didn't want to borrow a single nickel.'

5

On Friday he made a detour past Willie's garage to discuss repairs to his car. Having been guaranteed absolutely that it would be ready for collection by that evening, he left it there and went the rest of the way to his office on foot. He arrived fifteen minutes late, and Wolff had already gone out – to negotiate a contract with a newly opened hamburger restaurant, he gathered. He sat down at his desk and began to work his way through the day's post, which had just been brought in by Miss deWiijs. As usual, most of it was complaints about one thing or another, and confirmation of contracts and agreements that had already been fixed on the telephone or by fax, and after ten minutes he realized that he was sitting there humming that confounded tune.

He broke off in annoyance. Went out to fetch some coffee from Miss deWiijs's office instead, and became involved in a conversation about the weather, which soon came round to focus on four-footed friends. Cats in general, and Miss deWiijs's Siamese, Melisande de laCroix, in particular. Despite the regular ingestion of contraceptive pills and despite the fact that the frail creature hardly ever dared to stick her nose outside the door, for the last couple of weeks she had been displaying more and more obvious signs of being pregnant.

There was only one other cat in the whole of the block where Miss deWiijs lived – a thin, arthritic old moggy that as far as she knew was being taken care of by a family of Kurdish immigrants, although he preferred to spend the waking hours of day and night outdoors. At least when the weather was decent. How he had managed to get wind of the shy little Madame Melisande de laCroix was a mystery, to say the least.

A mystery and an absurdity. To be sure, Miss deWiijs had not yet been to the vet's and had the pregnancy confirmed. But all the signs pointed very clearly in that direction. As already indicated, and unfortunately.

Malik liked cats. Once upon a time they had owned two, but Ilse hadn't really been able to put up with them, especially the female, and when they discovered that Jacob was apparently allergic to furry animals they had disposed of them by means of two rational and guaranteed painless injections.

He liked Miss deWiijs as well. She radiated a sort of languid, feminine warmth that he had learnt to prize highly over the years. The only thing that never ceased to surprise him was that men had left her unmarried and untouched. Or rather, there was nothing to suggest that this was not the case; and the indications were that she would stay that way. She would be celebrating her fortieth birthday next May, and Malik and Wolff had already begun discussing how best that occasion should be marked. Needless to say, it was not a day that could be allowed to pass unnoticed. Miss deWiijs had been working for them for over ten years, and both Malik and Wolff knew that she was probably more vital to the survival of the firm than they were.

'What are you thinking of doing if you're right about the state of your cat?' he asked.

Miss deWiijs shrugged, setting her heavy breasts a-bobbing under her sweater.

'Doing?' she said. 'There's not much else one can do but let nature take its course. And hope there won't be too many of them. Besides, Siamese cats are easy to find homes for, even if they are only half-breeds.'

Malik nodded and finished off his cup of coffee. Clasped his hands behind his neck and thought about what else needed to be done today.

'I'll drive out to Schaaltze,' he decided. 'Tell Wolff I'll be back after lunch.'

★

It was only when he was in the lift on his way down that he remembered he didn't have a car. He recited an elaborate curse under his breath, wondering how he could be so absent-minded, and considered briefly going back up. Then he recalled that it was actually possible to get there by bus as well. It was unusual for him to travel by public transport nowadays, but he knew that Nielsen and Vermeer sometimes used to travel in on the number 23 from Schaaltze, and if the bus goes one way, surely it must go the other way as well?

The bus stop was on the other side of the shopping centre and post office, and he was about halfway there when he had the feeling that somebody was following him.

Or observing him, at the very least. He stopped dead and looked round. The pavement wasn't exactly teeming with pedestrians but, nevertheless, there were enough of them to prevent him from detecting or picking out anybody behaving oddly. He thought for a second or two, then continued towards the bus stop. Perhaps he was just imagining things, and in any case it would be sensible not to make it too obvious that he smelt a rat. He quickly convinced himself of this, lengthening his stride and trying to keep all his senses on the alert.

He was amazed by his reaction, and how quickly and

almost naturally he'd accepted the feeling and the suspicion. As if it were an everyday occurrence, almost.

Why on earth should anybody be following him? Ryszard Malik! Who the hell could be interested in such an everyday and insignificant person?

He shook his head and thrust his hands into his overcoat pockets.

What kind of stupid imagining was this? Ilse must have infected him with her silly nonsense, that must be it!

And yet . . . He knew it was true. Or sensed it, rather. There was somebody behind him. Not far away. Somebody dogging his steps. Perhaps it was somebody who'd walked past him, he thought, and then turned round and started following him, some ten metres or so behind. You would be bound to notice such a manoeuvre in some vague, intuitive way . . . Or had there been somebody standing in the reception area when he went out into the street? Somebody who'd been waiting for him? Good God, that would be worrying.

He came to the bus stop and paused. The bus had evidently just left, as there was nobody waiting. He backed into the little shelter and began surreptitiously watching passing pedestrians. Some were walking fast and purposefully, others more slowly. Occasionally somebody would stop. Step into the shelter beside him to wait for the bus, shielded to some extent from the wind. Stood there with that half-friendly, half-distant air that strangers on the same mission usually adopt. A young man with a black-and-yellow striped scarf that was almost brushing the ground. Two old women in threadbare coats, carrying shopping bags. A slightly younger woman in a blue beret, with a slim leather briefcase. A boy in his early teens with some kind of facial tic, scratching his groin continually without taking his hands out of his pockets.

Not especially likely candidates, he had to admit, none of them. When the bus came, everybody got on apart from the two old women. He let the others go first, paid somewhat awkwardly and managed to find an empty seat right at the back.

So that he wouldn't have anybody behind him, he told himself.

During the journey, which took barely twenty minutes – more or less the same as by car, he noted with a degree of surprise – his mind indulged in an unequal struggle with refractory and importunate questions.

What the hell am I doing? asked his thoughts, soberly. This is utter lunacy! Madness!

But there is something, insisted his emotions. Don't try to convince yourself otherwise.

I'm going barmy, maintained his thoughts. My life is so damned monotonous that I'll clutch at anything that might introduce a bit of excitement.

You are in danger, countered his emotions. You know you are, but you daren't admit it.

He looked out of the filthy window. The Richter Stadium with its pompous clock tower was just passing by.

Why do my thoughts say 'I' and my emotions 'you'? he asked himself, confused. No doubt it has something to do with my macho syndrome, or so Ilse would . . .

Then he suddenly realized that he was sitting there humming that tune again under his breath.

'The Rise and Fall of Flingel Bunt'. There was something about it. About that as well. Something quite specific. A memory of something he'd taken part in and was now drifting under the dark surface of the well of forgetfulness, without his being able to pin it down.

Not until he had got off the bus and was on his way over the street to the factory. Then it struck him, and as it did so he realized that he would do well not to dismiss suspicions and threats out of hand in the near future.

That was as far as Ryszard Malik's imagination and powers of insight stretched; but, as his son would say afterwards, the less he knew and suspected, the better, no doubt.

And what happened to Melisande de laCroix's presumed pregnancy and Miss deWijs's fortieth birthday were questions that, as far as Ryszard Malik was concerned, also disappeared rapidly into the dark void of the future.

6

Although it was a year and a half since Ilse Malik had resigned from her job at Konger's Palace, she still hadn't managed to develop much of a social life. She played tennis with an old girlfriend once a week – on Tuesday afternoons. She went to visit her sister in Linzhuisen – when her husband was away on business, which happened at least once a month. She was a member of the Save Our Rainforests association, and every spring and autumn she used to sign up for some evening study circle or other, but left after the first meeting.

That was all – apart from the season ticket for the theatre that all the hotel employees were given, of course, and which she still made use of even though she was no longer entitled to it, strictly speaking.

But nobody wanted to be strict, and this particular Friday (they always went on the Friday after the premiere) she was due to see *A Doll's House*. She had no idea how many times she'd seen it already, but it was one of her absolute favourites, and it would have taken a lot to prevent her from going.

Perhaps there might be a glass of wine and a bite of cheese afterwards, and a chat with Bernadette, the only one of her former colleagues with whom she had had and still had any kind of close contact.

As it turned out, she had more than just one glass of wine. The part of Nora had been played excellently by a young and very promising actress on loan from the Burgteater in Aarlach, and a new managing director had taken over at the hotel less than a month before. There was a lot to talk about. When Ilse Malik clambered aboard a taxi outside Kraus a few minutes after half past eleven (Bernadette lived close by, and preferred a short walk and a breath of night air), she felt unusually contented with the evening and with her existence in general, and promptly started a conversation with the taxi driver about films and plays. Unfortunately it ebbed out after a minute or so, when it transpired that he hadn't set foot inside a theatre since having been forced to attend a play by an over-zealous drama teacher at college over thirty-five years ago. Of all the films he had lapped up in recent years, he hadn't come across a single one that could measure up to *Creature from the Black Lagoon*.

In any case, shortly after twenty to twelve he pulled up

outside the Maliks' house in Leufwens Allé – the temperature had risen by some five degrees, thank goodness, and the roads were good. Ilse paid, and added a generous tip rounding it up to fifteen guilders despite the somewhat distressing lack of culture, and got out of the car.

The house was in darkness, which surprised her somewhat. Malik seldom went to bed before midnight, especially on a Friday night when he had a free run of the place. There wasn't even a light on in his study upstairs; but of course it was possible he was sitting in the darkened TV room, which was at the back facing the garden.

But the fact that he'd switched the light off in the hall when he knew that she hadn't come home yet was sheer stupidity. She made a mental note to make that clear to him as she fumbled in her handbag for her keys. He didn't normally lock the outside door when she was out, but something told her he'd done so this evening.

At least, that's the way she told herself she had been thinking. Later.

Afterwards. When she was trying to relive what had happened, and when everything was in chaos and one big black hole.

She inserted her key into the lock. Turned it and found to her surprise that the door wasn't in fact locked. Opened it. Reached out her hand and switched on the light in the hall.

He was lying just inside the door. On his back with his feet almost on the doormat. His white shirt was mainly dark red, as was the normally light-coloured pine floor. His mouth was wide open, and his eyes were staring intently at a point somewhere on the ceiling. His left arm was propped against the little mahogany chest of drawers used to store gloves and scarves, looking as if he had put his hand up in school to answer a question. One of the legs, the right one, of his grey gabardine trousers had slid up almost as far as his knee and exposed that ugly birthmark that looked like a little crocodile – she had been so fascinated by it when they were engaged. By the side of his right hand, half clenched, next to the shoe rack, was the *Telegraaf*, folded to reveal the partially-solved crossword puzzle. A fly was buzzing around his head, evidently unaware that it was January and that instead of being there it ought to have been hidden away in some dark crack, asleep for at least three more months.

She registered all this while standing with her keys dangling between her thumb and index finger. Then she closed the door behind her. Suddenly she felt dizzy and automatically opened her mouth to gasp for more air, but it wasn't enough. It was too late. Without a sound she fell head first, diagonally over her husband, hitting her eyebrow against the sharp edge of the shoe rack. Her own light-coloured, warm blood started trickling down to mingle with his, cold and congealed.

Some time later she came round. Tried in vain to shake some life into her husband, and eventually managed to crawl five more metres into the house, staining the floor, carpets and walls with blood, and phoned for an ambulance.

It was only after it had arrived and the crew established what had happened that the police were called. By then it was six minutes past one, and it was half an hour after that before the real police work got under way, when Detective Inspector Reinhart and his assistant Jung arrived at the crime scene with forensic technicians and a police doctor. By then Ilse Malik had lost consciousness again, this time as the result of an injection administered by the older and more experienced of the two ambulance men, with a modicum of necessary force.

By this time Ryszard Malik had been dead for more than five hours, and when Inspector Reinhart announced in some irritation that 'we're not going to solve this shitty mess before dawn, gentlemen', nobody even raised an eyebrow in protest.

THREE

20–29 JANUARY

7

He could have sworn that he'd disconnected the phone before going to bed, but what was the point of swearing? The telephone – that invention of the devil – was ensconced on his bedside table and was intent on etching its blood-soaked sound waves onto his cerebral cortex.

Or however you might prefer to express it.

He opened one reluctant eye and glared at the confounded contraption in a vain attempt to shut it up. It kept on ringing even so. Ring after ring carved its way through his dawn-grey bedroom.

He opened another eye. The clock on the aforementioned table indicated 07.55. Who in hell's name had the cheek to wake him up on a Saturday morning when he wasn't on duty, he wondered. Who?

In January.

If there was a month he hated, it was January – it went on and on for ever and ever with rain or snow all day long, and a grand total of half an hour's sunshine.

There was only one sane way of occupying oneself at this lugubrious time of year: sleeping. Full stop.

He stretched out his left hand and lifted the receiver.

'Van Veeteren.'

'Good morning, Chief Inspector.'

It was Reinhart.

'Why the flaming hell are you ringing to wake me up at half past five on a Saturday morning? Are you out of your mind?'

But Reinhart sounded just as incorruptible as a traffic warden.

'It's eight o'clock. If you don't want to be contacted, and refuse to buy an answering machine, you can always pull out the plug. If you'd like to listen, Chief Inspector, I can explain how you . . .'

'Shut up, Inspector! Come to the point instead!'

'By all means,' said Reinhart. 'Dead body in Leufwens Allé. Stinks of murder. One Ryszard Malik. The briefing's at three o'clock.'

'Three?'

'Yes, three o'clock. What do you mean?'

'I can get from here to the police station in twenty minutes. You could have phoned me at twelve.'

Reinhart yawned.

'I was thinking of going to bed for a bit. I've just left

there. Been at it since half past one . . . I thought you might like to go there and have a look for yourself?'

Van Veeteren leant on his elbow and raised himself to a half-sitting position. Tried to see out through the window.

'What's the weather like?'

'Pouring down, and windy. Fifteen metres a second, or thereabouts.'

'Excellent. I'll stay at home. I suppose I might turn up at three, unless my horoscope advises me not to . . . Who's in charge now?'

'Heinemann and Jung. But Jung hasn't slept for two nights, so he'll probably need a bit of rest soon.'

'Any clues?'

'No.'

'How did it happen?'

'Shot. But the briefing is at three o'clock, not now. I think it's a pretty peculiar set-up. That's why I rang. The address is Leufwens Allé 14, in case you change your mind.'

'Fat chance,' said Van Veeteren, and hung up.

Needless to say it was impossible to go back to sleep. He gave up at a quarter to nine and went to lie down in the bath instead. Lay there in the half-light and thought back to the previous evening he'd spent at the Mephisto restaurant with Renate and Erich.

The former wife and the lost son. (Who had still not returned and didn't seem to have any intention of doing so either.) It had been one of Renate's recurrent attempts to rehabilitate her guilty conscience and the family that had never existed, and the result was just as unsuccessful as one might have expected. The conversation had been like walking on thin ice over dark waters. Erich had left them halfway through the dessert, giving as an excuse an important meeting with a lady. Then they had sat there, ex-husband and ex-wife, over a cheeseboard of doubtful quality, going through agonies as they tried to avoid hurting each other any more than necessary. He had seen her into a taxi shortly after midnight and walked all the way home in the pious hope that the biting wind would whip his brain free from all the murky thoughts lurking inside it.

That had failed completely. When he got home he slumped into an armchair and listened to Monteverdi for an hour, drank three beers and had not gone to bed until nearly half past one.

A wasted evening, in other words. But typical, that was for sure. Very typical. Mind you, it was January. What else could he have expected?

He got out of the bath. Did a couple of tentative back

exercises in front of the bedroom mirror. Dressed, and made breakfast.

Sat down at the kitchen table with the morning paper spread out in front of him. Not a word about the murder. Naturally enough. It must have happened as the presses were rolling . . . Or whatever the presses did nowadays. What was the name of the victim? Malik?

What had Reinhart said? Leufwens Allé? He had a good mind to phone the inspector and ask a few questions, but pricks of conscience from his better self, or whatever it might have been, got the upper hand, and he desisted. He would find out all he needed to know soon enough. No need to hurry. Better to make the most of the hours remaining before the whole thing got under way, perhaps. There hadn't been a murder since the beginning of December, despite all the holidays, and if it really was as Reinhart said, an awkward-looking case, no doubt they would have their hands full for some time to come. Reinhart generally knew what he was talking about. More than most of them.

He poured himself another cup of coffee, and started studying the week's chess problem. Mate in three moves, which would presumably involve a few complications.

'All right,' said Reinhart, putting down his pipe. 'The facts of the case. At six minutes past one this morning, an ambulance driver, Felix Hald, reported that there was a dead body at Leufwens Allé 14. They'd gone there because the woman of the house, Ilse Malik, had phoned for an ambulance. She was extremely confused, and had failed to contact the police even though her husband was as dead as a statue . . . Four bullet wounds, two in his chest, two under the belt.'

'Under the belt?' wondered Inspector Rooth, his mouth full of sandwich.

'Under the belt,' said Reinhart. 'Through his willy, if you prefer that. She'd come home from the theatre, it seems, at round about midnight or shortly before, and found him lying in the hall. Just inside the door. The weapon seems to be a Berenger-75, all four bullets have been recovered. It seems reasonable to suspect that a silencer was used, since nobody heard anything. The victim is fifty-two years old, one Ryszard Malik. Part owner of a firm selling equipment for industrial kitchens and restaurants, or something of the sort. Not in our records, unknown to us, no shady dealing as far as we are aware. Nothing at all. Hmm, is that it, Heinemann, more or less?'

Inspector Heinemann took off his glasses and started rubbing them on his tie.

'Nobody noticed a thing,' he said. 'We've spoken to the neighbours, but the house is pretty well protected. Hedges, big gardens, that sort of thing. It looks as if somebody simply walked up to the door, rang the bell, and shot him when he opened up. There's no sign of a struggle or anything. Malik was alone at home, solving a crossword and sipping a glass of whisky while his wife was at the theatre. And then, it seems the murderer just closed the door and strolled off. Quite straightforward, if you want to look at it from that point of view.'

'Sound method,' said Rooth.

'That's for sure,' said Van Veeteren. 'What does his wife have to say?'

Heinemann sighed. Nodded towards Jung, who gave every sign of finding it difficult to stay awake.

'Not a lot,' Jung said. 'It's almost impossible to get through to her. One of the ambulance men gave her an injection, and that was probably just as well. She woke up briefly this morning. Went on about Ibsen – I gather that's a writer. She'd been to the theatre, we managed to get that confirmed by a woman she'd been with . . . A Bernadette Kooning. In any case, she can't seem to grasp that her husband is dead.'

'You don't seem to be quite with it either,' said Van Veeteren. 'How long have you been awake?'

Jung counted on his fingers.

'A few days, I suppose.'

'Go home and go to bed,' said Reinhart.

Jung stood up.

'Is it OK if I take a taxi? I can't tell the difference between right and left.'

'Of course,' said Reinhart. 'Take two if you need them. Or ask one of the duty officers to drive you.'

'Two?' said Jung as he staggered to the door. 'No, one will do.'

Nobody spoke for a while. Heinemann tried to smooth down the creases in his tie. Reinhart contemplated his pipe. Van Veeteren inserted a toothpick between his lower front teeth and gazed up at the ceiling.

'Hmm,' he said eventually. 'Quite a story, one has to say. Has Hiller been informed?'

'He's away by the seaside,' said Reinhart.

'In January?'

'I don't think he intends to go swimming. I've left a message for him in any case. There'll be a press conference at five o'clock; I think it would be best if you take it.'

'Thank you,' said Van Veeteren. 'I'll only need thirty seconds.'

He looked round.

'Not much point in allocating much in the way of resources yet,' he decided. 'When do they say his wife is likely to come round? Where is she, incidentally?'

'The New Rumford hospital,' said Heinemann. 'She should be able to talk this afternoon. Moreno's there, waiting.'

'Good,' said Van Veeteren. 'What about family and friends?'

'A son at university in Munich,' said Reinhart. 'He's on his way here. That's about all. Malik has no brothers or sisters, and his parents are dead. Ilse Malik has a sister. She's also waiting at the Rumford.'

'Waiting for what, you might ask?' said Rooth.

'Very true,' said Van Veeteren. 'May I ask another question, gentlemen?'

'Please do,' said Reinhart.

'Why?' said Van Veeteren, taking out the toothpick.

'I've also been thinking about that,' said Reinhart. 'I'll get back to you when I've finished.'

'We can always hope that somebody will turn himself in,' said Rooth.

'Hope lives eternal,' said Reinhart.

Van Veeteren yawned. It was sixteen minutes past three on Saturday, 20 January. The first run-through of the Ryszard Malik case was over.

Münster parked outside the New Rumford hospital and jogged through the rain to the entrance. A woman in reception dragged herself away from her crochet work and sent him up to the fourth floor, ward 42; after explaining why he was there and producing his ID, he was escorted to a small, dirt-yellow waiting room with plastic furniture and eye-catching travel posters on the walls. It was evidently the intention to give people the opportunity of dreaming that they were somewhere else. Not a bad idea, Münster thought.

There were two women sitting in the room. The younger one, and by a large margin the more attractive of the two, with a mop of chestnut-brown hair and a book in her lap, was Detective Inspector Ewa Moreno. She welcomed him with a nod and an encouraging smile. The other one, a thin and slightly hunchbacked woman in her fifties, wearing glasses that concealed half her face, was fumbling nervously inside her black handbag. He deduced that she must be Marlene Winther, the sister of the woman who had just been widowed. He went up to her and introduced himself.

'Münster, Detective Inspector.'

She shook his hand without standing up.

'I realize that this must be difficult for you. Please understand that we are obliged to intrude upon your grief and ask some questions.'

'The lady has already explained.'

She glanced in the direction of Moreno. Münster nodded.

'Has she come round yet?'

Moreno cleared her throat and put down her book.

'She's conscious, but the doctor wants a bit of time with her first. Perhaps we should . . . ?'

Münster nodded again: they both went out into the corridor, leaving Mrs Winther on her own.

'In deep shock, it seems,' Moreno explained when they had found a discreet corner. 'They're even worried about her mental state. She's had trouble with her nerves before, and all this hasn't helped, of course. She's been undergoing treatment for various problems.'

'Have you interviewed her sister?'

Moreno nodded.

'Yes, of course. She doesn't seem all that strong either. We're going to have to tiptoe through the tulips.'

'Hostile?'

'No, not really. Just a touch of the big sister syndrome. She's used to looking after little sister, it seems. And she's evidently allowed to.'

'But you haven't spoken to her yet? Mrs Malik, I mean.'

'No. Jung and Heinemann had a go this morning, but they didn't seem to get anywhere.'

Münster thought for a moment.

'Perhaps she doesn't have all that much to tell?'

'No, presumably not. Would you like me to take her on? We'll be allowed in shortly in any case.'

Münster was only too pleased to agree.

'No doubt it would be best for her to talk to a woman. I'll stay in the wings for the time being.'

Forty-five minutes later they left the hospital together. Sat down in Münster's car, where Moreno took out her notebook and started going through the rather meagre results of her meeting with Ilse Malik. Münster had spoken to Dr Hübner – an old, white-haired doctor who seemed to have seen more or less everything – and understood that it would probably be several days before the patient could be allowed to undergo more vigorous questioning. Always assuming that would be necessary, that is.

Hübner had called it a state of deep shock. Very strong medicines to begin with, then a gradual reduction. Unable to accept what had happened. Encapsulation.

Not surprising in the circumstances, Münster thought.

'What did she actually say?' he asked.

'Not a lot,' said Moreno with a sigh. 'A happy marriage, she claimed. Malik stayed at home yesterday evening while she went to see *A Doll's House* at the Little Theatre. Left home at about half past six, drank a glass of wine with that friend of hers afterwards. Took a taxi home. Then she starts rambling. Her husband had been shot and lay in the hall, she says. She tried to help him but could see that it was serious, so she called an ambulance. She must have delayed that for getting on for an hour, if I understand the situation rightly. Fell asleep and managed to injure herself as well. She thinks her husband is in this same hospital and wonders why she's not allowed to see him . . . It's a bit hard to know how to handle her: the nurse tried to indicate what had happened, but she didn't want to know. Started speaking about something else instead.'

'What?'

'Anything and everything. The play – a fantastic production, it seems. Her son. He hasn't time to come because of his studies, she says. He's training to be a banking lawyer, or something of the sort.'

'He's supposed to be arriving about an hour from now,' said Münster. 'Poor bastard. I suppose the doc had better take a look at him as well.'

Moreno nodded.

'He'll be staying with his aunt for the time being. We can talk to him tomorrow.'

Münster thought for a moment.

'Did you get any indications of a threat, or enemies, or that kind of thing?'

'No. I tried to discuss such matters, but I didn't get anywhere. I asked her sister, but she had no suspicions at all. Doesn't seem to hiding anything either. Well, what do we do next, then?'

Münster shrugged.

'I suppose we'd better discuss it on Monday with the others. It's a damned horrific business, no matter which way you look at it. Can I drive you anywhere?'

'Home, please,' said Ewa Moreno. 'I've been hanging around here for seven hours now. It's time to spend a bit of time thinking about something else.'

'Not a bad idea,' Münster agreed, and started the engine.

Mauritz Wolff opted to be interviewed at home, a flat in the canal district with views over Langgraacht and Megsje Bois and deserving the description 'gigantic'. The rooms were teeming with children of all ages, and Reinhart assumed he must have married late in life – several times, perhaps – as he must surely be well into his fifties. A large and somewhat red-faced man, in any case, with a natural smile that found it difficult not to illuminate his face, even in a situation like this one.

'You're very welcome,' he said. 'What an awful catastrophe. I'm really shocked, I have to say. I can't take it in.'

He shooed away a little girl clinging on to his trouser leg. Reinhart looked round. Wondered if a woman ought to put in an appearance from somewhere or other before long.

'Not a bad flat you have here,' he said. 'Is there anywhere we can talk in peace and quiet?'

'Follow me,' said Wolff, clearing a way through a corridor to a room that evidently served as a library and study. He closed the door and locked it. Invited Reinhart to sit down on one of the two armchairs by a low smoking table, and sat down heavily in the other one.

'Too awful,' he said again. 'Have you any idea about who might have done it?'

Reinhart shook his head.

'Have you?'

'Not the remotest.'

'Did you know him well?'

'Inside out,' said Wolff, holding out a pack of cigarettes. Reinhart took one. 'Would you like anything to drink, by the way?'

'No thank you. Go on!'

'Well, what can I say? We've worked together for sixteen years. Ever since we started the firm. And we knew each other before that.'

'Did you mix privately as well?'

'Do you mean families and so on?'

'Yes.'

'Well, not really. Not since I met Mette, my new wife, at least. It must be absolutely awful for Ilse. How is she? I've tried to call her . . .'

'Shocked,' said Reinhart. 'She's still in hospital.'

'I understand,' said Wolff, and tried to look diplomatic. Reinhart waited.

'She can be a bit nervy,' Wolff explained.

'I've heard it said, yes,' said Reinhart. 'How's the firm going?'

'So-so. We're keeping going. A good niche, even if it went better in the eighties. But what the hell didn't?'

He started laughing, then checked himself.

'Can it have something to do with work?' Reinhart asked. 'The firm, I mean?'

The question was badly formulated, and Wolff didn't understand it.

'Can the murder of Malik have some connection with your business?' Reinhart spelled it out.

Wolff shook his head uncomprehendingly.

'With us? No, how could that have been?'

'What do you think it could be, then? Did he have a mistress? Any dodgy business deals? You knew him better than anybody else.'

Wolff scratched the back of his head.

'No,' he said after a while. 'Neither of those things. If Malik had been seeing other women I'd have known about it. And I can't imagine him being involved in anything illegal.'

'So he's a model of virtue then,' Reinhart established. 'How long have you known him, did you say?'

Wolff tried to work it out.

'We met for the first time about twenty-five years ago . . . that was through work as well. We were both with Gündler and Wein, and eventually we pulled out and started up on our own. There were three of us to start with, but one left after six months.'

'What was his name?'

'Merrinck. Jan Merrinck.'

Reinhart made a note.

'Can you remember if anything unusual has happened recently? If Malik behaved oddly in some way or other?'

Wolff thought it over.

'No. No, there hasn't been anything as far as I can recall. I'm sorry, but there doesn't seem to be all that much I can help you with.'

Reinhart changed tack.

'What was his marriage like?'

'Malik's?'

'Yes.'

Wolff shrugged.

'Not all that good. But he hung in there. My first was worse, I reckon. Malik was strong. A confident and reliable man. A bit dry, perhaps. My God, I can't understand who could have done this, Inspector. It must be a madman, don't you think? Some lunatic? Have you got a suspect?'

Reinhart ignored the question.

'What time did he leave the office yesterday?'

'A quarter to five,' answered Wolff without hesitation. 'A bit earlier than usual as he had to collect his car from a repair workshop. I stayed there on my own until half past five.'

'And he didn't behave unusually in any way?'

'No. I've said that already.'

'This Rachel deWiijs who works for you. What have you to say about her?'

'Rachel? A treasure. Pure gold, through and through. Without her we wouldn't survive for more than six months . . .' He bit his lip and drew at his cigarette. 'But everything has changed now, of course. Bloody hell.'

'So Malik didn't have anything going with her, then?'

'Malik and Rachel? No, you can bet your life that he didn't.'

'Really?' said Reinhart. 'OK, I'll take you at your word. What about you yourself? Did you have any reason to want him out of the way?'

Wolff's jaw dropped.

'That was the most fucking . . .'

'There, there, don't get over-excited. You must realize that I have to ask that question. Malik has been murdered, and the fact is that most victims are killed by somebody they know. And you are the person who knew him best; I thought we'd agreed on that already?'

'He was my business partner, for Christ's sake. One of my best friends . . .'

'I know. But if you had a motive even so, it's better for you to tell us what it is yourself rather than leaving us to find out about it later.'

Wolff sat in silence for a while, thinking about that one.

'No,' he said eventually. 'Why the hell should I want to kill Malik? His share in the firm goes to Ilse and Jacob, and all that will do is to make a mess of everything. You must understand that his death is a shock for me as well, Inspector. I know I sometimes sound a bit brusque, but I'm grieving over his death. I'm missing him as a close friend.'

Reinhart nodded.

'I understand,' he said. 'I think we'll leave it at that for today, but you'll have to reckon with us turning up again before long. We are very keen to catch whoever did this.'

Wolff stood up and flung out his arms.

'Of course. If there's anything I can do to help . . . I'm at your disposal at any time.'

'Good,' said Reinhart. 'If anything occurs to you, let us know. Go back to the kids now. How many have you got, incidentally?'

'Six,' said Wolff. 'Three from before and three new ones.'

'Go forth and multiply, and replenish the earth,' said Reinhart. 'Isn't it a bit of a strain? Er, looking after them all, I mean.'

Wolff smiled and shook his head.

'Not at all. The tipping point is four. After that, it makes no difference if you have seven or seventeen.'

Reinhart nodded, and resolved to bear that in mind.

8

In their eagerness to sell a few extra copies to casual readers with nothing better to do at the weekend, the Sunday papers made a meal of the Ryszard Malik murder. Bold-print headlines on billboards and front pages, pictures of the victim (while still alive, smiling) and his house, and a double-page spread in both *Neuwe Blatt* and *Telegraaf*. Detailed and non-committal, but needless to say it was pitched about right – what the hell did people have to keep them occupied on a damp and windy day in January apart from sitting indoors and lapping up the story of somebody who had suffered even more than they were doing?

Van Veeteren had a subscription to both papers and had no need to stick his nose outside the door in order to buy one. Instead he stayed in all day, reading selected chapters of Rimley's *Famous Chess Games* and listening to Bach. He had paid a brief visit to Leufwens Allé on the Saturday evening and established that there was nothing useful for him to do there. The technicians and crime-scene boys had run a fine-toothed comb over both house and garden, and for him to imagine he would be able to find something they'd missed would be to overestimate his abilities. Although it had happened before.

And in any case, it was not even certain that he would need to bother about it. Hiller would no doubt decide when he emerged from the sea on Monday morning; perhaps he would judge it best for Reinhart and Münster to continue pulling the strings. That would be good, he had to admit. A blessing devoutly to be wished, he thought – if he'd been able to choose a month in which to hibernate or to spend in a deep-freeze, he would have gone for January without hesitation.

If he could pick two, he would take February as well.

On Monday his car refused to start. Something to do with damp somewhere or other, no doubt. He was forced to walk four blocks before he was able to scramble into a taxi, soaking wet through, at Rejmer Plejn; and he was ten minutes late for the run-through.

Reinhart, who was in charge, arrived a minute later, and the whole meeting was not exactly productive.

The forensic side was done and dusted, and had uncovered nothing they didn't know already. Or thought they knew. Ryszard Malik had been shot at some time between half past seven and half past nine on the Friday evening, with a 7.65 millimetre Berenger. As none of the neighbours had heard a shot, it could be assumed that the killer had used a silencer.

'How many Berengers are floating around town?' asked Münster.

'Le Houde guesses about fifty,' said Rooth. 'Anybody can get one in about half an hour if he has a bit of local knowledge. There's no point in starting to look, in any case.'

Van Veeteren sneezed and Reinhart carried on describing the wounds, the angles and similar melancholy details. The murderer had probably fired his gun at a distance of between one and one and a half metres, which could suggest that he hadn't even bothered to step inside first. The door opened inwards, and in all probability he'd have been standing ready to shoot the moment Malik opened it. Two shots in the chest, then, each of them would have been fatal, one through the left lung and the other through the aorta – hence the unusually large amount of blood.

And then two under the belt. From a bit closer.

'Why?' asked Van Veeteren.

'Well, what do you think?' said Reinhart, looking round the table.

Nobody spoke. Heinemann looked down at his crotch.

'A professional job?' asked Münster.

'Eh?' said Reinhart. 'Oh, you mean the fatal shots . . . No, not necessarily. A ten-year-old can shoot accurately with a Berenger from one metre away. Assuming you're ready for a bit of a recoil, that is. It could be anybody. But the shots under the belt ought to tell us something, or what do you think?'

'Yes, sure,' said Rooth.

Nobody spoke for a few seconds.

'Don't feel embarrassed on my account,' said Moreno.

'Could be a coincidence,' said Münster.

'There's no such thing as coincidence,' said Reinhart. 'Only a lack of knowledge.'

'So the shots in the chest came first, is that right?' Heine-mann asked, frowning.

'Yes, yes,' sighed Reinhart. 'The other two were fired when he was already lying on the floor – we've explained that already. Weren't you listening?'

'I just wanted to check,' said Heinemann.

'It doesn't seem to make much sense, shooting some-body's balls off after you've already killed him,' said Rooth. 'Seems a bit mad, I'd say. Sick, in a way.'

Reinhart nodded and Van Veeteren sneezed again.

'Are you cold, Chief Inspector?' Reinhart wondered. 'Shall we ring for a blanket?'

'I'd prefer a hot toddy,' grunted Van Veeteren. 'Is the

forensic stuff all finished? I take it they didn't find any fingerprints or dropped cigarette butts?'

'Not even a grain of dandruff,' said Reinhart. 'Shall we run through the interviews instead? Starting with the widow?'

'No, starting with the victim,' said Van Veeteren. 'Even though I assume he didn't have much to say for himself.'

'I beg your pardon,' said Reinhart, producing a loose sheet of paper from his notebook. 'Let's see now . . . Ryszard Malik was fifty-two years of age. Born in Chadów, but has lived in Maardam since 1960 or thereabouts. Studied at the School of Commerce. Got a job with Gündler and Wein in 1966. In 1979 he started his own firm together with Mauritz Wolff and Jan Merrinck, who jumped ship quite early on – Merrinck, that is. Aluvit F/B, and for God's sake don't ask me what that means. Malik married Ilse, née Moener, in 1968. One son, Jacob, born 1972. He's been reading jurisprudence and economics in Munich for several years now. Anyway, that's about it . . .'

He put the sheet of paper back where it came from.

'Anything off the record?' Rooth wondered.

'Not a dickie bird,' said Reinhart. 'So far, at least. He seems to have been a bit of a bore, as far as I can see. Bor-ing marriage, boring job, boring life. Goes on holiday to Blankenbirge or Rhodes. No known interests apart from crossword puzzles and detective novels, preferably bad ones . . . God only knows why anybody should want to kill him, but apart from that I don't think there are any unanswered questions.'

'Excellent,' said Van Veeteren. 'What about the widow? Surely there's a bit more substance to her, at least?'

Münster shrugged.

'We haven't been able to get much out of her,' he said. 'She's still confused and doesn't want to accept what's happened.'

'She might be hiding something, though,' said Heinemann. 'It's not exactly anything new to pretend to be mad. I recall a Danish prince—'

'I don't think she is,' interrupted Münster. 'Neither do the doctors. We know quite a lot about her from her sister and her son, but it doesn't seem to have anything much to do with the murder. A bit pitiful, that's all. Bad nerves. Prescribed drugs on and off. Taken in for therapy once or twice. Finds it hard to get on with people, it seems. Stopped working at Konger's Palace for that reason, although nobody has said that in so many words . . . As far as we can see Malik's firm produces enough cash to keep the family going. Or has done until now, I should say.'

Van Veeteren bit off the end of a toothpick.

'All this is more miserable than the weather,' he said, spitting out a few fragments. 'Has Moreno anything to add?'

Ewa Moreno smiled slightly.

'The son is rather charming, actually,' she said. 'In view of the circumstances, that is. He flew the nest early, it seems. Left home as soon as he'd finished secondary school and he doesn't have much contact with his parents, especially his mother. Only when he needs some money, or something similar. He admits that openly. Do you want to know about the sister as well?'

'Is there anything for us to get our teeth into?' asked Reinhart with a sigh.

'No,' said Moreno. 'Not really. She also has a stable but rather boring marriage. Works part-time in an old people's home. Her husband's a businessman. They both have alibis for the night of the murder, and it seems pretty unlikely that either of them could be involved – completely unthinkable, in fact.'

All was quiet for a while. Rooth produced a bar of chocolate from his jacket pocket and Heinemann tried to scrape a stain off the table with his thumbnail. Van Veeteren had closed his eyes, and it was more or less impossible to make out if he was awake or asleep.

'OK,' said Reinhart eventually. 'There's just one thing I want to know. Who the hell did it?'

'A madman,' said Rooth. 'Somebody who wanted to test his Berenger and noticed that the lights were on in the house.'

'I reckon you've hit the nail on the head,' said Heinemann.

'No,' said Van Veeteren without opening his eyes.

'Oh, really?' said Reinhart. 'How do you know that?'

'By the prickings of my thumb,' said Van Veeteren.

'Eh?' said Heinemann. 'What the hell does that mean?'

'Shall we go and get some coffee?' suggested Rooth.

Van Veeteren opened his eyes.

'Preferably a hot toddy, as I said before.'

Reinhart checked the time.

'It's only eleven,' he said. 'But I'm all for it. This case stinks like a shit heap.'

On the way home from the police station that gloomy Monday, Reinhart stopped off at the Merckx shopping centre out at Bossingen. It was really against his principles to buy anything in such a temple of commerce, but he decided to turn a blind eye to the crassness of it all today. He simply didn't feel up to running around from one little shop to the next in the centre of town, after rooting about in the unsavoury details of Ryszard Malik's background.

Half an hour later he had acquired a lobster, two bottles of wine and eleven roses. Plus a few other goodies. That would have to do. He left the inferno and a quarter of an hour later went through the front door of his flat in

Zuyderstraat. Put away his purchases in their appointed places, then made a phone call.

'Hi. I've got a lobster, some wine and some roses. You can have them all if you get yourself here within the next hour.'

'But it's Monday today,' said the woman at the other end.

'If we don't do anything about it, it'll be Monday for the rest of our lives,' said Reinhart.

'OK,' said the woman. 'I'll be there.'

Winnifred Lynch was a quarter Aboriginal, born in Perth, Australia, but grew up in England. After a degree in English language and literature at Cambridge and a failed and childless marriage, she'd landed a post as guest lecturer at Maardam University. When she met Reinhart at the Vox jazz club in the middle of November, she'd just celebrated her thirty-ninth birthday. Reinhart was forty-nine. He went home with her, and they made love (with the occasional pause) for the next four days and nights – but unusually (to the surprise of both of them, given their previous experience) it didn't end there. They carried on meeting. All over the place: at concerts, restaurants, cinemas and above all, of course, in bed. As soon as the beginning of December it was clear to Reinhart that there was something special about this slightly brown-skinned, intelligent woman, and when she went back to England for the Christmas holiday he felt withdrawal symptoms, the like of which he hadn't experienced for nearly thirty years. A sudden reminder of what it was like to miss somebody. Of the fact that somebody actually meant something to him.

The feeling scared him stiff, no doubt about that; it was a warning, but when she came back after three weeks he couldn't help but go to meet her at the airport. Stood waiting with a bunch of roses and a warm embrace, and of course it started all over again.

This Monday was the fifth – or was it the sixth? – occasion since then, and when he thought about it he realized that it could hardly have been more than ten days since the last time.

So you could bet your life that he'd got something special going.

'Why did you become a policeman?' she asked as they lay back in bed afterwards. 'You promised you'd tell me one day.'

'A trauma,' he said after a moment's thought.

'I'm human, you know,' she said.

'What do you mean by that?'

She didn't answer, but after a while he imagined that he understood.

'All right,' he said. 'It was a woman. Or a girl. Twenty years old.'

'What happened?'

He hesitated, and inhaled deeply twice on his cigarette before answering.

'I was twenty-one. Reading philosophy and anthropology at the university, as you know. We'd been together for two years. We were going to get married. She was reading languages. One night she was going home after a lecture and was stabbed by a lunatic in Wollerim's Park. She died in hospital before I got there. It took the police six months to find her killer. I was one of them by that time.'

If she has the good sense to say nothing, I want to spend the rest of my life with her, he thought out of the blue.

Winnifred Lynch put her hand on his chest. Stroked him gently for a few seconds, then got up and went to the bathroom.

That does it then, Reinhart acknowledged in surprise.

Later on, when they'd made love again and then recovered, he couldn't resist asking her a question.

'What do you have to say about a murderer who fired

two shots under the belt of a victim who's already lying dead?'

She thought for a moment.

'The victim's a man, I take it?'

'Yes.'

'Then I think the murderer is a woman.'

Well, I'll be damned, Reinhart thought.

9

The weekend spent by a stormy sea had evidently had an invigorating effect on Police Chief Hiller, and when he returned to work on Monday morning he had promptly ordered full steam ahead on the Malik case.

What that meant in practice was no fewer than six CID officers, with Van Veeteren in charge, plus whatever foot-soldiers happened to be around at the time, all of them expected to work full-time on finding the murderer. Senior officers in addition to Van Veeteren were Reinhart, Münster, Rooth, Heinemann and Moreno. Jung had succumbed to influenza after his succession of sleepless nights and was expected to be sidelined for several more days yet. DeBries was on holiday.

Van Veeteren had nothing in principle against having so many people working on the case. The only problem was that there wasn't very much for them to do that made sense. Trying to trace the murder weapon via narks and contacts in the so-called underworld was a hopeless,

Sisyphean task, he knew that. In order to increase the chances of success to twenty-five per cent, it would mean assigning a hundred police officers to that job for a hundred days – plus generous overtime money. That kind of staffing was only resorted to when a prime minister had been murdered. It was widely believed by the senior officers that Ryszard Malik had not been Prime Minister.

That left the wife. Van Veeteren charged Moreno and Heinemann with keeping an eye on Ilse Malik's gradual return to full consciousness and emergence from the shadows. It was decided that they might as well have somebody at the hospital round the clock, seeing as they had enough officers available for once. You could never tell, and if there was anybody who might be able to come up with something relevant to this business, she was the one.

The only other thing to do was to cast bread upon the waters. That was always a possibility. Call on anybody who had any kind of link with Malik – neighbours, business acquaintances, old and new friends – and ask them questions. In accordance with the proven method used with pigs searching for truffles, i.e. if you continue rooting around in the ground for long enough, sooner or later you'll come across something edible.

Van Veeteren gave this less than stimulating task to Rooth and Reinhart to begin with (together with at least three otherwise unoccupied probationers of somewhat variable ability). Van Veeteren was naturally well aware that there was little point in telling Reinhart what to do, but as Hiller was revelling in his newly awakened zeal and wanted a sheet of paper on his brightly polished desk no later than Tuesday afternoon, that is of course what he would get.

Despite a rather troublesome cold, Van Veeteren himself went to play badminton with Münster. This was not mentioned on the list of duties on the document placed before the chief of police.

By the time Hiller's full steam ahead was throttled back on Friday and the team was reduced, due to an armed robbery resulting in a fatality in the suburb of Borowice, nothing much had been discovered. Under the supervision of Rooth and Reinhart – and later Münster as well – some seventy interviews had taken place, and the only outcome was that the image of Malik as a somewhat wooden but also reliable person used to taking responsibility had been reinforced and fully established. Eighty kilos of decency with two left brains, as Reinhart preferred to express it.

And precisely in line with Dr Hübner's forecast, Ilse Malik had begun to float up towards the surface of the real world out at the New Rumford, even if it was a somewhat precarious journey. In any case, on the Wednesday morning she had finally accepted as fact the murder of her husband. Her memories of that Friday evening consequently became a little more consistent in outline, and she was also able to tell them relatively coherently what she had been doing during the day of the murder. It is true that she occasionally relapsed into attacks of hysterical sobbing, but what more could one expect? Her son Jacob was present by her side more or less all the time, and if what Moreno had suggested was true – that he had cut himself loose from his mother's apron strings somewhat precipitately – he now seemed to be making up for his youthful rebellion. Needless to say, he had little choice but to make the most of the hand that fate had dealt him.

On Thursday morning something new crept into Ilse Malik's memory. To be sure, the son maintained forthwith – in conversation with Heinemann and Moreno, who had also taken up residence at the bedside, with at least one of them permanently present – that it was a typical example of his mother's paranoia. He had heard about similar things before and recommended strongly that the officers shouldn't pay too much attention to it.

However, what Ilse Malik claimed was that somebody had clearly had designs on her husband's life in the week before that fatal Friday. In the first place they had received strange telephone calls – on two different occasions: on the Tuesday and Thursday, if she remembered rightly. Some unknown person had phoned without saying a thing – all she could hear in the receiver was some music, despite her protests and strong words, especially the second time. Ilse Malik had no idea what the music was and what it was supposed to mean, but she was pretty sure that it was the same tune both times.

Whether or not her husband had received similar calls she had no idea. He certainly hadn't said anything about it.

The other evidence of a plot to take Ryszard Malik's life consisted of a white Mercedes that had attempted to kill him by crashing into his Renault as he was on his way home from work. For want of anything else to follow up, this information was also checked; but in view of the relatively slight damage done to Malik's car, both Heinemann and Moreno decided that the suspicions had no foundation in fact. The owner of the Mercedes in question was a sixty-two-year-old professor of limnology from Geneva, and when they contacted the Swiss police they found no reason to suspect that he might have had murderous intentions when he skidded into Malik's rear end.

As for the rest of Mrs Malik's revelations, they were mainly a distinctly humdrum description of a humdrum life and marriage, and in view of the changed circumstances with regard to staffing, Van Veeteren decided on Friday to cancel the hospital watch. By this time both Heinemann and Moreno were so bored by the job they had been given that they both volunteered to join the bank robbery team, which was being led by Reinhart, who was also released from the Malik case – for the time being, at least. Jung and Rooth were also transferred to the newly established team, despite the strong objections, especially from the latter, to the prospect of having to work over the weekend.

Which left Van Veeteren and Münster.

Also left was the necessity of attempting to achieve something that could be reminiscent of a result.

'Have you got any ideas?' ventured Münster as they sat over an early Friday evening beer at Adenaar's.

'None at all,' muttered Van Veeteren, glaring at the rain pattering against the window pane. 'I don't normally have any ideas in this accursed month of the year. We'll have to wait and see.'

'Yes, I suppose so,' said Münster. 'A funny business, though. Reinhart maintains that the killer is a woman.'

'Very possible,' sighed the chief inspector. 'It's always hard to find a woman. Personally, I've been trying to find one all my life.'

Coming from Van Veeteren and on an occasion such as this, that was almost to be regarded as a heroic attempt at humour. Münster was obliged to cough away a smile.

'At least we can have the weekend off,' he said. 'It's a relief that we weren't set on the trail of the bank robber.'

'Maybe. It's a relief for him as well not to be pestered by us.'

'I expect they'll get him even so,' said Münster, draining his glass. 'There were witnesses, after all. Anyway, I'd better be heading for home. Synn will have left for work by now, and the babysitter gets paid by the hour.'

'Oh dear,' said Van Veeteren. 'There's always a cloud on the horizon.'

On Monday it became clear that Münster's prediction had been correct. The bank robber – an unemployed former traffic warden – had been arrested by Rooth and Heinemann early on Sunday morning, following a tip-off from a woman who had been extremely well dined in one of the best restaurants in town on the Saturday evening. The confession came after less than an hour, thanks to some unusually effective interrogation by Reinhart, who was evidently keen to get home as quickly as possible as something important was awaiting him there.

There had been no developments in the Malik case, apart from the fact that Jacob Malik had returned to his studies in Munich. His mother had been on a short visit to her sister's, where she would also be staying until the funeral, which had been fixed for 3 February. Some twenty tip-offs had been received from the general public, but none of them were considered to be of any significance for the investigation. When the general run-through and reports took place in the chief of police's leafy office, it was decided to reduce the level of activity to routine, with Van Veeteren in charge. On Saturday there had been a robbery at a city centre jeweller's – this time, luckily, nobody had been injured; a racist gang had run amok through the immigrant district beyond Zwille and caused a certain amount of damage; and in the early hours of Monday morning an unhappy farmer out at Korrim had shot dead his wife and twelve cows. Obviously, all these incidents required careful investigation.

By now Ryszard Malik had been dead for nearly ten days, and just about as little was known about who had killed him as on the day he died.

Absolutely nothing, zilch.

And January was still limping along.

10

The feeling of satisfaction was greater than she had expected.

More profound and genuine than she could ever have imagined. For the first time in her adult life she had discovered meaning and equilibrium – or so she imagined, at least. It was hard to put her finger on exactly what it was, but she could feel it in her body. Feel it in her skin and in her relaxed muscles; a sort of intoxication that spread among her nerve fibres like gently frothing bubbles, and kept her at a constantly elevated level of consciousness, totally calm and yet with a feeling of being on a high. As high as the sky. An orgasm, she thought in a state of exhilaration, an orgasm going on for an absurdly long period of time. Only very slowly and gently did it ebb away, subsiding lazily into expectation and anticipation of the next occasion. And the one after that.

To kill.

To kill those people.

Some years ago she had been touched by religion, had been on the point of joining one of those religious sects that were springing up like mushrooms from the soil (or like mildew from the brain, as somebody had said), and she recognized her state from the way she had felt then. The only difference was that the religious bliss had passed over. Three or four days of ecstasy had given way to regret and a hangover, just like any other intoxication.

But not now. Not this time. It was still there after ten days. Her whole being was filled with strength, her actions with determination and significance; on every occasion, no matter how trivial – like eating an apple, cutting her nails or standing in line at the checkout of the local supermarket. Awareness and determination characterized everything she did, for even the most insignificant action was of course also another step on the way, another link in the chain leading ultimately to the next killing.

To kill, and to kill. And eventually to close the circle that had been her mother's past and her own life. Her mission. There was a point to everything, at last.

She read about her first deed in the newspapers. Bought the *Neuwe Blatt, Telegraaf* and several others, and lay in her room studying all the speculations. She was surprised by all the attention it had attracted. How much would they write next time? And the time after that?

She was slightly annoyed at the fact that she didn't have

a television set; she even toyed with the idea of buying a little one, but decided not to. Or at least, to postpone doing so; perhaps she would be unable to resist the temptation of seeing and hearing about herself on the news on the next occasion, but it was best to bide her time. She could have sat in a cafe and watched, of course, but that didn't feel sufficiently attractive. Not sufficiently private.

Because no matter what – this was a private affair, all of it. Between herself and her mother.

Just her, her mother, and the names on the list.

She had crossed one of them out now. Drawn a red circle round the one next in line. Late on the Monday evening, she decided that the period of waiting should come to an end now. The scene was set. The stage design completed. Time to go out again. First the preludes, and then the act itself.

The killing.

A feeling of well-being spread underneath her skin, and when she closed her eyes, through the yellowish, fading glimmer, she could make out her mother's face.

Her tired, but imperative expression.

Do something, my girl.

FOUR

30 JANUARY TO 1 FEBRUARY

11

When Rickard Maasleitner woke up on the Tuesday morning, the headmaster's words were still ringing in his ears; and of course there was good reason to suspect that he had been dreaming about them all night.

'You must understand that your being off work sick is not only a result of your allergy problems. It is also an opportunity for you to think things over. I want you to consider – and to consider very carefully indeed – whether or not you really want to continue working at our establishment!'

He had pushed his glasses down to the tip of his nose and leaned forward over his desk as he talked. Tried to look as fatherly and understanding as possible, despite the fact that they were more or less the same age and had known each other since they had first joined the teaching staff. During the Van Breukelen era.

'You have plenty of time,' he had added. Put an arm round Maasleitner's shoulders for a moment as he left the room, and mumbled something about idealism and upbringing. In bad taste.

Plenty of time?

He turned over and checked the alarm clock on the bookcase. A quarter to ten.

A quarter to ten on a Tuesday morning in January. Still in bed. A strange feeling, to say the least. Off sick for three weeks with allergy problems. Ah well – what it really meant was that he had been suspended from teaching for dragging a cheeky fifteen-year-old out into the corridor and telling him to go to hell. Or back to the country he came from, wherever that was. And boxed the ears of another one of similar ilk.

And not regretted it for one moment.

That was the crux of the matter. He had not apologized. Refused to crawl up to the cross. Both incidents had taken place during the hectic exam period at the beginning of December, and since then the wheels had been turning.

Protests by pupils. The parents' association. A couple of articles in the newspapers. All the time there had been a door open for him, and, of course, he had been well aware of it – an escape route which would have enabled everybody concerned to draw a line under the whole business, if he would only acknowledge his guilt and beg for forgiveness.

If he would regret it, in other words.

Everybody had expected that to be what happened. Needless to say. Maasleitner would do the sensible thing, do the decent thing and give way. If not before the Christmas holidays, then during them. Obviously . . . he would be filled with misgivings after due consideration, and all that.

But that was not what happened at all. He had come to a dead end instead. At quite an early stage he had known that he was not going to back down this time. He had done that before, pleaded guilty and begged to be forgiven for actions he knew deep down, and without a shadow of doubt, were correct and justified.

This time that was more obviously the case than ever. In both cases. The two young thugs he had come into conflict with had received only a fraction of the treatment they really deserved. An ounce of justice for once. And now he was suspended, more or less. As yet they weren't calling it that, and he was still being paid; but of course it was only a matter of time before the whole thing was made rather more official. The sack, in other words.

Three weeks, to be precise. Rickard Maasleitner knew the rules of the game. Understood them and didn't like them. Never had. A safety net for cretins and blackguards. Hell and damnation, he thought as he kicked off the covers. Justice!

He had barely got out of bed when the telephone rang.

If it's somebody from school, I'll hang up on them, he decided.

But it wasn't somebody from school. It was a woman's voice. A quite low-pitched and slightly gruff voice.

'Do you recognize this tune?' it said.

That was all. Then the music started. Something instrumental. Or a long intro, perhaps. A bit long in the tooth, by the sound of it. But a nice tune.

'Hello,' he said after listening for about ten seconds. 'Is this some kind of quiz?'

No answer. The music kept on playing.

He held the receiver some way from his ear and thought for a moment.

'If you think you can throw me off balance by this kind of nonsense, you're very much mistaken!' he said, and hung up.

Scum of the earth, he thought. What the hell's this world coming to?

He put on his dressing gown and went to the kitchen to make breakfast.

During the rest of the day he received at least eight more telephone calls – he lost count some time in the early afternoon.

The same music. No singing, just a band playing, something from the sixties, he thought – he seemed to recognize it vaguely, but couldn't remember what it was called. Nor the band playing it.

Obviously he considered several times pulling out the plug and putting a stop to the nonsense, but for some reason he didn't. Instead, each time the phone rang he broke off his reading or his work on the index of the teaching book he was busy with. Answered, listened to the music and stared out over the rooftops and the naked black trees, wondering what the hell was going on. Didn't say a word from the third call onwards.

At first he had been convinced that it had something to do with school, that there was probably some pupil or other behind it; but the longer it went on, the more doubtful he became. Strangely enough his irritation seemed to drain away . . . drain away and change into something else, probably an equal mixture of curiosity and another ingredient he didn't really want to acknowledge. He was reluctant to admit that it was probably fear.

There was something disturbing about the whole business. Something he couldn't grasp or understand. Sophistication, perhaps? The woman's voice from the first call never came back, only the music, nothing else. The same pop tune, no words . . . Quite well played, that had to be said, and, he thought, from the early sixties, if he wasn't much mistaken.

But even if the voice never returned, he remembered what the woman had said.

'Do you recognize this tune?'

It was something he ought to remember. Isn't that what she implied? The music meant something, and of course the point was that he should know what it meant. Surely that was what she implied?

'Hell and damnation,' he muttered as he replaced the receiver for the fifth or sixth time. 'What is it all about?'

It would be some time before Rickard Maasleitner became fully aware of that. But on the other hand, by then it was all the more obvious.

12

Enso Faringer was nervous. That was beyond question. The moment they sat down at their usual table in Freddy's, he had started squirming around and scratching at the ugly rash on his neck he always had in the winter. He also gulped down his beer, and managed to smoke two cigarettes before the food was served.

The conversation was floating round in circles, and Maasleitner could see that his colleague didn't really know what leg to stand on. Or rather, what chair to sit on. He had tried to get Faringer to eat out with him on Tuesday evening, but had only received an obvious excuse for an answer – an old friend was due to make a visit, or some such thing.

So he was supposed to believe that Enso Faringer had some friends, was he? Maasleitner had a good mind to enquire further about the alleged visit while he had him trapped on the line; but he had swallowed the lie with a wry smile. No point in stirring things up. He played with the idea of putting his colleague on the spot now as well, but let it pass. He didn't want to be awkward. Faringer was a contact, after all. Somebody who had insight into what was going to happen at the Elementar school, even if he was hardly capable of drawing conclusions of his own. Or influencing them in one way or another.

Come to that, Faringer was his only contact. There was nobody else he could rely on. In a situation like the one he was in, Maasleitner would have to make do with whatever was available.

They had a kebab, as usual, and Faringer gossiped tentatively about a few pupils and teachers he knew Maasleitner didn't like. A bit about his aquarium as well, and his father who had been in a mental hospital for several years, but never wanted to die despite the fact that he was over ninety-five years old. Enso was in the habit of visiting him about four times a week.

That was also a sign of his nervousness, of course. The fact that he was gossiping. Faringer's mouth seemed to be ticking over in neutral, as if he were talking to his fish, or to a classroom of pupils when he didn't need to think too hard about what he was saying. Maasleitner was tired of his company after only ten minutes.

'Whose side are you on?' he asked when Faringer had been served and taken a swig at his third beer.

'What do you mean?'

'You know what I mean.'

'No . . . well, yes, maybe. No, you'd better explain. I'm not quite with you.'

'I'm going to get the sack three weeks from now. Or two and a half, to be precise. What do you say to that?'

Faringer swallowed.

'You can't be serious? That can't be allowed to happen. I must have a word with . . .'

He fell silent.

'Have a word with whom?'

'I don't know. But you're surely not going to leave? It'll sort itself out somehow or other.'

'Don't talk rubbish. Don't try and tell me that you don't know the score. It's as clear as day, for Christ's sake.'

'Well . . .'

'I'm going to get the boot because I gave those fucking thugs what they deserved. Haven't you grasped that? What the hell do you mean by sitting here mumbling on and pretending you don't know what's going on?'

His anger had spilled over much sooner than he'd expected, and he could see that Faringer was scared. He tried to smooth things over a bit.

'There must have been some sort of reaction among the staff. Are they just going to stand by and let things take their course, or . . . or am I going to get some sort of support? What are they saying? That's all I want to know.'

'I see.'

Faringer looked relieved.

'So if you could keep your ear to the ground . . . Listen to what's going on. I mean, you're good at interpreting moods. You have more insight than a few of the others, there's no need to hide your light under a bushel . . .'

It was a very clumsily expressed compliment, but he could see that it was effective. Enso Faringer leant back in his chair and lit a cigarette. Narrowed his eyes and tried to look as if he were thinking hard.

Perhaps he really is, Maasleitner thought.

'You'd like me to take a few soundings, is that it?'

Maasleitner nodded.

'Maybe start a little . . . campaign?'

'Well, why not?'

It was obvious that the beer was starting to affect his colleague's confused mind now, and it dawned on Maasleitner what a waste of time it all was. Needing to turn for help to the likes of Enso Faringer! Sitting here and asking for favours from this universally despised and ignored laughing stock. *Herr Fräulein*, as the pupils used to call him.

Besides, he wasn't at all sure what he hoped to get out of it. Just a chance to let off steam, presumably. Give vent to his irritation and his feeling of being trampled underfoot. A stubborn old fool with a bee in his bonnet, was that what he would end up becoming? Slowly but surely he could feel exhaustion and pointlessness grasping him by the throat, and when he saw the little German teacher frown and take a ballpoint from his inside pocket, he had the feeling that everything was being enacted in the theatre of the absurd.

A farce.

Was Faringer going to work out tactics on his paper napkin? Or sketch out a manifesto, perhaps? An appeal?

Bloody hell, Maasleitner thought. Who are all these people I'm surrounded by?

Or are they all like this, if you scrape a bit at the surface?

It was hardly a new question. Barely even a question, come to that.

More of a statement.

More beer, he thought. Might as well blur a few edges. Inertia, come and embrace me!

When they staggered out of the little basement restaurant some considerable time later, the mood was significantly more relaxed. Maasleitner even found it necessary to place his arm round his colleague's shoulders in order to assist his attempts to negotiate the steps leading up to street level. Faringer missed one step altogether, grabbed hold of the iron rail and roared with laughter; and when they shortly afterwards managed to flag down a taxi, it transpired that he had left his wallet on the table. Maasleitner went back to retrieve it while Faringer lay slumped in the back seat, singing a rude song for the scarcely amused but decidedly chastened driver.

As Maasleitner watched the taxi's rear lights vanish round the corner by the printing works, he wondered how on earth Enso Faringer would be able to summon up the strength to face his classes the next day.

As far as he was concerned that was no longer a consideration that he needed to take into account, and thanks to the alcohol flowing sweetly through his veins he suddenly had the feeling that, despite everything, all was well with the world. A nice, comfortable lie-in was in store for him next morning, and then perhaps a little excursion. To Weimarn? Why not? Provided the weather turned out to be reasonable, of course.

It wasn't too bad at the moment. The rain had died away. A warm, gentle breeze caressed its way through the town, and as he slowly began to wander through the familiar, narrow alleys that would lead him home to Weijskerstraat, he had the strong impression that there was not really much point in worrying about the future.

As if to confirm this feeling, at about the same time a lone figure emerged from the dark shadows enveloping the Keymer church a little further down the same street.

It followed him about thirty paces behind; discreetly and silently, over the rounded cobbles, over Wilhems-graacht, into Weijskerstraat and right up to the front door, which Maasleitner was somewhat surprised to find was standing ajar, and that there appeared to be some-thing wrong with the lock. Despite his euphoric state, he paused for a few moments to mutter away about the circumstances – while his pursuer waited patiently in another doorway diagonally over the narrow street. Then Maasleitner shrugged, stepped inside and took the lift up to the fourth floor.

He hadn't been home for long, hadn't even had time to get undressed, when there was a ring at the door. The clock over the cooker in the kitchen said a few minutes past mid-night, and as he went to open up he wondered who on earth it could be, visiting him at this time of night.

Then it dawned on him that it must be Enso Faringer, whose drunken high had doubtless enabled him to come up with some crazy idea or other; and there was a tolerant smile on his lips as he opened the door.

Some sixteen hours later his seventeen-year-old daughter opened that same door, and if only the circumstances had not been so grotesque, it would probably have still been perfectly possible to see the traces of that smile on his face.

FIVE

1–7 FEBRUARY

13

'So there's no doubt, then?' said Heinemann.

'Not really,' said Münster. 'Same ammunition – 7.65 millimetre. The technical boys were more or less certain that it was the same weapon, but we won't know that for sure until tomorrow.'

'Two bullets in the chest, two under the belt,' said Rooth, looking at the photograph lying on the table in front of him. 'I'll be damned if it isn't the same thing all over again, more or less. A copy of Ryszard Malik.'

'Of course it's the same culprit,' said Moreno. 'There hasn't been a word in the papers about the bullet under the belt.'

'Correct,' muttered Van Veeteren. 'Sometimes the muzzle we put on journalists actually works.'

He looked up from the document he was holding and had just read. It was a very provisional medical statement Miss Katz had popped in to hand over, and suggested that Rickard Maasleitner had probably died between eleven and twelve o'clock the previous night, and that the cause of death was a bullet that had penetrated the heart muscle. The other shots would not have brought about instant death; not taken one at a time, that is – possibly in combination, as a result of blood loss.

'A bullet in the heart,' said Van Veeteren, passing the sheet of paper on to Münster, who was sitting next to him.

'He didn't leave Freddy's until shortly after half past eleven,' said Moreno. 'It takes at least a quarter of an hour to walk to Weijskerstraat. The murderer can hardly have struck before midnight.'

'Between twelve and two, then,' said Rooth. 'Ah well, we'll have to find out if anybody saw anything.'

'Or heard,' said Heinemann.

Rooth stuck his index finger into his mouth, then withdrew it with a plopping sound.

'Did you hear that?' he asked. 'That's about as much noise as is made when you use a silencer. He must have done, or he'd have woken up the whole building.'

'OK,' said Heinemann. 'We'll assume that, then.'

Van Veeteren broke a toothpick in half and looked at the clock.

'Nearly midnight,' he said with a deep sigh. 'We might as well go home now and get some sleep but, so help me God, we'd better make some progress tomorrow. We have quite a few threads to pull at, this time round; and there's no reason why we should be left floundering. The sooner we solve this business, the better.'

He paused briefly, but nobody took advantage of the opportunity to speak. He could see in his colleagues' faces the same mixture of intense concentration and weariness that he could feel inside his own head. Best to rest for a few hours, no doubt about that. Besides, there wouldn't be much point in waking people up in the middle of the night to answer a few questions. The police had a bad enough reputation as it was: there was no need to make it any worse.

'This is what we'll do tomorrow,' said the chief inspector. 'Reinhart and deBries will continue interviewing the neighbours. The whole block, if there's time. I assume they're still at it now, and I suppose they might as well carry on. It could be that somebody has seen something – the murderer must have called round twice, for God's sake. Once to tamper with the lock, and once to kill. It might be that nobody noticed anything, but we'll have to see . . . Heinemann.'

'Yes.'

'I want you to dig into the background. We have details of the whole of Malik's life. Find out when his and Maasleitner's paths crossed. There must be a link.'

'Let's hope so,' said Heinemann.

'Münster and Rooth will take his family. Or rather, the family that used to be his. I have a list of them here. Moreno and Jung will go to the Elementar school . . .'

'Oh my God,' said Jung. 'That's the school I used to go to . . .'

Van Veeteren raised his eyebrows.

'When was that?' he asked.

Jung tried to work it out.

'Eighteen years ago,' he said. 'Just one term in the seventh class, then we moved house in the spring. I hardly recall a single teacher. I didn't have Maasleitner in any case.'

'A pity,' said Van Veeteren. 'Talk to the headmaster and some of the staff even so, but tread carefully. They're usually very wary of anybody who intrudes on a seat of learning like that. Remember what happened at Bunge?'

'I certainly do,' said Münster. 'Lie low, that's my advice.'

'I'll bear it in mind,' said Jung.

'But leave that Faringer character alone,' said Van Veeteren. 'I intend to have a little chat with him myself.'

'A bit of an oddball,' said Münster.

'Of course,' muttered Van Veeteren. 'All teachers are. If they're not odd to start with, they become so as the years go by.'

He rummaged in his empty breast pocket and looked round the room.

'Any questions?'

Rooth yawned, but nobody spoke.

'OK,' said the chief inspector and started collecting his papers together. 'We'll meet for a run-through at three o'clock tomorrow afternoon. Make sure you make the most of the time until then. This time we're going to get him.'

'Or her,' said Münster.

'Yes, yes,' said Van Veeteren. '*Cherchez la femme*, if you really must.'

When he got home and had gone to bed, he realized that his tiredness had not yet overcome the tension in his brain once and for all. The image of Rickard Maasleitner's bullet-ridden body kept cropping up in his mind's eye at regular intervals, and after ten minutes of vainly trying to fall asleep, he got up and went to the kitchen instead. Fetched a beer from the refrigerator and sat down in the armchair with a blanket round his knees and Dvořák in the loud-speakers. He allowed the darkness to envelop him, but instead of the unease and disgust he ought to have felt, in view of the two unsolved murders they were struggling with, another sensation altogether took possession of him.

It was a feeling of movement. Of hunting, in fact. The feeling that the drive had begun now, and that the prey was somewhere out there in the hustle and bustle of town, and it was only a matter of time before he would be able to get his teeth into it. Bring down the murderer.

Oh, shit! he thought as he took a swig at his beer. I'm beginning to lose the plot. If I weren't a police officer I'd probably have become a murderer instead.

It was only a random thought, of course, but nevertheless, somewhere in some obscure corner of his brain, he realized that there was more meaning in it than would be sensible to acknowledge. It had something to do with the concept of the hunt . . .

In the beginning, at least.

Only in the beginning, if truth be told. Somewhere along the line came the peripeteia, the volte face, and when he eventually – usually much, much later – stood there with his prey, with the perpetrator, what generally possessed him were exclusively feelings of loathing and disgust. The excitement – the stimulation – was only theoretical.

And in the beginning.

For when you had dug down sufficiently deep into dire reality, his stream of thought told him, when you had dug down as deep as the soil layer of the crime itself, all there was to see was of course the black and hopeless dregs. The causes. The maggot-ridden roots of warped society.

The back side.

Not that he believed the society in which he lived had higher or lower moral principles than any other. It was simply the way things were – two to three thousand years of culture and law-making bodies were unable to do anything about it. The veneer of civilization, or whatever you preferred to call it, could begin to crackle at any moment, crumble away and expose the darkness underneath. Some people might have imagined that Europe would be a protected haven after 1945, but Van Veeteren had never been one of them. And then things had turned out as they did. Sarajevo, Srebrenica, and all the rest of it.

And of course it was in the same underlying darkness that his own hunting instincts were based. In any case, he had always found it difficult to associate his police activities with any kind of noble deeds. Nemesis, rather. The inexorable goddess of revenge with blood on her teeth . . . Yes, that was more like it, there was no denying it.

And at some point, the game always turned deadly serious.

In this particular case it had taken two murders for him to begin to feel involved. Were his senses becoming duller, he wondered. What would he be like a few years from now? What would be needed by then to start the notorious Chief Inspector Van Veeteren firing on all cylinders?

Butchered women? Children?

Mass graves?

When would cynicism and world weariness have overcome his determination to fight once and for all? For how much longer would the moral imperative have the strength to continue screeching in the darkness of his soul?

Good questions. He felt his self-disgust rising and cut off the train of thought. No doubt it had been the contrary nature of January that had made him a little sluggish at the start. Now it was February. February the second, to be precise. What was this Maasleitner business all about?

He started thinking about what had happened that afternoon.

The alarm had sounded just as he was preparing to pack up for the day. Half past four. He and Münster had been at the flat in Weijskerstraat a quarter of an hour later, more or less at the same time as the forensic boys and the medical team. Rickard Maasleitner was lying in exactly the same posture as Ryszard Malik had been some . . . how long ago was it now? Two weeks, more or less? Yes, that was correct.

He had been convinced from the very first glance that it was the same killer. And that the method had been the same.

A ring on the doorbell, and then shots the moment the door opened.

A sound method, Rooth had said.

Most certainly. Once it was done, all that remained was to close the door and walk away. What sort of time was involved? Ten seconds? That would probably be long enough. You could fire four shots from a Berenger in half that time, if needs be.

He emptied his glass.

And then?

Well, then everything got under way, of course. Police tape round the crime scene, a thorough search, taking care of the poor daughter who had found him. And so on.

Questions.

Questions and answers. No end to it already. And yet it was just the beginning. As already stated.

But if one were to look a little more closely at the whole business, one thing stood out, of course. Only one so far, that is. There was an enormous difference between the risk involved in the two murders.

In the case of Malik, the chances of being seen were as minimal as it is possible to be; but yesterday, all it needed was for somebody to happen to go out with a rubbish bag, or to glance out through a half-open door.

It had been night time, of course; but even so.

Ergo:

Either there were witnesses. Or there weren't.

Perhaps, and this was much to be desired, somebody (or several people) had seen the killer on one of the two occasions when he must have visited the flats – while he was fiddling with the lock (because it must surely be the murderer who was responsible for that?), or when the shooting took place. Either on the way there or while leaving.

Or while he was standing waiting?

A case of either–or, then. If Reinhart and deBries did their job properly, we should know tomorrow. And even if the neighbours, or Reinhart and deBries, had missed something, there was still a good chance of striking lucky. A press release had been issued at ten o'clock, and would be in all the main newspapers and in the radio and television news bulletins in the morning. Everybody who thought they might have some relevant information, or had merely been in the Weijskerstraat area around midnight on Wednesday evening, was urged to get in touch with the police immediately.

So there were grounds for hope.

Having come thus far in his deliberations, Van Veeteren gave in to temptation and lit a cigarette. It was time to address the big question, and that would no doubt need a bit of extra effort.

Why?

Why in hell's name should anybody march up to somebody's door, ring the bell and shoot whoever opened it?

What was the motive?

What was the link between Ryszard Malik and Rickard Maasleitner?

And furthermore: what would have happened if somebody else had opened the door? Could the murderer be one hundred per cent certain who it would be? Was it all the result of meticulous planning, or was coincidence involved?

There's no such thing as coincidence, Reinhart had once said, and that was no doubt basically true. Nevertheless, there was a hell of a difference between some causes and others. Between some motives and others.

Why had Malik and Maasleitner been singled out by the murderer?

Dvořák fell silent, and Van Veeteren could feel the weariness behind his eyes now. He stubbed out his cigarette and heaved himself up out of the armchair. Switched off the CD player and went to bed. The blood-red digital numbers on the clock radio showed 02.21, and he realized that he had less than five hours' sleep to look forward to.

Ah well, he'd been through worse in the past, and no doubt would be faced with worse situations in the future as well.

When Detective Inspector Reinhart snuggled down under the covers on his big iron-frame bed, the night had ticked its way through twenty more red minutes; but even so, he considered phoning Miss Lynch and asking her if she felt like popping over. In order to exchange a few words, if nothing else; and to remind her that he loved her.

However, something – he was confident it had to do with his good character and upbringing – restrained him from submitting to his desires, and instead he lay for a while thinking about their efforts during the course of the evening, and the way in which people seemed to notice nothing of what was happening round about them.

Or their stupidity, as some people would doubtless have expressed it.

In any case, a lack of awareness. In the old, well-maintained 1930s block of flats where Rickard Maasleitner lived, there were no less than seventy-three inhabitants. In flats off the relevant staircase – 26B – there were seventeen tenants at home at the time of the murder, in addition to the victim himself. At least eight of those had been awake when the murderer fired the fatal shots (assuming that the incident took place before one in the morning). Five of those had been on the same floor. One had come home at ten minutes to twelve.

Nobody had noticed anything at all.

As for the front door lock, which the murderer had sabotaged by jamming a piece of metal between the bolt and the drum, at least three persons had noticed that there was something amiss, but none of them had done anything about it, or drawn any conclusions.

Stupid idiots! Reinhart thought.

Then again, of course, he knew that this was not an entirely fair judgement. He himself hadn't the slightest idea what his neighbours got up to of an evening – he hardly knew what they were called, never mind anything else – but after seven hours of interrogation, and with so many possible witnesses among them, one would surely have been justified in expecting a rather more positive outcome.

Or any outcome at all, to be honest.

But there had not been any.

What was pretty clear, however, was the time sequence. The front door of Weijskerstraat 26 was locked automatically at 22.00 every evening. In order to tamper with the lock in the way the murderer had done, he (or she, as Winnifred Lynch maintained) must have waited until after that time; presumably somewhere inside the building. And then, when the automatic locking took place, he or she must have calmly opened the door from the inside and inserted the piece of metal. The alternative was that the murderer must have stood hidden somewhere in the shrubbery outside the front door, and slipped in when one of the residents went in or came out. A pretty risky operation, and hence not very likely, as deBries and Reinhart had agreed.

What the murderer did after that was impossible to say, of course; but when Maasleitner came home at about midnight after his night out with Faringer, he (or she) had presumably wasted no time hanging around. Everything suggested that Maasleitner hadn't been at home for more than a few minutes before the doorbell rang.

And then four bullets. Two in the chest, and two below the belt. Exactly the same as the previous occasion. Close the door and melt away. And no witnesses.

Good God, thought Reinhart with a shudder. It was so simple, enough to make you afraid of the dark.

Nevertheless he stretched out his arm and switched off the light. And as he did so remembered that there were a couple of straws to grasp. Two of the flat owners had been at home during the night in question, but had not been available for interview. What is more, one of them – a certain Mr Malgre – lived next door to Maasleitner; and for want of anything better, Reinhart made up his mind to attach his best hopes for the next day's interviews to the one with him. This was scheduled for midday, when Malgre would be back from a conference in Aarlach. DeBries was due to interrogate him.

Now, if Malgre was the type used to attending conferences, Reinhart thought, he was bound to be a person with a high level of awareness. Not your usual thickie.

As he registered that idea, the usual flag of protest was raised in the back of his mind, condemning such prejudiced thoughts. But his exhaustion had the upper hand. Reinhart sighed, turned onto his side and fell asleep.

By that time the minutes had ticked their way forward to 03.12, and all evening and subsequent night he hadn't devoted a single second to thinking about the motive.

That would have to wait until tomorrow.

He'd been working today. Tomorrow he would start using his brains.

14

Baushejm was only a few stone's throws away from the suburb where Münster lived, and he drove straight there on the Friday morning, if for no other reason than to save time. Wanda Piirinen (formerly Maasleitner) had a job to do – she was a secretary at one of the town's most reputable law firms – and despite the murder of her ex-husband, she had no intention of taking any more leave than necessary. Half a day, to be precise.

The children – three of them, aged seventeen (the girl who had found her father murdered the previous day), thirteen and ten – had been allowed an extended weekend, and when Münster was shown into the well-kept villa, they had just been collected by an aunt, and would be spending at least two days with her and their cousins out at Dikken.

'We divorced eight years ago,' explained Wanda Piirinen. 'It was not a good marriage, and relations have not improved since then. I don't have any feelings, although I know I ought to have.'

'You have three children together,' said Münster, devoting a rapid thought to his own two.

She nodded and gestured towards the coffee pot on the table. Münster poured himself a cup.

'That's the only reason why we still remain in contact. Or used to, perhaps I should say.'

Münster took a sip of coffee and observed her covertly over the edge of his cup. An elegant lady, that was for sure. Round about forty-five, he thought; fit-looking and sun-tanned despite the time of year, but also displaying signs of ruthlessness which she had difficulty in concealing.

Perhaps she doesn't want to, Münster thought. Perhaps she wants her independence and strength to be noticed immediately. To deter men from getting any inappropriate ideas or taking liberties. Her thick, ash-blonde hair was skilfully plaited, and her make-up seemed to be fastidious and understated. He guessed that she spent rather a long time at the dressing table every morning. Her nails were long and well-manicured, and it was a little difficult to believe that she had been solely responsible for bringing up three children. On the other hand, of course, this is what people working in a law firm should look like – efficiency and well-directed energy radiated from her like an aura, and he realized that he would have to deal with what Reinhart generally called a modern woman.

Or possibly post-modern?

'Well?' she said, and he became aware that he had lost himself in thought.

'Describe him!' he said.

'Rickard?'

'Yes, please.'

She gave him a searching look.

'I don't think I want to.'

'Why not?'

'I would only have negative things to say. It doesn't seem appropriate for me to disclose my feelings about my former husband when he has just been murdered. Please excuse me.'

Münster nodded.

'I understand. How was contact with the children? Between him and the children, I mean.'

'Bad,' she said, after a moment's hesitation. 'At first they used to go and stay with him occasionally. Every other weekend, and sometimes during the week. We live in the same town, after all. It ought to have been a practical possibility to arrange something along those lines, but after a year I realized that it would be better for them to live with me all the time. They needed a home, not two homes.'

'Did he protest?' Münster asked.

'Not really. Just a little bit, for appearances' sake. He no doubt thought it was a bit of a nuisance, having them in his house. That is . . . was . . . his attitude towards quite a lot of people.'

'What do you mean?'

'I'm sure you understand. If you talk to some of his colleagues, you will soon get a clear idea about that. And his friends, always assuming that he has any left . . .'

'We shall do that, of course,' said Münster.

He looked around the modern fitted kitchen. There was very little to show that four people must have recently had breakfast there, but no doubt there are painless routines for that kind of thing, he assumed.

Why am I feeling so aggressive? he wondered, slightly surprised. What's the matter with me?

He had managed to find time to make love to Synn, take a shower and have breakfast before leaving home, so he ought not to be so irritated. Surely she wasn't all that dangerous?

'What do you think about it?' he asked.

'About the murder?'

'Yes.'

She leant back and gazed out of the window.

'I don't know,' she said, and for the first time there was a trace of doubt in her voice. 'A lot of people don't like Rickard, that is no secret; but that anybody would want to murder him . . . No, I'd never have thought that.'

'Why didn't people like him?'

She thought for a moment, searching for the right words.

'He could see no further than himself,' she said. 'Contemptuous of everybody and everything that didn't suit his taste. Or didn't fit in with his way of thinking.'

'And what was that?'

'Excuse me?'

'His way of thinking.'

She hesitated slightly again.

'I think it can be traced back to his upbringing,' she said. 'He was an only child from the age of ten onwards. He had an elder brother who drowned at the age of fourteen. After that, his parents devoted all their care and attention to Rickard, but they were totally blind to the fact that he might have any faults or shortcomings. Yes, that was the basis of it all, of course.'

'Why did you marry him?' Münster asked, wondering if he might be being impertinent.

But she smiled for the first time.

'Feminine weakness,' she said. 'He was handsome and I was young.'

She took a sip of coffee, and sat for a few moments with the cup in her hand.

'He was overflowing with manly attributes,' she said eventually. 'They are best in the early stages. By the age of forty they have somehow changed. I hope you don't mind my saying that.'

'Not at all,' said Münster. 'I'm forty-three. But that isn't what we should be talking about. You don't have any suspicions, I take it?'

She shook her head.

'And he hasn't mentioned anything?'

'No. But we very rarely talked to one another. A telephone call once a week, perhaps. He had a life of his own.'

'What was your daughter doing there? When she found him, that is.'

'She'd gone to fetch some books. She was the one most in touch with him. They could talk to each other, I think, and her school is only a couple of blocks away from Weijskerstraat. She used to go there to study sometimes. When she had a free period, for instance.'

'And she had a key?'

Wanda Piirinen nodded.

'Yes. It's worst for her, that's for sure. It'll take time . . . A pity she should have to be the one who found him as well.'

She bit her lip.

'Please be gentle with her, if you have to interview her several times. She didn't sleep much last night.'

Münster nodded.

'We talked to her quite a lot yesterday. A smart girl.'

Suddenly Wanda Piirinen had tears in her eyes, and he wondered if he had misjudged her slightly. He felt it was about time to take his leave.

'Just one more thing,' he said. 'Ryszard Malik – does that name mean anything to you?'

'He's the one who was shot on the previous occasion, isn't he?'

'Yes.'

She shook her head.

'No,' she said. 'I've never heard the name before, I'm quite sure.'

'OK, many thanks,' said Münster, rising to his feet. 'I hope you'll get in touch if you think of anything you consider might be of interest to us.'

'Of course.'

She showed him out. For some reason she remained in the doorway until he had clambered into his car in the street outside. When he started the engine, she raised her hand as a sort of farewell gesture before disappearing into the house.

That's that then, Münster thought. Another insight into another life. And as he did a U-turn in the deserted sub-urban street, he suddenly felt something dark and sombre stick its claws into him.

'Hell and damnation,' he muttered. It must be something to do with the time of year . . .

'Fired!' said Jung. 'Can you believe that he was actually in the process of being fired? For Christ's sake, I thought it was impossible for a teacher to get the boot!'

They were in the car again, on the way back to the police station. The visit to the Elementar school had taken up three hours of their time, but the outcome was not bad at all. After a short introductory conversation with Greitzen, the headmaster, they had spent most of the time with the school's so-called staff-welfare group – three women and three men – and the picture of Rickard Maasleitner that had emerged was undoubtedly a colourful one.

He was evidently one of those pedagogues who should have chosen a different career. That was soon clear to Jung. A job in which he didn't have such good opportunities to take advantage of his position of power. To use and misuse his power.

The incidents in December had not been the first ones. By no means. Maasleitner's twenty-five-year teaching career had been littered with similar intermezzos. What had kept him in his job were *esprit de corps*, misguided solidarity on the part of colleagues, interventions by school leaders and others; but it was crystal clear that many people were sick and tired of him. Not to say everybody.

'There are two types of teacher,' a hardened and chain-smoking counsellor had explained. 'Those who solve conflicts, and those who create them. Unfortunately, Maasleitner belonged to the latter category.'

'Belonged to?' a gently ironic but confidence-inspiring female language teacher had commented. 'He was their uncrowned king. He could hardly walk across the school playground without stirring up trouble. He could pick an argument with the flagpole.'

Moreno had wondered if Maasleitner had enjoyed any kind of support from the staff even so, and what the outcome of his suspension would have been, if it had progressed to a natural conclusion, as it were. Needless to say the problem had been discussed in the staff-welfare group – whose function and remit were to deal with delicate matters like the problems caused by Maasleitner – and there was a surprisingly firm agreement that they would have let it take its natural course. They would have left Maasleitner to dig his own way out of the hole he had created himself, as best he could.

That indubitably said quite a lot about the situation. And about Maasleitner.

'But he must surely have had a few allies?' Jung had suggested.

But not a single name was mentioned. Perhaps that was a way of presenting a united front, it had occurred to Jung afterwards. Perhaps it was only natural. But then again, it was rather odd. Maasleitner had just been murdered, after all . . . Don't speak ill of the dead, and all that. But here the opposite seemed to be the case.

Terrible, he thought. If the people you have been working with every day – in some cases for more than twenty years – had nothing but shit to throw at a man lying helpless on the ground, well . . . It indicated that he hadn't been anybody's favourite, that was definite.

They had spoken to some of the pupils as well. Six of them, to be precise; one at a time. These somewhat younger witnesses displayed rather more consideration and respect for the dead. To be sure, Maasleitner had been a pain: but it was going over the top for somebody to go and shoot him. Kick him – yes! Kill him – no, no! As one young man put it. A couple of the girls had even tried hard to find the odd nice thing to say about him, although their efforts gave the distinct impression of being rather strained and forced.

He was knowledgeable, and sometimes fair, he didn't have any particular favourites – those were among the good qualities they mentioned. (In other words, he thought just as badly about all of them, Jung thought to himself.)

In the end they had gone back to the headmaster's study

again. He served them coffee and wondered if they needed any further information – and hoped that if so, they could arrange to dig deeper outside school hours.

Neither Moreno nor Jung thought they had much more to ask about at this stage. Apart from what could have caused his murder and who did it, of course; but the headmaster had merely shaken his head in response to that.

'You mean, can I think of anybody who would want to eliminate him? No. I assume you are not looking for a young murderer. Our oldest pupils are sixteen years of age. I can't imagine that any member of staff would . . . No, that's out of the question. He wasn't exactly well liked, but it's completely out of the question.'

'What do you think?' asked Moreno as they waited at a red light down by Zwille.

'Well,' said Jung, 'I wouldn't like to be the headmaster and need to say a few words at the funeral. Good Lord no.'

'It's wrong to tell lies in church,' said Moreno.

'Exactly.'

'And Malik doesn't seem to have had any connection with the school at all. No, I think we can leave them in peace and let them get on with their studies.'

Jung said nothing for a while.

'How about going for lunch somewhere instead?' he said as the police station loomed up in front of them. 'There's two hours to go before our meeting.'

Ewa Moreno hesitated.

'OK,' she said. 'At least they won't have us getting in the way if we do that.'

DeBries started the tape recorder even before Alwin Malgre had settled down in the visitor's chair.

deB: Welcome, Mr Malgre. I'd like to ask you a few questions about Wednesday evening.

M: So I understand.

deB: So, your name is Alwin Malgre, and you live at Weijskerstraat 26B?

M: That's correct.

deB: Would you mind speaking a bit louder, please?

M: Why?

deB: I'm recording our conversation on this tape recorder.

M: Oh . . .

deB: Anyway. I take it you are aware that a murder was committed in the block of flats where you live at some time between midnight and one in the morning last Wednesday night?

M: Maasleitner, yes. It's terrible.

deB: Your flat is next door to his, I understand. Can

you please tell me what you were doing the
night before last?

M: Er, let me see . . . Yes, I was at home, reading . . .

deB: Do you live alone in the flat?

M: Yes, of course.

deB: And you didn't have any visitors?

M: No.

deB: Please go on.

M: I was at home reading all evening. Swotting,
perhaps I should say. I had to attend that seminar
because Van Donck didn't have time—

deB: Who's Van Donck?

M: My boss, of course.

deB: What is your work, and what exactly was this
conference? Is that where you were yesterday?

M: Yes, in Aarlach. I work at the Stamp Centre. Van
Donck is my boss . . . Well, there's just the two
of us in the firm. You could say that I'm his
assistant.

deB: You sell postage stamps, is that right?

M: And buy. Are you interested in philately, Mr . . .
Mr . . . ?

deB: DeBries. No. What was this conference all about?

M: More of a seminar, really. Seminar and auction.
About the problems resulting from the collapse
of the Soviet Union. This time it was mainly the

stamps issued by the Baltic states that we were discussing. I don't know if you realize the chaos that has been caused in philately by the formation of all these new states . . . It's a gold mine for us as well, of course, depending on how speculative you want to be.

deB: Naturally. Anyway, we can go into that some other time. Wednesday evening, if you wouldn't mind.

M: Well, I don't know what to say. I came home at half past six or thereabouts. Had my evening meal and started reading. Had a cup of tea at about half past nine, I should think it was . . . Watched the nine o'clock news on the telly as well, of course. Well, and then I suppose I sat up until about half past eleven, roughly.

deB: So you were asleep from half past eleven, is that right?

M: No, I carried on reading until about a quarter to one. In bed, that is. Van Donck had acquired two new books that same afternoon, and obviously I didn't want to go to Aarlach under-prepared. I'd have a bit of time on the train as well, naturally, but . . .

deB: Did you notice anything?

M: Excuse me?

deB: Did you notice anything unusual during the
evening?

M: No.

deB: You didn't hear anything around midnight?

M: No . . . No, I was in bed by then. The bedroom
faces the courtyard.

deB: So you didn't notice when Mr Maasleitner came
home?

M: No.

deB: Nothing else around that time either?

M: No.

deB: Do you usually hear noises from inside
Maasleitner's flat?

M: No, the building is extremely well insulated.

deB: We've gathered that. Were you well acquainted
with your neighbour?

M: Maasleitner, you mean?

deB: Yes.

M: No, not at all. We said hello if we bumped into
each other on the stairs, but that's all.

deB: I understand. Is there anything else you saw or
heard that you think might be connected with
the murder?

M: No.

deB: Nothing you noticed that you think we ought to
know about?

M: No – what are you referring to?

deB: Anything at all. Something unusual that has happened recently, for instance?

M: No . . . no, I can't think of anything.

deB: You don't know if Maasleitner had any visitors these last few days?

M: No, I've no idea. You'd better ask the other neighbours. I'm not all that observant . . .

deB: We can't very well expect you to be. Anyway, many thanks, Mr Malgre. If anything occurs to you, please get in touch with us without delay.

M: Of course. Thank you very much. That was most interesting.

Extremely productive, deBries thought after Malgre had left the room. He lit a cigarette, stood by the window and gazed out over the town.

Three hundred thousand people, he thought. There sometimes seemed to be pretty high walls between all of them. While one of them gets shot and killed, his neighbour is in bed ten metres away, reading up on Estonian postage stamps.

But that's no doubt what was meant by the concept of privacy.

★

It took Van Veeteren about a minute to discover that having lunch while reconstructing what had happened was not a good idea. When he entered Freddy's bar and restaurant through the low door, Enso Faringer was already sitting at their reserved table, and his nervousness was obvious from a distance.

Van Veeteren sat down and produced a pack of cigarettes: Faringer took one and dropped it on the floor.

'So,' the chief inspector began, 'we might as well have a bite to eat, seeing as we're sitting here.'

'Sounds good.'

'So this is where you spent Wednesday evening, is it?'

Faringer nodded and adjusted his spectacles, which evidently had a tendency to slide down his shiny nose.

'I understand you are a German teacher.'

'Yes,' said Faringer. 'Somebody has to be.'

Van Veeteren was not sure if that was meant as a joke or not.

'You presumably knew Maasleitner well?'

'Er . . . not really, no.'

'But you used to meet, I gather?'

'Only sporadically. We'd go out for a beer now and then.'

'Such as last Wednesday?'

'Yes, like last Wednesday.'

Van Veeteren said nothing for a while in order to give

Faringer an opportunity of saying something off his own bat; but it was a waste of time. His eyes were moving ceaselessly behind his thick glasses, he was wriggling and squirming in his chair and fiddling with the knot of his tie.

'Why are you so nervous?'

'Nervous?'

'Yes. I have the impression you're frightened of something.'

Faringer emitted a very short laugh.

'No, I'm always like this.'

Van Veeteren sighed. The waiter came with the menu and they spent a few minutes perusing it before deciding on today's special.

'What did you talk about on Wednesday?'

'I can't remember.'

'What do you mean?'

'I don't recall. We had a bit too much to drink, and I often get these black holes in my memory.'

'But you must remember something, surely?'

'Yes, I know that Maasleitner asked me about the situation at school. He was in a bit of a mess. He asked me to help him.'

'How?'

Faringer scratched at his neck, where he had some kind of a rash.

'Oh, I don't know. Keep my eyes open, I assume.'

'He didn't ask you to take the initiative?'

'The initiative? No. How would I be able to take the initiative?'

No, Van Veeteren thought. That would be out of the question, of course. Enso Faringer wasn't the type to take initiatives.

The lunch lasted for forty-five minutes, despite the fact that Van Veeteren cancelled dessert and coffee; and by the time he sat down in the driving seat of his car, he was convinced of one thing. Faringer had been telling the truth. The little German teacher had no recollection of the measures he and Maasleitner had drawn up to save the world during the evening of the murder. Van Veeteren had also talked to the staff at Freddy's, and nobody found it the least bit strange that the 'little Kraut' had lost his memory. On the contrary.

It had simply been one of those evenings.

So that was that, Van Veeteren thought. Deep down he was also rather grateful – having to sit there and listen to Enso Faringer's account of a whole evening of drunken rambling would hardly have constituted an unmissable experience.

When he was about halfway back to the police station he found himself with something else to think about. It had started raining again, and it was clear that if he didn't do something about replacing that damned windscreen wiper as soon as possible, something nasty was likely to happen.

But then again, he knew that the moment he did something about replacing a broken part, something else would break.

His car was like that, that's all there was to it.

A bit reminiscent of life itself.

15

'Why did you give Heinemann the job of sifting the background?' wondered Reinhart. 'I mean, he needs a week in order to have a shit.'

'Could be,' said Van Veeteren. 'But at least he's meticulous. Let's start without him. Somebody pour out the coffee. Miss Katz promised to serve us something tasty.'

'Sounds good,' said Rooth.

'Let's start with the scientific guff,' said the chief inspector, distributing a set of photocopies. 'I don't think you'll find anything sensational there.'

The seven detectives present each read through the brief reports from the pathologist and the forensic team (apart from Van Veeteren, who had already digested them, and Reinhart, who preferred to fill his pipe), and the consensus was that, sure enough, they didn't contain anything new. Generally speaking, they merely confirmed what was already known – cause of death, time of death (now made more precise, assigned to the period 23.45–01.15), the weapon (a 7.65 millimetre Berenger, 99 per cent certainly the same gun used for the murder of Ryszard Malik). No fingerprints had been found, no trace of anything unusual; the piece of metal used to jam the lock was made of stainless steel, available all over the place and impossible to trace.

'All right,' said Van Veeteren. 'Let's record the crap, so that Hiller can use it as a lullaby to send him into dreamland over the weekend.'

He started the tape recorder.

'Run-through of the case Rickard Maasleitner, Friday, 2 February, 3.15 p.m. Those present: Van Veeteren, Münster, Rooth, Reinhart, Moreno, deBries and Jung. Reinhart and deBries first.'

'Pass,' said Reinhart.

'We've got nowhere,' deBries explained. 'We've interviewed over seventy people at number 26 and the building opposite. Nobody's seen or heard a squeak. The light over the front door of 26B had fused, by the way, so it would have been hard to get an image of the murderer anyway.'

'Did he smash that as well?' asked Moreno.

'Probably not, but it's hard to say. It's been out of order for the past six days.'

'Nothing else?' asked Van Veeteren.

'No,' said Reinhart. 'The transcripts of the interrogations

are at your disposal if you want something guaranteed to send you to sleep over the weekend.'

'Good,' said Van Veeteren. 'Well done, everybody.'

'Thank you,' said deBries.

The rest of the meeting proceeded in more or less the same way. As far as the character and general reputation of the deceased were concerned, a number of reports came up with the same conclusion. Rickard Maasleitner was a shit. A bully and a self-centred know-all of the very worst sort, it seemed. Even so, it was difficult to see that anybody would have had sufficient cause to kill him. As far as was known he hadn't had any affairs – indeed, it was not at all clear if he'd had a single relationship with a woman since his divorce eight years ago. He might possibly have resorted to prostitutes occasionally, but this was pure speculation that couldn't be confirmed or disproved. He had no debts. No commitments. No shady deals.

And nobody had been close to him.

His former wife had nothing positive to say about him, nor had anybody else. His children were naturally a bit shocked; but any sorrow they may have felt would no doubt be able to be assuaged successfully, according to both amateur and professional diagnoses.

Both Rickard Maasleitner's parents were dead, and one

could be forgiven for thinking that his last real ally had been buried three years ago, in the shape of his mother.

'A right bastard!' was Reinhart's summary of the victim's character. 'He seems to have been so awful, it would have been interesting to meet him.'

Van Veeteren switched off the tape recorder.

'A good finishing line,' he explained.

'Wouldn't it be possible to track down the weapon?' Jung asked.

Van Veeteren shook his head.

'DeBries, tell the assembled masses how one goes about getting hold of a gun. You've been looking into this.'

'By all means,' said deBries. 'Pretty straightforward, in fact. You get in touch with somebody who gives the impression of being just outside the reach of the law – some seedy-looking type hanging around Central Station or Grote Square, for instance. You say you need a gun. He tells you to wait, and a quarter of an hour later he comes back with an envelope. You slip him a hundred guilders for his services, then you go home and open the envelope. The instructions are inside. You have to send money – let's say a thousand guilders – to a poste restante address. Müller, General Post Office, Maardam, for instance. You do as bidden, and a week or so later you receive a letter with a key inside it. It's for a safe-deposit box at Central Station.

You go there, open the box, and – hey presto! – you find a little box containing a gun . . .'

'Then all you need to do is get off your arse and start killing,' said Van Veeteren.

'A sound method,' said Rooth again.

'Devilishly clever,' said Reinhart. 'But we have to assign Stauff or Petersén to the job of looking into that. Just to be sure.'

Van Veeteren nodded. He reached over the table and took a cigarette out of deBries's pack.

'And what are the rest of us supposed to do then?' asked Münster.

'Jung,' said the chief inspector, when he'd finally managed to light his cigarette. 'Could you go and search for Heinemann. It'll be a right cock-up if we can't nurse a single gee-gee over the winning line today.'

'Sure,' said Jung, rising to his feet. 'Where is he?'

Van Veeteren shrugged.

'Somewhere in the building, I assume. In his office, if you're lucky.'

Ten minutes later Jung returned with Heinemann in tow.

'Sorry,' said Heinemann, flopping down onto the empty chair. 'I was a bit delayed.'

'You don't say,' said Reinhart.

Heinemann put a large envelope on the table in front of him.

'What have you got there?' asked Münster.

'The connection,' said Heinemann.

'What do you mean?' wondered Rooth.

'I was supposed to look for the connection, wasn't I?'

'Well, I'll be damned!' said deBries.

Heinemann opened the envelope and took out an enlarged photograph. He handed it to Van Veeteren.

The chief inspector studied it for a few seconds, looking bewildered.

'Explain,' he said eventually.

'Of course,' said Heinemann, taking off his glasses. 'The photograph is of the leaving class – that really is what they call it – from the United Services Staff College in 1965. Third from the left in the bottom row is Ryszard Malik. Second from the right in the middle row is Rickard Maasleitner.'

You could have heard a pin drop. Van Veeteren passed round the photograph of thirty-five formally dressed young men in grey-green military shirts with innocent expressions on their faces.

'1965, did you say?' asked Münster when everybody had seen it.

'Yes,' said Heinemann. 'They were called up in April '64, and left at the end of May '65. Anyway, that's what

I've found . . . Apart from the fact that they have the same initials, of course, but I expect you've thought about that?'

'What?' said Rooth. 'My God, you're right! . . .'

'R.M.,' said Reinhart. 'Hmm, I don't suppose it means anything.'

'Have you got the names of all of them?' asked Van Veeteren.

Heinemann dug down into the envelope and produced a sheet of paper.

'Just the names and dates of birth so far, but Krause and Willock are working on that. It'll take a while, as you'll appreciate.'

'The main thing is that it's done scrupulously,' said Reinhart.

Silence again. Münster stood up and walked over to the window, turning his back on the others. Van Veeteren leant back and sucked in his cheeks. Moreno took another look at the photograph.

'Well,' said deBries after a while, 'this is worth thinking about, I reckon.'

'Presumably,' said Van Veeteren. 'We'll take a break now. I need to contemplate. Come back here half an hour from now, and then we can decide where to go from here. DeBries, can you let me have a cigarette?'

★

'Where exactly is this military college?' asked Moreno when they had reassembled.

'Up in Schaabe nowadays,' said Heinemann. 'It was moved from here in Maardam at the beginning of the seventies – it used to be out at Löhr.'

'Did you find any other connections?' Münster wondered.

'No, not yet. But I think this one is spot on. If there are any others, they will probably be further back in the past.'

'How should we go about this, then?' asked Rooth.

Van Veeteren looked up from the list of names.

'This is what we'll do,' he said, checking how many of them there were. 'There are eight of us. Each of us will take a share of the names and track them down over the weekend. It ought to be possible to find at least two out of four. You can check addresses and suchlike with Krause and Willock. They can distribute the names among you as well. On Monday morning I want comprehensive reports, and if you come across anything significant before then, get in touch.'

'Sound method,' said Reinhart.

'Exactly what I was going to say,' said Rooth. 'When will Krause and Willock be ready?'

'They'll be working all evening,' said Van Veeteren. 'Joensuu and Klempje have been roped in as well. You can all go home and then ring here and get your names tonight, or tomorrow morning. OK? Any questions?'

'One more thing, perhaps,' said Reinhart.

'Of course, dammit,' said Van Veeteren, tapping at the photograph with his index finger. 'Tread carefully. It's by no means certain that these are the ones we're looking for. Don't forget that!'

'Should we release this information to the general public?' Münster asked.

Van Veeteren thought for three seconds.

'I think we should be extremely careful not to do that,' he said eventually. 'Bear that in mind when you ask your questions as well – don't say too much about what's going on. I don't think Hiller would be too pleased if thirty-three people suddenly turned up and demanded police protection round the clock.'

'Mind you, it would be fun to see his face if they did,' said Reinhart.

'If they did,' said Van Veeteren.

Russian roulette? Münster thought as he was sitting with the kids on his knee an hour later, watching a children's programme on the telly. Why do the words Russian roulette keep coming into my head?

It could be a coincidence, of course, Van Veeteren thought
as he settled down in the bath with a burning candle on the
lavatory seat and a beer within easy reach. Pure coincidence, if Reinhart hadn't already banned that expression.
Two people living in the same town might well end up
sooner or later in the same photograph, whether they want
to or not.

Wasn't that more likely than their not doing so?

God only knows, Van Veeteren thought. In any case,
we'll find out eventually.

16

Saturday, 3 February began with warm south-westerly winds and a misleadingly high and bright sky. Van Veeteren had already made up his mind in principle to attend Ryszard Malik's funeral, but when he stood in the balcony doorway to check the weather situation at about nine o'clock, he realized that he also had the gods on his side.

Still standing there, he tried to establish what had led him to make that decision. Why he felt it was so necessary for him to be present at the burial ceremony in the Eastern Cemetery, that is. And, to his horror, it dawned on him that it was because of an old film. Or several films, rather. More specifically that classic introductory scene with a group of people dressed in black round a coffin that was being lowered slowly into a grave. And then, a short distance away, two detectives in their crumpled trench coats observing the mourners. They turn up their collars and begin a whispered conversation about who's who . . . Who is that lady with the veil, half turned away from the grave; why isn't the widow crying; and which of the bastards is it who pumped a bullet into the head of the stinking rich Lord ffolliot-Pym?

What reasoning! Van Veeteren thought as he closed the balcony door. Downright perverse! But then, there's nothing one won't do . . .

Out in the windswept cemetery later that day there seemed to be a distinct shortage of possible murderers. The one who behaved most oddly was without doubt a large man in a green raincoat and red rubber boots; but he had been instructed to attend by the chief inspector.

PC Klaarentoft was known as the force's most skilful photographer, and his task on this occasion was to take as many pictures as he possibly could. Van Veeteren knew that he had stolen this idea from another film, namely *Blow-Up* from the mid sixties. Antonioni, if he remembered rightly? The theory was, of course, that somewhere among all these faces, which would slowly emerge from the police photographic laboratory, would be the murderer's.

Ryszard Malik's and Rickard Maasleitner's murderer.

He recalled seeing the film – which was a pretty awful mish-mash – three times, simply to observe how the face of a killer could be plucked out of the lush greenery of an English park.

Another kind of perversion, of course, and Klaarentoft had evidently not seen the film. He traipsed around between the graves, snapping away to his heart's content, totally ignoring Van Veeteren's instruction to be as unobtrusive as possible.

The fact that he managed to take no less than twelve pictures of the clergyman conducting the ceremony suggested that he might not have grasped the point of his contribution.

On the other hand, of course, the group that followed Ryszard Malik to his final resting place was on the sparse side, so there was a shortage of motifs. Van Veeteren counted fourteen people present – including himself and Klaarentoft – and during the course of the ceremony he was able to identify all of them, apart from two children.

He was unable to detect furtive observers keeping some distance away from the grave (there were a few people tending other graves in the vicinity, of course, but none of them behaved strangely or alerted his famous intuition in the slightest), and when the rain started to fall and he had managed to give Klaarentoft discreet instructions to go away and snap something else, he had long been aware that there was not much point in his hanging around.

And an hour or so later, when he had finally managed to sink a glass of mulled wine at the Kraus bar, he realized that the cold he had succeeded in keeping at bay over the last few days had now got second wind.

The next funeral will be my own, he predicted.

*

'It's Saturday. Do you really have to do that today?' he had asked.

'Today or tomorrow. Don't you think it's best if I get it out of the way as soon as possible?'

'Yes, of course,' he'd replied and turned over in his bed. 'I'll see you this evening.'

It wasn't an especially unusual exchange. Nor unexpected. As she sat in the bus she felt a nagging pain at the back of her head, like a bad omen. She had been with Claus Badher for fifteen months now – maybe sixteen, it depended on what criteria you used – and it was probably the best relationship she'd ever been involved in. In fact, it certainly was. It involved love and mutual respect, shared values and interests, and everything else one could reasonably expect.

Everything in the garden was lovely. Pure bliss. All their friends thought they ought to take things further. Move in together permanently, with all that implied. Claus thought so too.

There was just that little irritation. That tiny little snag that frightened her. That might be rooted in contempt, despite everything, and if so was destined to grow and become even more worrying. She didn't know. Contempt for her job. Needless to say he was extremely careful not to make it obvious – probably didn't even realize it himself – but sometimes she couldn't help but notice. It just crept up on her, flashed briefly on the surface, then vanished; but she knew it was there. As in the little exchange they'd just had, for instance, which wasn't really significant in itself as yet . . . But she suspected it could grow into something really threatening as the years passed by.

A threat to their equal status. And to her life.

Claus Badher worked as a foreign exchange broker in a bank, and was on his way up. She worked as a detective inspector and was on the way . . . Where was she on the way to?

She sighed. At the moment she was on the way to a house in Dikken, where she was due to meet a fifty-two-year-old lawyer and ask him about his time as a National Serviceman.

Absurd? Of course it was absurd. She often thought that Claus was absolutely right. Always assuming that was what he was thinking, of course . . .

She got off the bus and walked the hundred metres or so to the house. Went in through the gate and was greeted by two enthusiastically barking and stumpy tail-wagging boxer puppies. She paused on the gravel path to stroke them. Looked up at the big two-storey house in dark brown English brick with green shutters. Behind one of the gable ends she could just make out a swimming pool, and some wire netting she assumed must be surrounding a tennis court.

Why not? she thought. If I really had to, I suppose I might manage to cope with living like this.

'Ewa Moreno, detective inspector. I'm sorry to trouble you. I just have a few questions I'd like to ask you.'

'No problem. I'm at your disposal.'

Jan Tomaszewski was wearing something she assumed must be a smoking jacket – and, indeed, the rest of him seemed to belong to another age. Or in a film. His dark hair was powdered and immaculately combed, and his slim body gave the distinct impression of being aristocratic. Leslie Howard? she wondered. He reached out over the smoke-grey glass table and served her tea from a charmingly sculpted silver pot.

Another world, she thought. I'd better get going before I swoon.

'Thank you,' she said. 'As I mentioned, I need to ask you about the time you spent during your National Service at the Staff College in Löhr. I think that was 1964 to '65 – is that right?'

He nodded.

'That's correct. Why on earth should you be interested in that?'

'I'm afraid I can't tell you that. And I'd appreciate it if you would be discreet about our conversation as well.

Perhaps we can meet again at a later stage if you want to know more.'

That was a formulation she had thought out in advance, and she could see that it had fallen on fruitful ground.

'I understand.'

'Anyway, we are mainly interested in a couple of your fellow students at the college. Ryszard Malik and Rickard Maasleitner.'

She took the photograph out of her briefcase and handed it to him.

'Can you point them out?'

He smiled and took a pair of glasses from his breast pocket. Scrutinized the photograph for some thirty seconds.

'Maasleitner isn't a problem,' he said. 'We were in the same barrack room nearly all the time. I'm not so sure about Malik, but I think that's him.'

He pointed and Moreno nodded.

'Correct. Can you tell me what you remember about them?'

Tomaszewski took off his glasses and leant back in his chair.

'I can hardly remember Malik at all,' he said after a while. 'We were never in the same group and we didn't mix when we were off duty. He was a bit introspective and pretty anonymous, I think. I should mention that I'm not completely unaware of what has happened . . .'

Moreno nodded.

'Do I take it that you think this is the link? The connection between the two of them, I mean?'

'We're following up several different lines of inquiry,' Moreno explained. 'This is just one of them. Obviously, we need to follow up every possibility.'

'Of course. Anyway, I recall Maasleitner in a bit more detail. We were frequently in the same class during training – telegraphy, general staff work and so on. I have to say I didn't much like him. He was a bit dominant, if you know what I mean.'

'How do you mean, dominant?' Moreno asked.

'Well . . .' Tomaszewski flung out his arms. 'Big mouthed. Young and arrogant. A bit unbalanced – but he probably wasn't all that bad.'

'Was he generally disliked?'

Tomaszewski thought that one over.

'I think so. Not that it was a real problem. It was just that he had something about him that could be a bit trying. But of course there's bound to be one or two like that in such a big group.'

'Did you mix at all when you were off duty?'

Tomaszewski shook his head.

'Never.'

'Do you know if Malik and Maasleitner did?'

'I've no idea. I wouldn't have thought so, but of course I can't swear to it.'

'Do you know if any of the others were close to them? To either one of them, that is?'

Tomaszewski studied the photograph again. Moreno produced a list of names and handed it to him. Drank a little tea and took a chocolate biscuit while he was thinking about it. Looked around the whitewashed walls, crammed full with rows of colourful, non-figurative paintings, almost edge-to-edge. Her host was evidently something of a collector. She wondered how much money was hanging here.

Quite a lot, most probably.

'Hmm,' he said eventually. 'I'm afraid I can't be of much help to you. I can't think of any link between them. I can't associate Malik with anybody else at all. I think Maasleitner occasionally hung around with them.'

He pointed to two faces in the back row.

'Van der Heukken and Biedersen?' Moreno read the names from her list.

Tomaszewski nodded.

'As far as I can recall. You realize that it's over thirty years ago?'

Moreno smiled.

'Yes,' she said. 'I realize that. But I understood that time

158

spent on National Service had an ineradicable effect on all young men who underwent it.'

Tomaszewski smiled.

'No doubt it did on some. But most of us try to forget all about it, as far as possible.'

Charming was the word that stuck in her mind after the visit to Tomaszewski. The discreet charm of the bourgeoisie, she recalled, and she had to admit that on the whole there were worse ways of spending an hour on a Saturday morning.

She had not expected her trip to Dikken to produce anything substantial for the investigation, and the same applied to the next name on her list: Pierre Borsens.

When she got off the bus in Maardam, she had succeeded in thrusting aside the morning's gloomy thoughts and made up her mind to call in at the covered market and buy a couple of decent cheeses for the evening meal. Pierre Borsens lived only a block away from the market, and it wasn't yet quite half past twelve.

The man who sat down at the table brought with him an aroma that Jung had some difficulty in identifying. It had the same crudely acidic quality as cat piss, but it also had an unmistakable tang of the sea. Rotten seaweed scorched by the sun, or something of the sort. Most probably it was a combination of both these ingredients.

And more besides. Jung hastily moved his chair back a couple of feet, and lit a cigarette.

'I take it you are Calvin Lange?' he asked.

'I certainly am,' said the man, reaching out a grubby hand over the table. Jung leant forward and shook it.

'My place is in a bit of a mess at the moment,' the man explained. 'That's why I thought it would be better to meet here.'

He smiled, and revealed two rows of brown, decayed teeth. Jung was grateful to hear what the man said. He would prefer not to have been confronted by the mess.

'Would you like a beer?' The question was rhetorical.

Lange nodded and coughed. Jung gestured towards the bar.

'And a cigarette, perhaps?'

Lange took one. Jung sighed discreetly and decided it was necessary to get this over with as quickly as possible. It was always problematical to arrange reimbursement for beer and cigarettes, that was something he'd discovered a long time ago.

'Do you recognize this?'

Lange took the photograph and studied it while drawing deeply on his cigarette.

'That's me,' he said, placing a filthy index finger on the face of a young, innocent man in the front row.

'We know that,' said Jung. 'Do you remember what those two are called?'

He pointed with his pen.

'One at a time,' said Lange.

The waitress arrived with two glasses of beer.

'Cheers,' said Lange, emptying his in one gulp.

'Cheers,' said Jung, pointing at the photograph again.

'Let's see,' said Lange, peering awkwardly. 'No, no fucking idea about him. Who else?'

Jung pointed at Maasleitner with his pen.

'Seems familiar,' said Lange, scratching his armpit. 'Yes, I recognize that bugger, but I've no idea what he's called.'

He belched, and looked gloomily at his empty glass.

'Do you remember the names Malik and Maasleitner?'

'Malik and . . . ?'

'Maasleitner.'

'Maasleitner?'

'Yes.'

'No, is that him?'

He plonked his finger on Malik.

'No, that's Malik.'

'Oh, shit. What have they done?'

Jung stubbed out his cigarette. This was going brilliantly.

'Do you remember anything at all from your year as a National Serviceman?'

'National Service? Why are you asking about that?'

'I'm afraid I can't go into that. But we're interested in these two people. Staff College 1965 – that's right, isn't it?'

He pointed again.

'Oh, shit,' said Lange, and had a coughing fit. 'You mean this picture is from the Staff College? Fuck me, I thought it was the handball team. But there were too many of 'em.'

Jung thought about this for three seconds. Then he returned the photograph to his briefcase and stood up.

'Many thanks,' he said. 'You're welcome to my beer as well.'

'If you twist my arm,' said Lange.

Mahler advanced a pawn and Van Veeteren sneezed.

'How are things? Under the weather again?'

'Just a bit, yes. I was out in the rain at the cemetery for a bit too long yesterday afternoon.'

'Stupid,' said Mahler.

'I know,' sighed Van Veeteren. 'But I couldn't just walk away. I'm rather sensitive about that kind of thing.'

'Yes, I know how you feel,' said Mahler. 'It was that Malik, I gather. How's the case going? They're writing quite a lot about it in the newspapers.'

'Badly,' said Van Veeteren.

'Have you found a link yet?'

Van Veeteren nodded.

'But I'm not sure it's the right one. Well, I suppose I am really . . . But that doesn't mean very much yet. You could say that I'm looking for a stone and I've found the market square.'

'Eh?' said Mahler.

Van Veeteren sneezed again.

'For Christ's sake,' he said. 'Looking for a star and I've found a galaxy, how about that? I thought you were supposed to be the poet.'

Mahler chuckled.

'I know what you mean,' he said. 'But isn't it an incident that you're looking for?'

Van Veeteren picked up his white knight and sat there for a few seconds, holding it in his hand.

'An incident?' he said, placing the knight on C4. 'Yes, that's probably not a bad guess. The problem is that such a lot is happening.'

'All the time,' said Mahler.

17

Of the three people eventually allocated to Inspector Münster, it turned out that one lived in central Maardam, one in Linzhuisen barely thirty kilometres away, and one down in Groenstadt, a journey of some two hundred kilometres. On the Saturday afternoon Münster conducted a short telephone interview with the latter – a certain Werner Samijn, who worked as an electrical engineer and didn't have much to say about either Malik or Maasleitner. He had lived in the same barrack room as Malik and remembered him most as a rather pleasant and somewhat reserved young man. He thought Maasleitner was a more cocksure type (if the inspector and the man's widow would excuse the expression), but they had never mixed nor got to know each other.

Number two on the list, Erich Molder, failed to answer the several phone calls Münster made to his house in Guyderstraat; but number three, Joen Fassleucht, agreed to meet Münster at the former's home late on Sunday afternoon.

Münster's son, Bart, aged six and a half, objected strongly to this arrangement, but after some discussion it was decided that Bart could go along in the car, provided he promised to stay in the back seat reading the *Monster* comic while his father carried out his police duties.

It was the first time Münster had agreed to anything of this nature, and as he sat in Fassleucht's living room nibbling at biscuits, he became aware that it did not have a particularly positive influence on his powers of concentration.

But perhaps that didn't matter so much on this occasion – it was hardly an important interrogation, he tried to convince himself. Fassleucht had mixed with Malik quite a lot during his National Service: they were both part of a group of four or five friends who occasionally went out together. Went to the cinema, played cards, or simply sat round the same table in the canteen and gaped at the goggle-box. After demob, all contact had ceased; and as for Maasleitner, all Fassleucht could do was to confirm the opinion expressed by Samijn the previous day.

Overbearing and rather cocky.

Münster had been apprehensive, of course, and when he returned to his car after about half an hour he saw immediately that Bart had disappeared.

A cold shudder ran down his spine as he stood on the pavement wondering what the hell he should do; and, of course, that was the intention. Bart's dishevelled head suddenly appeared in the back window – he had been lying on the floor hidden under a blanket – and his broadly grinning face left no doubt about the fact that he considered it an unusually successful joke.

'You really looked shit scared!' he announced in glee.

'You little bastard,' said Münster. 'Would you like a hamburger?'

'And a Coke,' said Bart.

Münster drove towards the centre in search of a suitable establishment for the provision of such goods, and decided that his son would have to grow several years older before it was appropriate to take him along on a similar assignment.

'There's an in-depth article about your case in the *Allgemejne* today,' said Winnifred Lynch. 'Have you read it?'

'No,' said Reinhart. 'Why should I do that?'

'They try to make a profile of the perpetrator.'

Reinhart snorted.

'You can only make a perpetrator profile in the case of a serial killer. And even then it's a decidedly dodgy method. But it sounds good in the press, of course. They can write and make up stories about murderers who don't exist. A green light for any fantasies you like. Much more fun than reality, naturally.'

Winnifred Lynch folded up the newspaper.

'Isn't it a serial killer, then?'

Reinhart looked hard at her over the edge of his book.

'If we go and take a bath I can tell you a bit more about it.'

'Good that you have such a big bath tub,' commented Winnifred ten minutes later. 'If I do take you on, it'll be because of the bath tub. So don't imagine anything else. OK?'

'The murderer?'

'Yes.'

'Well, I don't know,' said Reinhart, sinking down further into the bubbles. 'Of course it's possible that there's going to be a series, but it's almost impossible to judge after only two. And then, what kind of a series is it? Continue this series of numbers: 1, 4, . . . – then what? There are all kinds of possibilities.'

'And the former National Servicemen have nothing useful to say?'

Reinhart shook his head.

'I don't think so. Not the ones I spoke to in any case. But

the key might well be there somewhere, even so. It's so damned easy to hide something, if you want to. If there's something you don't want stirring up, then all you do is say nothing about it. It was thirty years ago, after all . . .'

He leant his head against the edge of the bath and thought for a while.

'It's going to be extremely difficult to solve this case, no matter what. If there are no more after these two, that is. There's a bit of difference in the work input, I can assure you.'

'What do you mean?'

Reinhart cleared his throat.

'Well, hypothetically. Let's say I make up my mind to kill somebody, anybody at all. I get up at three o'clock on a Tuesday morning. I get dressed in dark clothes, hide my face, go out and find a suitable place and wait. Then I shoot the first person to come past, and go home.'

'Using a silencer.'

'Using a silencer. Or I stab him with a knife. What chance is there of my being found out?'

'Not a lot.'

'Next to none. But if I do it even so, how many working hours do you think it costs the police? Compared with the hour it took me.'

Winnifred nodded. Stuck her right foot into Reinhart's armpit and started wiggling her toes.

'That's nice,' said Reinhart. 'When war breaks out, can't we just come here and lie like this?'

'By all means,' said Winnifred. 'But what about a motive? That's what you're getting at, I take it?'

'Exactly,' said Reinhart. 'It's because of this imbalance that we have to look for a motive. A single thought on the right lines can save thousands of working hours. So you can see why I'm such a trump card at the police station.'

She laughed.

'I can imagine it. But you haven't had that thought on the right lines in this case, is that it?'

'Not yet,' said Reinhart.

He found the soap and started lathering her legs.

'I think it's a wronged woman,' said Winnifred after a while.

'I know that's what you think.'

He thought for half a minute.

'Would you be able to fire those other two shots?'

She thought about it.

'No. Not now. But I don't think it's impossible. You can be driven to it. It's hardly inexplicable, let's face it. On the contrary, in fact.'

'A mad woman who goes around shooting the willies off all men? With good reason?'

'For specific reasons,' said Winnifred. 'Specific causes. And not just any old willies.'

'Perhaps she's not mad either?' said Reinhart.

'Depends on how you look at it, I suppose. She's been wronged, as I said. Affronted, perhaps . . . No, let's change the subject, this is making me feel ill.'

'Me too,' said Reinhart. 'Shall I do the other leg as well?'

'Yes, do that,' said Winnifred Lynch.

Van Veeteren had arranged to meet Renate for a while on Sunday afternoon, but when he got up at eleven o'clock, he was pleased to discover that his cold had deteriorated to such an extent that he had a perfectly good excuse for cancelling the meeting. All his respiratory passages seemed to be blocked by something thick and slimy and more or less impenetrable, and the only way in which he could breathe at all was by walking around with his mouth wide open. For a few painful seconds he observed what this procedure looked like in the hall mirror, and he recognized that today was one of those days when he ought not to force his presence on another human being.

Not even an ex-wife.

It was bad enough putting up with himself, and the day progressed in a fashion reminiscent of a seal travelling through a desert. At about ten in the evening he slumped over the kitchen table with his feet in a bubbling footbath and a terry towel draped over his head – in the vain hope that the steam from an aromatic concoction in a saucepan would banish the slime in his frontal cavities. It certainly had an effect: fluid poured out from every orifice, and he was covered in sweat.

Bugger this for a lark, he thought.

And then the telephone rang.

Van Veeteren recalled Reinhart's early morning call the other day, and formed a rapid but logical conclusion: if I didn't wish to receive any calls, I ought to have pulled out the plug.

I haven't pulled out the plug, and therefore I'd better answer.

'Hello. Enso Faringer here.'

For a few blank seconds he hadn't the slightest idea who Enso Faringer was.

'We met down at Freddy's and talked about Maas-leitner.'

'Yes, of course. What do you want?'

'You said I should give you a call if I remembered anything.'

'And?'

'I've remembered something.'

Van Veeteren sneezed.

'Excuse me?'

'It was nothing. What have you remembered?'

'Well, I remember Maasleitner talking about that music.'

'What music?'

'Somebody had telephoned him over and over again, and played him a tune, it seems.'

'A tune?'

'Yes.'

'Why?'

'I don't know. It had annoyed him in any case.'

A diffuse memory began to stir in the back of the chief inspector's brain.

'Hang on a minute. What kind of music was it?'

'I don't know. He never said what it was – I don't think he knew.'

'But why did this person call him? What was the point?'

'He didn't know. That's what irritated him.'

'Was it a man or a woman?'

'I don't think he said. I think it was just music, all the time.'

Van Veeteren thought for a moment.

'When exactly was this?'

Faringer hesitated.

'The same day we went to Freddy's, I think. When he was shot. Or maybe the day before.'

'And this call was repeated several times?'

'Yes, it seems so.'

'Did he try to do anything about it?'

'I don't know.'

'And he didn't know who it was behind it?'

'I don't think so. No, he was angry, mainly because he'd no idea what it was all about.'

Van Veeteren thought again.

'Mr Faringer,' he said eventually, 'are you sure you remember this correctly? You're sure you haven't got hold of the wrong end of the stick?'

He could hear some coughing at the other end of the line, and when the little German teacher's voice returned, there was no doubt that he was rather offended.

'I know I was slightly drunk, but I can remember this as clear as day.'

'I understand,' said Van Veeteren. 'Is there anything else you remember?'

'Not yet,' said Faringer. 'But if I do, I'll be in touch again.'

'I'll probably be in touch again as well,' said the chief inspector before hanging up.

Well, what the devil does this mean? he wondered as he poured the liquid from the foot bath and the concoction of herbs down the sink.

And what was it he almost remembered that somebody had said a few weeks ago?

18

It was late on Tuesday afternoon before they succeeded in tracking down all thirty-three staff NCOs (which was their official military status) of the 1965 vintage. Thirty-one of the group were still alive, the youngest of them now fifty, the eldest fifty-six. Five of them turned out to be resident abroad (three in other European countries, one in the USA, one in South Africa); fourteen were still in the Maardam police district, and the remaining twelve in other parts of the country.

Heinemann was in charge of this aspect and kept a register of all those concerned. He also made an effort to systematize the results of the interrogations, without finding an entirely successful method. When he handed the documentation over to Van Veeteren at about half past six in the evening, he devoted some considerable time to an attempt to enlighten his boss about all the cryptic signs and abbreviations, but in they end they both realized that it was a waste of time.

'You can explain it orally instead when we meet tomorrow to run through the current situation,' Van Veeteren decided. 'It'll be just as well for everybody to get the information at the same time.'

There had been a rumour to the effect that the chief of police himself intended to turn up for this meeting, which was due to take place at 10 a.m. on Wednesday, but when the time came he was unable to attend. Whether this was due to something important that had cropped up or was the desire to re-pot some plants in his office, was something nobody was in a position to say – but the fact that February is the most sensitive month for all plants was something that Reinhart at least was fully conversant with.

'Eight wise heads is a good score,' he said. 'If we had Hiller's as well, that would reduce the number to seven. Let's get started!'

Heinemann's summary – with questions and interruptions and comments – took almost an hour, despite the fact that there were no real links nor justifiable suspicions to report.

Opinions of Ryszard Malik had been more or less unanimous. A rather reticent, somewhat reserved person; friendly, reliable, without any striking characteristics or interests – that seemed to be the general impression. His social intercourse with his fellow students had been restricted to a group of four or five, generally speaking; but even among those there was nobody able to give any interesting tips of use to the investigation.

Needless to say, it was not easy to have any idea about what any such tips might have constituted; but without denigrating anybody's efforts it would be fair to say that comments made about Malik failed to bring the question of who murdered him a single centimetre closer to a solution.

The same could probably also be said of Maasleitner. The perception of him as a somewhat overbearing, self-centred and not very likeable young man was universal. He had belonged to a group of eight to ten people who frequently went around together, in their free time as well as during duty hours. Quite an active group, it seems, with a few questionable escapades on the programme for some evenings, not to say nights, as Heinemann put it.

'Questionable evening and night escapades?' said Reinhart, raising his eyebrows. 'Is that a formulation you made up yourself?'

'No,' said Heinemann unexpectedly. 'It's a quotation from the Koran.'

'I don't believe that for a moment,' said Rooth.

'Go on,' said Van Veeteren, clearly irritated.

'It must also be pointed out,' said Heinemann, 'that not a single one of those questioned managed to think of any links at all between Malik and Maasleitner, which surely undermines our hypotheses to some extent. We need to ask ourselves two questions. Firstly: is this really the background to the murders? Were Ryszard Malik and Rickard Maasleitner really murdered because they were on the same course when they did their National Service thirty years ago?'

He paused. Van Veeteren blew his nose into a paper tissue, which he then dropped on the floor under his desk.

'Secondly: if we say yes to the first question, what form does that connection take? There are two possibilities. Either the murderer is one of the others in the photo . . .'

He tapped on the photograph with the frame of his spectacles.

'. . . or is there an outsider who has some kind of relationship with the group?'

'Who intends to murder all thirty-five of them,' said Rooth.

'There are only thirty-one left,' deBries pointed out.

'Great,' said Rooth.

Heinemann looked round, waiting for comments.

'OK, we've made a note of that,' said Reinhart, clasping

his hands behind his head. 'Where do we go from here then?'

Van Veeteren cleared his throat and leant forward over the table, resting his head on his clenched hands.

'We have an extremely important question to ask ourselves,' he said, speaking slowly to emphasize the significance. 'I know it's a bit hocus-pocus, but never mind. Anyway, did any of you smell a rat when you spoke to these people? Something they weren't telling us about? Just a little trace of a suspicion, you know what I mean . . . No matter how illogical or irrational it might seem. If so, speak up now!'

He looked round the table. Nobody spoke. Jung looked as if he were about to, but changed his mind. DeBries might also have been on the way to saying something, but decided to hold back. Moreno shook her head.

'No,' said Reinhart in the end. 'I usually recognize murderers, but this time I saw no trace of one.'

'There were several of them we interviewed over the phone,' said Münster. 'It's almost impossible to get the kind of impression we're talking about if we don't have them sitting in front of us.'

Van Veeteren nodded.

'Perhaps we should have another chat with the lads who were a bit familiar with Maasleitner. It couldn't do any harm. If the murderer is an outsider who nevertheless has some sort of link with that group . . . Well, there are all kinds of possibilities, needless to say. I think we should try to find out if there was something that happened . . . something that could have been traumatic, somehow or other—'

'Traumatic?' said Rooth.

'It ought to have cropped up during our interviews, if there had been anything like that,' said deBries.

'Possibly,' said Van Veeteren. 'But you never know. We have a few more interviews to conduct in any case. I have an old colonel and a couple of company commanders in store.'

'Where?' asked deBries.

'One here,' said Van Veeteren. 'Two up in Schaabe, unfortunately.'

'I know a girl in Schaabe,' said Rooth.

'OK,' said Van Veeteren, 'you can take those two.'

'Thank you,' said Rooth.

'What about that music?' said deBries.

'Yes,' said Van Veeteren with a sigh. 'God only knows what it means, but it seems that both Malik and Maasleitner received strange telephone calls shortly before their time was up. Somebody who didn't say a word, but just played a tune . . .'

'What kind of a tune?' wondered Jung.

'We don't know. Mrs Malik evidently took two such calls; she mentioned it when she was in hospital, but we didn't take her all that seriously. I went to see her yesterday – she's still staying with her sister, and won't be leaving there any time soon I suspect. She confirms that it actually happened, but she had no idea what the music was, nor what it might signify.'

'Hmm,' said Reinhart. 'What about Maasleitner?'

'He evidently also received lots of calls the same day, or the day before. He told that little Kraut teacher about it, but he was wallowing in alcohol up to his armpits more or less, and doesn't remember all that much about it.'

'But it must have been the same music, no matter what,' said Münster.

'Yes,' muttered the chief inspector. 'We can take that for granted. But it would be interesting to know what the point of it was.'

Nobody spoke.

'Didn't *they* understand, at least?'

Van Veeteren shook his head.

'It seems not. Maasleitner didn't, in any case. We don't know if Malik received any calls himself. He didn't say anything to his wife, but that's understandable.'

'Very understandable,' said Rooth.

Reinhart took out his pipe and stared at it for a while.

'It seems that we have a worthy opponent this time, don't you think?'

Van Veeteren nodded glumly.

'We certainly do. Anyway, I have no intention of mentioning this telephone music to the media . . . Not yet, at least. But, obviously, we have to warn the remaining thirty-one.'

'Those who have still survived,' said deBries.

'Münster can write a letter that we can send round to them. Be careful about the wording, and I want to see it before it goes out.'

'Of course,' said Münster.

'I suppose we'll have to cut back on the number of officers on the case,' said the chief inspector, blowing his nose for the twentieth time in an hour. 'Let's discuss how to divide the jobs to be done after coffee.'

'There's a right time for everything,' said Reinhart.

Reinhart sat down opposite the chief inspector and stirred his coffee slowly.

'It feels a bit worrying,' he said.

Van Veeteren nodded.

'Do you think there'll be more?'

'Yes.'

'So do I.'

They sat in silence for a while.

'It might be just as well,' said Reinhart. 'We'll never solve it otherwise.'

Van Veeteren said nothing. Rubbed his nose with a paper serviette, breathing heavily. Rooth came to join them, carrying an overloaded tray.

'What's preferable?' Reinhart continued. 'Two victims and a murderer who gets away with it? Or three victims and a murderer who gets caught?'

'Or four?' said Van Veeteren. 'Or five? There always has to be a limit.'

'Or, at least, one has to be imposed,' said Reinhart. 'That's not quite the same thing.'

'It would be best if there weren't any victims at all,' interposed Rooth. 'And no murderer either.'

'Utopia,' Reinhart snorted. 'We deal with reality.'

'Oh, that,' said Rooth.

That evening, ensconced in an armchair and wrapped up in two blankets with Handel in the loudspeakers, Van Veeteren thought back to the conversation in the canteen. He noted that it was almost exactly a week since Rickard Maasleitner was murdered. Nearly three since the first murder.

And he also noted that the police had hardly earned any

laurels thus far. Had he used the resources available to him as best he could?

Should he not have arranged some kind of protection? Ought he not to have put more resources into tracing the weapon? Should he not . . . ?

He picked up the photograph and studied it for the thousandth time since Heinemann first produced it. Studied the faces of those formally dressed young men, one after the other.

Thirty-five young men full of optimism as they began to make their way out into the world. Every one of them looking with confidence as far into the future as it was possible to see, or so it seemed.

The future? he thought.

Was one of them next in line?

He thought so. But who?

SIX

8–14 FEBRUARY

19

When the call finally came, Karel Innings had been waiting for it for six days.

Ever since he had sat reading his newspaper that morning and drawn the horrific conclusions, he had known that it must come.

Something must be done. He had twice tried to get in touch himself, but Biedersen had been away. The message on his answering machine said he would be back home by the sixth, but the same message was there when he tried to phone again on the seventh.

The most obvious course would be for Biedersen to make the first move. Without needing to think any further about it, he knew that to be the case. That's what the relationship had been, quite simply – Biedersen and Maasleitner, Malik and Innings. In so far as there had been any relationships at all, that is.

The next most obvious course – and for every hour that passed during these ominous, grey February days, he could feel that this solution was becoming more and more inevitable – was clearly to contact the police. The timid detective inspector who had been to see him inspired warmth and confidence, and he acknowledged that in different circumstances he would scarcely have hesitated before telling all.

Perhaps he also realized that the special circumstances were in fact just an excuse. There were always special circumstances. You always had to take things into account. Consideration for others – false and genuine – always had to be taken into account and, naturally, awkward situations were constantly a possibility. But whose life could cope with something like this becoming public knowledge? A horrendous skeleton suddenly falling out of the cupboard after more than thirty years of silence.

Probably nobody's. When he lay awake at night and felt Ulrike's warm body by his side, he knew that at this moment in time it was an impossibility.

She must be spared this.

And of course it was not only his life with Ulrike that was at stake, even if she was beyond doubt the most important part. The whole of his new life, this incredibly placid and harmonious existence that was now beginning its second year, with Ulrike and their three children – his own and her two . . . No doubt it could have tolerated crises, but not this. Not this nauseating, abhorrent bombshell from the past.

It had evidently decided to haunt him yet again. It never gave up, and could never be atoned.

The two-edged fear gnawed constantly at him during these waking hours. On the one hand, the fear of being exposed – and on the other something even worse. During the day, the thought gave him hardly a moment of peace. It was as if every part of his body, wound up like a spring by worry and tension and lack of sleep, was in acute pain as he sat in the editorial office and tried to concentrate on the routines and tasks he had known inside out for more than fifteen years. Was it obvious to the others? he kept asking himself more and more frequently. Could they see?

Probably not. Given the non-stop hustle and bustle and stress, it was possible for a colleague to more or less collapse on the spot under the weight of personal problems, without anybody else noticing a thing. It had actually happened. It was even worse with Ulrike and the children, of course. They lived in such close contact, and they cared. He could blame it on his bad stomach, and did so. Sleepless nights need not necessarily mean that something serious was wrong.

And simply belonging to the group was an acceptable reason for being worried. The group originally comprising thirty-five National Servicemen. For the uninitiated, that was no doubt bad enough.

He was still managing to keep control of himself then. But it was inevitable that things would get progressively worse; and when at last he heard Biedersen's broad accent over the phone on Thursday afternoon, he had the feeling that the call had come in the nick of time. He couldn't have kept going for much longer.

Not much longer at all.

Even if it was not easy to take everything seriously, he had entertained the thought that his telephone might be bugged, and evidently Biedersen thought so as well. He didn't even say who was calling, and but for the fact that Innings had been expecting it and recognized Biedersen's accent, he would have had little chance of identifying the voice.

'Hi,' was all Biedersen said. 'Shall we meet briefly tomorrow evening?'

'Yes,' said Innings. 'It would probably be as well.'

Biedersen suggested a restaurant and a time, and that was that.

It was only after Innings had replaced the receiver that it occurred to him that there was an unanswered question in this disturbing game.

What exactly would be involved if he entered into discussions with Biedersen?

And later that night as he lay awake in bed, wandering through the no-man's-land between sleep and consciousness, it suddenly dawned on him.

The new image for his fear was a trident.

20

Rooth had set off early and was in Schaabe by noon. As his first meeting was not until two hours later, he treated himself to a long and nourishing lunch at the station restaurant before heading for the Staff College.

Captain Falzenbucht turned out to be a short, thin, little man with a strange low, husky voice. (He'd no doubt been standing too long on the barrack square, shouting his head off, Rooth assumed.) He had passed the age of sixty several years ago, and so ought to be leading a life of leisure in retirement – but as he pointed out several times: as long as the college needed his services, it was naturally his duty to stay on. As a good soldier. As a man. As a citizen.

As a human being? Rooth wondered.

Oh yes, of course he could recall the cohort of 1965. They had been his second brood as a sub lieutenant, and when Rooth produced the photograph he proceeded to identify several individuals by name.

So he's had enough sense to do his homework, thought

Rooth, whose own military career was not suitable to be brought into the light of day on an occasion like this. Nor on any other, come to that.

'Anyway, the ones we are most interested in at this stage are Malik and Maasleitner,' he said. 'Can you point them out?'

Falzenbucht duly did so.

'I take it you know what's happened?'

'Of course,' croaked Falzenbucht. 'Murdered. A shocking story.'

'We've spoken to all the rest,' said Rooth.

'Are they all still alive?' Falzenbucht wondered.

'No, but we concentrated on those who are. Nobody can think of a link between Malik and Maasleitner, and nobody has any idea what might lie behind it all.'

'I understand,' said Falzenbucht.

'Have you any ideas?'

Falzenbucht assumed an expression that suggested deep thought.

'Hmm. I'm not surprised to hear that nobody could come up with anything. There is nothing. It has nothing – absolutely nothing at all – to do with the college and the education we provide here. I ought to make that clear.'

'How can you know that?' said Rooth.

'We'd have known about it if it had.'

Rooth considered this military logic for a few seconds.

'So what you don't see doesn't exist?' he said.

Falzenbucht made no reply.

'What do you think it's about, then?'

'I've no idea. But find out, you police officers.'

'That's why I've come here.'

'I see. Hmm.'

For a few brief moments Rooth toyed with the idea of putting his foot down: picking up this growling, poker-backed little man, putting him in the car and subjecting him to a thorough interrogation in some poky, smelly little cell at the Schaabe police station – but his good nature won out in the end, and he let it pass.

'Is there anything,' he said instead, 'anything at all, that you can tell me that you think might be of use to us in this investigation?'

Falzenbucht stroked his thumb and index finger over his well-trimmed moustache.

'None of the others in this group can have done it,' he said. 'They're lovely lads, every one of them. The murderer is somebody from the outside.'

The devil himself, perhaps? Rooth thought. He sighed discreetly and checked his watch. There was over half an hour to go before his next appointment. He decided to waste another five minutes on Falzenbucht, and then find the canteen for a cup of coffee.

★

Major Straade proved to be roughly twice the size of Falzenbucht, with rather less of a military bearing; but he had just as little to contribute to the investigation. Nothing, zilch. Like the captain, he was inclined to think that the background to the affair was to be found outside the barrack gates – the now closed-down barracks at Löhr, on the outskirts of Maardam, that is.

Something that happened outside working hours. In the men's free time. Somewhere in town. Always assuming that the link really did have to do with the Staff College. Was that certain? Had it been confirmed? Why imagine that the Staff College had anything to do with it at all?

They were questions that Straade kept coming back to, over and over again.

When Rooth had returned to his car and sat in the car park, he tried to assess all these guesses and judgements, but needless to say it was not easy to decide what they were really based on.

Sound and experience-based intuition? Or merely an anxious and bone-headed determination to protect the good name and reputation of the college?

Whatever, he found it hard to comprehend the military code of honour, and the obvious conclusion to draw was that the visit to Schaabe had resulted in absolutely nothing of value at all.

As far as the investigation was concerned, that is.

He checked the time and spread out a town plan on the empty seat beside him.

Van Kuijperslaan, is that what she'd said?

She opened the door, and he noted immediately that her warm smile had not cooled down over the years.

He removed the paper and handed over the bouquet. She smiled even more broadly as she accepted it. Showed him into the hall and gave him a hug. He responded gladly and with as much enthusiasm as he considered advisable at this early stage, but then he noticed from the corner of his eye a dark-haired man – about the same age as himself – coming out of the kitchen with a bottle of wine in his hand.

'Who the hell's this?' he hissed into her ear.

She let go of him and turned towards the man.

'This is Jean-Paul,' she said cheerfully. 'My boyfriend. I'm so glad he managed to get home in time for you to get to know him.'

'Great,' said Inspector Rooth, trying to smile as well.

21

As Innings was about to enter Le Bistro, he was stopped at the door by a porter who gave him an envelope and suggested he might like to go back out into the street. Somewhat bewildered, Innings did as he was told, opened the envelope and found inside the address of another restaurant.

It was located some three blocks up the street, not far from the church; and as Innings made his way there he thought over the fact that Biedersen was evidently approaching the situation in a serious frame of mind, and leaving nothing to chance. He tried to come to terms with his own attitude and think about what to say; but when he got there and saw Biedersen sitting in a booth about as far away from the door as possible, his dominant emotion was relief – and a strong desire to leave everything in somebody else's hands.

There didn't seem to be any doubt that Biedersen was willing to provide those hands.

'Long time no see,' he said. 'You are Innings, I presume?'

Innings nodded, and sat down. Closer inspection suggested that Biedersen had changed rather less than he had expected. The last time they'd met was by pure chance some ten years ago – but they hadn't really spent time together since those days in June 1976.

The same powerful, sturdy figure. Rugged face, sparse reddish hair, and eyes that seemed to burn. They were never still. He recalled that some people had been afraid of them.

Perhaps he had been one of them.

'So, here we are,' he said. 'I tried to get hold of you several times. Before you rang, that is.'

'Have you gathered what's going on?' said Biedersen.

Innings hesitated.

'Yes, er, well, I don't know . . .'

'The other two have been murdered.'

'Yes.'

'Somebody has killed them. Who do you think it is?'

Innings recognized that somehow or other he had succeeded in avoiding that question so far, goodness knows how.

'Her,' he said. 'It must be her . . .'

'She's dead.'

Biedersen spoke just as a waiter came to take their

orders, and there was a pause before he was able to expand on what he had said.

'She's dead, as I said. There must be somebody else acting on her behalf. I think it's her daughter.'

To his surprise, Innings noticed a trace of fear in Biedersen's voice. The same broad, off-putting accent, certainly; but with the addition of something forced, a touch of nervousness.

'Her daughter?' he said.

'Yes, her daughter. I've tried to trace her.'

'And?'

'She doesn't exist.'

'Doesn't exist?'

'Impossible to pin down. She vacated her flat in Stamberg in the middle of January, and nobody knows where she's gone to.'

'You've tried, you say . . .'

'A bit.' He leant forward over the table. 'That bloody bitch isn't going to get us as well!'

Innings swallowed.

'Have you received any of these music calls?'

Innings shook his head.

'I have,' said Biedersen. 'It's a right bastard. But you must have had a letter from the police?'

'This morning,' said Innings. 'It looks like it's you next.'

It slipped out of him before he could stop it, and he was well aware that the relief he felt for a brief moment was a very transitory phenomenon.

First Biedersen. Then him. That's what was planned.

'You could be right,' said Biedersen. 'But don't feel too secure, that's all. We have to put a stop to her – I mean, that's why we're sitting here.'

Innings nodded.

'We've got to get her before she gets us. I take it you're on board?'

'Yes . . .'

'Are you hesitating?'

'No, no, I'm just wondering what we ought to do.'

'I've already thought that through.'

'You don't say. What do you mean?'

'Like with like. There's a bag under the table, can you feel it?'

Innings felt around with his feet and felt something next to the wall.

'Yes?' he said.

'Your weapon's in there. You owe me eight hundred for the trouble.'

Innings felt a wave of dizziness envelop him.

'But . . . er, haven't you thought about . . . er, another possible alternative?'

Biedersen snorted.

'Huh. What might that be?'

'I don't know . . .'

Biedersen lit a cigarette. A few seconds passed.

'Shall we go and look for her?' Innings said. 'Or just sit here and wait?'

'For Christ's sake!' Biedersen snorted. 'We don't even know what she looks like! But if you're prepared to travel to Stamberg and try to get hold of a photo of her, by all means. But how the hell do we know that she's not wearing a wig? And other stuff? You must know how easy it is for a fucking woman to change her appearance!'

Innings nodded.

'It could happen tonight, do you realize that? Or tomorrow. The next person to ring your doorbell could be her. Have you thought of that?'

Innings didn't reply. The waiter came with their food, and they started eating in silence.

'That music . . . ?' said Innings after a while, wiping his mouth.

Biedersen put down his knife and fork.

'Twice,' he said. 'Somebody's called a couple of times and hung up when my wife answered. But it's that bloody tune in any case . . . I can't remember what it's called, but we were playing it all the time. But I suppose I don't need to tell you that – you were pretty sober.'

'I wasn't sober,' said Innings. 'You know I wasn't. I'd never do anything like that . . .'

'All right, all right, we don't need to go through all that again. What was the band called?'

'The Shadows?'

'Yes, that's it. You remember it. I've looked, but I don't seem to have the record any more.'

'Isn't it possible to trace the phone calls?'

'For God's sake,' said Biedersen. 'You don't seem to understand this. Naturally we can bring in the police and get as much bloody protection as we like – I thought we'd agreed not to do that?'

'OK,' said Innings. 'I'm with you on that.'

Biedersen stared hard at him.

'I don't know what your circumstances are,' he said, 'but I've got a family, have had for twenty-five years. A wife, three kids, and a grandchild as well. I have my own firm, good friends, business contacts . . . For Christ's sake, I have a whole world that would collapse like a house of cards! But if you're doubtful, just say. I can manage this on my own if needs be. I just thought it would be beneficial if we collaborated a bit. Shared the responsibility.'

'Yes . . .'

'If you don't want to play along, just say.'

Innings shook his head.

'No, I'm with you. Sorry. What do you think we should do?'

Biedersen flung out his hands.

'Maybe just wait,' he said. 'Be ready with the gun. You'd hardly need to explain why you acquired it either – everybody will believe us. A man must have the right to protect his life, for God's sake.'

Innings thought for a moment.

'Yes,' he said. 'It would be self-defence, of course.'

Biedersen nodded.

'Sure,' he said. 'But we have to keep in touch as well. We have no other allies, and there could come about a situation in which it wouldn't do any harm if there were two of us. We might get wind of her, for instance. Malik and Maasleitner never had a chance really.'

Innings thought about that.

'How?' he said. 'Keeping in touch, I mean.'

Biedersen shrugged.

'Telephone,' he said. 'We have to risk it, anything else would take too long. If we get through, all we need do is to arrange to meet somewhere. If necessary, spell it out . . . I mean, she must be hanging around us for some time first, and . . . well, if you notice you're being followed by a woman, all you need do is phone.'

'It takes two hours to drive up to where you live, is that right?'

'About that,' said Biedersen. 'An hour and three quarters if you're lucky. Yes, it might well be my turn next, so you can stand by to set off.'

Innings nodded. They continued eating in silence again. Toasted each other without speaking, and when Innings swallowed the cold beer he again felt a moment of dizziness. Carefully, he placed his foot on the bag with the ominous contents, and wondered how on earth he would be able to explain something like that to Ulrike.

A gun.

If he was forced to use it, he'd have to tell her the same story as he told the police, of course – she would naturally be upset, but his precaution would have been proved to be justified, so why the hell should there be any reason to think otherwise?

But for the time being he decided to keep its existence a secret. That would naturally be the easiest way.

And hope he would never have to use it.

Rely on Biedersen to do his duty.

'I must pay you,' he said. 'I don't think I've got as much as eight hundred on me, though . . .'

'All in good time,' said Biedersen. 'If we can sort out this lunatic, we can settle what we owe as well.'

Innings nodded, and they sat quietly for a while.

'There's one thing I've been thinking about, and that bothers me a bit,' said Biedersen, when they had been served with coffee and each lit a cigarette. 'She's behaved in exactly the same way twice now. Surely she can't be so bloody stupid as to do so again?'

No, Innings thought as he left the restaurant five minutes after Biedersen. That's right. Surely she can't be as stupid as that.

22

The persistent cold – in combination with the occasional beer and hot toddy too many during recent days – meant that it didn't turn out to be much of a match. Perhaps also an accumulated and unsatisfied need for more sleep played a role as well.

In any case, during the third set Münster toyed with the idea of changing hands and playing with his left for a few games; things were not normally as bad as that. However, he knew that if he did so it could be interpreted as an insult to his opponent, and so he refrained.

Be that as it may, the final scores were 15–5, 15–5, 15–3, and afterwards the chief inspector looked as if he needed to be placed in a respirator as quickly as possible.

'I must buy a new racket,' he croaked. 'There's no spring left in this old mallet.'

Münster had nothing to say about that suggestion, and they made their way slowly to the changing rooms.

*

After a shower, a change of clothes and a walk up the stairs to the reception area of the badminton hall, Van Veeteren suddenly felt that he was incapable of staggering as far as his car unless they paused for a beer in the cafe.

Münster had no choice, of course. He looked at his watch and sighed. Then he rang the babysitter, announced his delayed arrival time, and slumped down opposite the chief inspector.

'Hell and damnation,' announced Van Veeteren when his face had resumed its normal colour with the aid of a copious swig of beer. 'This case annoys me. It's like a pimple on the bum, if you'll pardon the expression. It just stays where it is, and nothing happens . . .'

'Or it grows bigger and bigger,' said Münster.

'Until it bursts, yes. And when do you think that will be?'

Münster shrugged.

'I don't know,' he said. 'Haven't Rooth and deBries discovered anything new?'

'Not a dickie bird,' said Van Veeteren. 'The military types seem to be a bit worried about the college's reputation, but they don't appear to be holding back any information.'

'And nobody has reported any phone calls with musical accompaniment?'

Van Veeteren shook his head.

'A few have asked for police protection, that's all.'

'Really?'

'I said we'd keep an eye on them.'

'You did?' said Münster. 'Shall we, in fact?'

Van Veeteren grunted.

'Needless to say, we keep an eye on all citizens. It's part of a police officer's duty, if you recall.'

Münster took a swig of beer.

'The only thing that's actually happening in this confounded case,' Van Veeteren continued, lighting a cigarette, 'is that Heinemann is sitting in some cubbyhole searching for a link.'

'What sort of link?'

'Between Malik and Maasleitner, of course. It seems that he's feeling a bit guilty because the Staff College connection was so unproductive. Ah well, we'll see.'

'I expect we shall,' said Münster. 'He's good at stumbling over things and finding gold. What do you think?'

Van Veeteren inhaled deeply and blew out the smoke through his nostrils. Like a dragon, Münster thought.

'I don't know what I think. But I do think it's damned inconsiderate of a murderer to take such a long time. Something has to happen soon, that's as obvious as can be.'

'Is it?' Münster wondered.

'Can't you feel it?' asked Van Veeteren, raising an eyebrow in surprise. 'Surely you don't imagine it's all over after these two? Malik and Maasleitner? The vaguer the link between the two of them, the more likely it is that they must be a part of a broader context – you don't need to complete the whole jigsaw puzzle in order to discover if it comprises a hundred or a thousand pieces.'

Münster thought that one over.

'What is it, then? The broader context, that is.'

'A good question, Inspector. There's two guilders for you if you can answer it.'

Münster finished his beer and started buttoning up his jacket.

'I really must be going now,' he said. 'I promised the babysitter I'd be home in half an hour.'

'All right,' sighed the chief inspector. 'All right, I'm coming.'

'What shall we do?' Münster asked as he turned into Klagenburg. 'Apart from waiting, I mean.'

'Hmm,' said Van Veeteren. 'I suppose we'll have to have another chat with the group comparatively close to Maasleitner. Given the absence of anything else, so far.'

'More questions then?'

'More questions,' said the chief inspector. 'A hell of a lot more questions, and no sign of a good answer.'

'Well, we mustn't lose heart,' said Münster, bringing the car to a halt.

'Ouch,' said Van Veeteren as he started to get out of the car. 'I'll be damned if I haven't pulled a muscle.'

'Where?' asked Münster.

'In my body,' said Van Veeteren.

23

It gradually dawned on him that he'd seen her for the first time at the football match on Sunday. Even if he didn't realize it until later.

He'd gone to the match with Rolv, as usual, and she'd been sitting diagonally behind them, a couple of rows back – a woman with large, brown-tinted glasses and a colourful scarf that hid most of her hair. But it was dark, he remembered that distinctly: a few tufts had stuck out. Thirty years of age, or thereabouts. A bit haggard, but he didn't see much of her face.

Later on, when he made an effort to think back and try to understand how he could recall her, he remembered turning round three or four times during the match. There had been a troublemaker back there, shouting and yelling and slagging off the referee, making people laugh part of the time, but they were urging him to shut up as well. Biedersen had never really established who it was; but it must have been then, when he kept turning round and was distracted from the game itself, that he saw her.

But he didn't know at the time. Hadn't registered and committed to memory what she looked like.

But she was wearing a light-coloured coat, just like when she turned up the next time.

Apart from that, almost everything else was different. No glasses, no colourful scarf; her dark hair in a bun; and it was astonishing that he could know nevertheless that it must be her. That was the moment he reacted. The new image was superimposed over the old one, and the penny dropped.

Monday lunchtime. As usual, he was at Mix, with Henessy and Vargas. She came in and stood for ages at the desk, looking round – trying to give the impression that she was looking for an empty seat, presumably, but she wasn't. She was looking for him, and when she'd found him – which must have been at least a minute after he'd seen her – she continued to stand there.

Just stood there. Smiled to herself, it seemed, but continued looking round the premises. Pausing to look more closely at him now and then, for a second or two; and thinking back, he found it hard to recall how long this had gone on. It could hardly have been more than a few minutes, but somehow or other that short period of time was made to feel longer: and afterwards, it seemed to him longer than the whole lunch. He hadn't the slightest recollection of what he'd been talking to Henessy and Vargas about.

In so far as there were still any doubts, they were cast aside by what happened on Tuesday morning.

It was about half past ten when he went to the post office in Lindenplejn to collect a parcel – and also to send advertising material to a few prospective customers in Oostwerdingen and Aarlach. Miss Kennan had been off work with flu since the previous Monday and there were things that couldn't be allowed to fester for ever and ever.

He didn't see when she came in – there were a lot of people in the queues formed in front of the various windows. But he suddenly became aware of her presence – he sensed that she was somewhere behind him, just as she had been at the football match.

He slowly turned his head, and identified her right away. In the queue next to his. A few metres behind his back, three or four at most. She was wearing the scarf and the glasses again, but had on a brown jacket instead of the overcoat. She stood there without looking at him – or, at least, not during the brief moment he dared to look at her – but with a slight, introverted smile. He chose to interpret the situation almost as a secret signal.

After a short discussion with himself, Biedersen left his place in the queue. Walked quickly out through the main entrance, continued over the street and entered the newsagent's on the other side. Hid inside there for a few minutes, head down and leafing through a few magazines; then he returned to the post office.

She was no longer there. There was no other change in the queue she'd been standing in. The man in the black leather jacket who'd been in front of her was still there. As was the young immigrant woman behind her. But the gap between them had closed.

Biedersen hesitated for several seconds. Then he decided to put off whatever it was he was going to do, and return to his office instead.

He double-locked the door and flopped down behind his desk. Took out his notebook and a pen, and started drawing more or less symmetrical figures – a habit he'd formed while still at school, and had resorted to ever since when faced with a problem.

And as he sat there, filling page after page then tearing them out, he asked himself if he'd ever been confronted by a bigger problem than this one. His realization that this woman was in fact following him – that it must be her – did not mean that the outcome was a foregone conclusion, no way. Having identified her meant that he had a chance: a trump card he must be careful not to waste. The main thing, he convinced himself, was that he didn't let on that he had noticed her. Didn't let her realize that he knew who she was, and what was involved. That was obvious.

The fact that he would have to kill her was another conviction that came early to him. The inevitability of this conclusion became clearer, the more he thought about it – although you could say he had known that from the start. He phoned Innings, but there was no reply. Perhaps that was just as well. He wouldn't have known how much to tell him, or what to instruct him to do.

It would be better to continue off his own bat to start with, he decided. The first couple of steps or so, at least. But no rush – the whole business was so delicately balanced. The main thing was to keep a cool head. The fact that he would have to kill her before she killed him didn't mean, of course, that he should just shoot her at the first opportunity. In broad daylight. He soon realized that there were only two possible alternatives: either he would have to shoot her in self-defence – wait until the last moment, as it were, with all that implied regarding risks and uncertainties – or else . . . Or else he would have to find a way of getting rid of her without it being possible for him to be suspected.

To murder her, in other words.

It didn't need much in the way of consideration before he concluded that the latter was the best way to proceed.

That's simply the kind of man I am, he decided. And this is an appropriate situation.

He could feel that something inside him came alive as he reached these conclusions. A new source of energy, a new source of inspiration. In fact, he had known this all the time. This is what he had to do. He opened his desk drawer and took out the bottle of whisky he always had concealed there. Took two deep swigs and felt the determination spreading throughout his body.

This is the sort of man I am . . . A new source of inspiration?

It hadn't been all that hard to make up his mind; but of course it would be much harder to decide how to proceed. Nevertheless, when he left his office at four that afternoon, he thought he had a good idea of what he was going to do.

In outline, at least.

It could hardly have been more than a pious hope on the part of Biedersen that he would come across her again that same evening; but when she turned up in the rain outside Kellner's, he had the feeling that something had short-circuited inside him. As if his heart had skipped a beat or two.

He closed his eyes and took a deep breath. Raised his newspaper so that it hid his face, and hoped that she hadn't seen him through the window.

After a short pause she came in through the revolving doors. Looked around the quite large and well-attended restaurant, and eventually found a vacant table so far back that it was almost out of sight for Biedersen. Nevertheless, by turning his chair a fraction and leaning back, he could keep an eye on what she was up to. It was obvious that she intended to eat – Biedersen had only ordered a beer. He watched her hang her jacket over the back of her chair, subject the menu to lengthy scrutiny, and eventually order something complicated from the Indian waiter.

Meanwhile, Biedersen paid his bill; and when the Indian waiter came to serve her meal, Biedersen made the most of the opportunity to slip into the Gents with his bag. Locked the door, and proceeded to make use of the contents of his bag: a wig (that had been packed away in his cellar ever since he'd taken part in a jokey charade when a good friend got married over twenty years ago), an American military parka (that he'd forbidden Rolv to wear when he still lived at home) and a pair of round spectacles of uncertain origin.

And also a pistol; a Pinchman, loaded with six bullets.

He checked his appearance in the scratched mirror, and

as far as he could make out, his disguise was just as effective as it had been when he tried it out in the bathroom mirror at home a couple of hours earlier.

There was no obvious reason to assume that this superannuated hippy was in fact identical with the locally well-known and successful businessman W. S. Biedersen.

No reason at all.

For safety's sake he decided to wait for her in the square outside. For almost an hour he wandered up and down in the wind and the light, driving rain. After a while he bought a packet of cigarettes at the kiosk, and a hamburger shortly afterwards. Phoned Innings from a call box as well. Got through without delay but restricted himself to saying that something might well be about to happen and he would ring again later. Since meeting Innings the previous Friday, he had been unable to decide if his former colleague was a help or a hindrance, and wondered if it would be best to ignore him altogether. That was his inclination at the moment.

There were not very many people out and about on a wet and windy evening like today, but his appearance and behaviour seemed not to attract curious looks. He realized that people took him for a drifter, a natural if regrettable background figure in any town or any street scene anywhere in the world. The perfect camouflage. At one point he was even greeted by another of the same sort: an unpleasant-smelling elderly man with one hand in an incredibly dirty bandage – but he only needed to tell him to piss off in order to be left in peace without more ado.

The clock on St Mary's church had just struck nine when she came out. She looked left and right several times, then walked rapidly over the square, passing by only a few metres away from him, and boarded one of the buses waiting outside the station.

Biedersen hesitated for a few seconds before getting on the bus as well. He gathered it was going to Hengeloo, and bought a ticket to there. He had barely sat down six rows behind her when the bus shuddered and set off.

It struck him how close he had been to losing her altogether, how small the margins were in this kind of situation, and made up his mind to stick as close to her as possible in future.

They were travelling westwards. Through Legenbojs and Maas. There were about a dozen passengers on board from the start, mostly elderly women with bulging plastic carrier bags and shopping baskets in their laps. A few youths were half asleep at the back with personal stereos turned up so that the high notes hovered over the muffled rumble of the engine like a cloud of buzzing insects. The driver occasionally stopped to pick up new passengers; a few got off as well, but not many – until after twenty-five minutes or so they came to the square at Berkinshaam, when over half the passengers stood up and prepared to alight.

He lost sight of her for a moment as a pair of old women stood up and fumbled around with their bags and baskets, and when they finally moved away he saw to his dismay that her seat was empty.

He stood up and scanned the front part of the bus, but it was clear that she must have left via the doors next to the driver. When he tried to look out through the side windows, all he could see was his own unrecognizable face and other items reflected from inside the bus.

As panic welled up inside him, he made a dash to get off the bus. He emerged into the dimly lit square and was lucky enough to see – what he assumed was, at any rate – her back as she turned into a narrow alley between high, dark gable ends.

He slung his bag over his shoulder and rushed to follow her; and when he came to the narrow entrance, he once again just caught sight of her back turning into another alley some twenty metres ahead. He swallowed. Realized that it was hardly a good idea to go careering after her now. He also managed to overcome his agitation and slow down his pace. He put his hand into his bag to check that the pistol was still there. Released the safety catch and left his hand in the bag.

When he came to the inadequate street lamp on the corner, he found that what she had turned into was a twenty-metre-long cul-de-sac culminating in a firewall. The tall building on the left appeared to be a factory or a warehouse, without a single illuminated window. Nor could he make out an entrance or doorway on that side of the street; the only entrance of any description was a portal leading into the four-or five-storey-high property on the right-hand side. He investigated and discovered that it was the entrance to a sort of tunnel running through the building and emerging into an inner courtyard, dimly lit by lights from various windows.

Biedersen paused. Took a few steps into the tunnel, then paused again. An unpleasant smell was forcing its way into his nostrils. Something rotten, or at least damaged by damp. He listened, but all he could hear was rain falling on a tin roof somewhere in the courtyard. And the faint sound of a television set evidently standing close to an open window. On one of the upstairs floors facing the street, presumably. A cat appeared and rubbed up against his legs.

Oh hell, he thought, clutching the pistol.

And he acknowledged that the feeling bubbling up inside him was fear, nothing else.

Pure, unadulterated fear.

24

When Innings got home after the restaurant meal with Biedersen, the first thing he did was to hide the bag containing the gun in a chest of drawers full of odds and ends in the garage. He knew that the risk of Ulrike or the children finding it was more or less negligible, and he hoped sincerely that it would remain hidden there for ever. Or at least until he had an opportunity to get rid of it.

His mind felt like a playground for a mass of the most divergent thoughts and ideas. As he sat on the sofa with Ulrike, watching a Fassbinder film, he tried to assess the most likely outcome of – or escape from – this nightmare. It seemed even harder now than it had been before. His thoughts seemed to be tossed around like a straw in the wind, and he soon began to wish that he could simply switch off his brain. For a short while, at least, in order to gain some breathing space.

When it came to wishes and hopes, the situation was much more straightforward. The most welcome development from his point of view would be that Biedersen simply sorted the whole business out by himself. Tracked down this madwoman and rendered her harmless, once and for all. Without any involvement on the part of Innings.

In view of what he had discovered at the restaurant – regarding the telephone music and so on – this was surely not an altogether unlikely outcome?

Innings kept coming back to this conclusion over and over again, but his assessment of it, like all the rest of his thoughts, kept swinging back and forth between hope and something that was most reminiscent of deepest despair.

In fact – and this gradually became the only consolation he could find – there was only one thing he could be absolutely sure about.

Something would happen soon.

This period of suspense would soon come to an end.

In a few days – a week or so, perhaps – it would all be over.

Any other outcome was unthinkable.

Given these hopes – which Innings began to cherish even before he went to bed on the Friday evening – there is no denying that it was very stressful to have to accept that nothing in fact happened.

On Saturday and half of Sunday they had visitors – Ulrike's brother with his wife and two children – and all the practical things that needed doing plus the conversation helped to keep the worry at a distance. For part of the time, at least. But things became much worse after they had left, and peace and quiet returned to the house on Sunday afternoon.

It was worse still on Monday, which seemed to float by in a cloud of listlessness and worry. That night he had barely a wink of sleep, and when he left the editorial office at about four on Tuesday afternoon, he had the distinct impression that several of his colleagues were wondering about his state of health.

He had told Ulrike that he was a bit upset because of the murder of two of his former colleagues when he was a National Serviceman, and she seemed to accept this as a reasonable explanation for his occasional preoccupation.

And then, on Tuesday evening, the telephone call came at last from Biedersen. Something might be about to happen, he said, but there was no reason for Innings to do anything. Not yet, at least.

That was all he said. Promised to ring again later. And although this call more or less corresponded to what Innings had been hoping for deep down, it increased his nervous tension even more – with another sleepless night as the outcome.

Needless to say, his sensitive stomach reacted accordingly; and when he phoned in on Wednesday morning to report sick, at least he had a legitimate physical excuse.

Perhaps he also felt emotionally calm when he settled down with his newspaper after Ulrike and the kids had left, but it didn't last long. He realized that subconsciously he'd been hoping to find something in the news – the discovery of a woman killed in mysterious circumstances up in Saaren, or something of the sort – but, of course, there wasn't a single word about any such incident. Besides, it was obvious that the morning papers wouldn't have had time to carry any such news. Biedersen had phoned at about half past eight. No matter what had happened next, the papers wouldn't have had time to print it. Innings had been working in the trade for nearly thirty years, and so he should know.

The broadcast journalists would have had a better chance. He switched on the radio and didn't miss a single bulletin all morning. But nothing. Not a single word.

Something might be about to happen, that's what Biedersen had said.

What?

I'll be in touch.

When?

Minutes passed. As did hours. It wasn't until five minutes past twelve that the telephone rang.

It was the police. For one confused second this fact almost caused him to lose control of himself. He was on the point of coming out with the whole story, but then he realized that, of course, this was how he would be informed of what had happened.

If this woman really had been found shot up in Saaren, and there was even the slightest of links to the other murders, this was naturally how the police would react.

They would be in touch with all thirty-one and try to winkle out if anybody knew anything.

He came round to this conclusion while talking to the police officer, and then when he sat waiting, he was pretty confident that he hadn't given himself away.

He had expressed surprise, obviously. Why would the police want to question him again? Routine questions? OK, fair enough.

But while he waited, the other possible scenario dawned on him.

Biedersen might not have succeeded in killing the woman.

If the opposite had been the case – if it was Biedersen who had been killed – well, there was every reason for the police to come visiting.

Every reason. He could feel his guts tying themselves in knots as this possibility became a probability.

Even more reason, in fact, than if Biedersen had succeeded in what he had set out to do; and when he opened the door and let in the woman who identified herself as a detective constable, he was convinced he knew why Biedersen hadn't been in touch later, as he had promised.

I must keep a straight face, he thought. No matter what has happened, I must keep a straight face.

It felt like clutching at straws. Thin and worn-out straws. But he knew that there wasn't anything else to clutch at.

She sat down on the sofa. Held her notebook at the ready while he served up tea and biscuits. She didn't seem to be about to come out with something devastating, and he succeeded in calming down a bit.

'Help yourself!'

He flopped down into the armchair opposite her.

'Thank you. Well, there are a few questions we'd like you to answer.'

'Has something happened?'

'Why do you ask that?'

He shrugged. She took a tape recorder out of her bag.

'Are you going to record this? That's not what happened last time.'

'We all have our own ways of working,' she said with a little smile. 'Are you ready?'

He nodded.

'OK,' she said, switching on the tape recorder. 'Do you recognize this music?'

SEVEN

15–23 FEBRUARY

25

If there was anything that Chief Inspector Van Veeteren hated, it was press conferences.

The similarity with sitting in the dock during a trial was too striking, and the defence you were most often able to come up with was certainly very reminiscent of a guilty man's excuses and dodgy evasions. There was something about the very atmosphere on these occasions that seemed to him to express both the general public's latent (and now often openly expressed) fear of all the violence inherent in modern society, and its lack of faith in the ability of the police force to put an end to it.

It was just the same this time round. The conference room on the first floor was full to overflowing with journalists and reporters, sitting, standing, taking photographs and trying to outdo one another in the art of asking biased and insinuating questions.

He had been press-ganged into accompanying Hiller and sitting behind a cheap, rectangular table overloaded with microphones, cables and the obligatory bottles of soda water, which for some unfathomable reason were always present whenever high-ranking police officers made statements in front of cameras – Reinhart maintained that it had something to do with sponsorship, and it was not impossible that he was right about this as well.

Reinhart was often right.

However, the sponsorship Van Veeteren received from the chief of police was virtually non-existent. As usual, once the questions started to come, Hiller leant back in his chair with his arms crossed and a sphinx-like expression on his face. He was only too happy to leave all the answers to the chief inspector, who – he was careful to stress – was the person responsible for the investigation. Hiller was merely the administrator and coordinator.

But he provided the introductory information himself, formally dressed in his midnight-blue suit and emphasizing each point by means of forceful tapping on the table with a silver ballpoint pen.

'The murder victim is a certain Karel Innings,' he explained. 'According to what we have been able to ascertain he was shot dead in his home in Loewingen at some time between half past twelve and half past one yesterday, Wednesday. Innings happened to be alone in the house, being on sick leave with a stomach complaint, and so far we have no definite clues concerning the killer. The victim was hit by a total of five bullets – three in the chest and two below the belt – and the weapon appears to have been a Berenger-75. There are clear indications that the gun was the same one as was used in two previous cases during the last few weeks . . . The murders of Ryszard Malik and Rickard Maasleitner.'

He paused for a moment, but it was obvious that he had more to say and no questions were fired at him as yet.

'It is thus possible that we are dealing with a so-called serial killer; but there is also a clear link between the people who have lost their lives so far. All three are members of a group who spent their military service in the years 1964 and 1965 at the Staff College here in Maardam, an institution that was later relocated to Schaabe. Our efforts are currently concentrated on trying to discover the precise significance of this link, and of course also providing the best possible level of protection for the remainder of that group.'

'Have you any clues?' interrupted a young woman from the local radio station.

'All questions will be answered shortly by Chief Inspector Van Veeteren, who is sitting here beside me,' Hiller explained with a smile. 'But before I throw the meeting open to the floor, just let me point out that you will be given access to all the information we possess at present, and I sincerely hope that we are all on the same side in the hunt for the ruthless murderer we are evidently up against. Thank you.'

The chief of police had said his piece. Van Veeteren leant forward over the table and glared at the audience.

'Fire away,' he said.

'Was it the same method in this case as well?' said somebody.

'How come that the police hadn't provided some kind of protection, if it was known that the victim would be one of that group?' asked somebody else.

'With regard to the method—' Van Veeteren began.

'Has the level of protection been increased?' interrupted a third.

'With regard to the method,' Van Veeteren repeated, unperturbed, 'it was a little different this time. The victim, Innings that is, evidently invited the perpetrator into his house and offered him tea . . . Or her. This naturally suggests—'

'What does that suggest?' yelled a red-haired reporter in the third row.

'It could suggest that he was acquainted with the murderer. At any rate, it seemed that he was expecting him to call.'

'Is it one of the others in the group?' asked somebody from the *Allgemejne*.

'We don't know,' said Van Veeteren.

'But you have interrogated the whole group?'

'Of course.'

'And will do so again?'

'Naturally.'

'Protection?' somebody repeated.

'We don't have unlimited resources,' explained Van Veeteren. 'It obviously requires vast manpower to keep thirty people under observation all round the clock.'

'Is it a madman?'

'A person is presumably not totally sane if he goes out and kills three people.'

'Was there any sign of a struggle at Innings's place? Had he tried to defend himself or anything like that?'

'No.'

'What theories do you have? Surely you have more than just this to go on?'

'Do you have a suspect?' the red-head managed to inter-ject.

Van Veeteren shook his head.

'At this stage we don't have a suspect.'

'Is it a man or a woman?'

'Could be either.'

'What's all this about music being played over the tele-phone?'

'There are indications that suggest the murderer keeps calling his victims for some time before shooting them.

He calls them and plays a particular tune over the phone to them.'

'What tune?'

'We don't know.'

'Why? Why does he ring?'

'We don't know.'

'What do you think?'

'We're working on various different possibilities.'

'Had Innings received one of these phone calls?'

'We haven't clarified that as yet.'

'If he had, surely he'd have contacted the police?'

'You would think so.'

'But he hadn't?'

'No.'

There was a pause. Van Veeteren took a sip of soda water.

'How many police officers are working on this case at the moment?' asked Würgner from *Neuwe Blatt*.

'All available officers.'

'How many is that?'

Van Veeteren did the calculation.

'About thirty. Of various ranks.'

'When do you think you'll be able to close the case?'

Van Veeteren shrugged.

'It's not possible to say.'

'Has it got something to do with the armed forces? The link seems to suggest that.'

'No, I would hardly think so,' said Van Veeteren after a moment's thought.

An elderly and unusually patient editor of a crime magazine programme on one of the television channels had been waving his pen for a while, and now managed to get his oar in.

'What exactly do you want help with? Pictures and stuff?'

Van Veeteren nodded.

'Yes,' he said. 'We'd like you to publish photographs and names of all the men in the group, and to write about the telephone calls. Ask the general public to pass on to us any possible tips they may have.'

'Why didn't you release the pictures and so on earlier? You must have known about it after the second murder, surely?'

'It wasn't definite,' said Van Veeteren with a sigh. 'It was only an indication.'

'But now it's definite?'

'Yes.'

A gigantic man with a long, grey beard – Van Veeteren knew him to be Vejmanen on the *Telegraaf* – stood up at the back of the room and bellowed in a voice reminiscent of thunder.

'OK. The interviews with Innings's relatives and friends! What results have they produced?'

'We are still conducting them,' said Van Veeteren. 'You'll get the details tomorrow.'

'How kind of you,' thundered Vejmanen. 'And when do you think we'll have the next victim?'

Van Veeteren blew his nose again.

'Our intention is to pick up the killer before he strikes again,' he explained.

'Excellent,' said Vejmanen. 'So shall we say that you are in no particular hurry? This business is going to be news-worthy for four or five days at least . . . Possibly a whole week.'

He sat down, and appreciative laughter could be heard here and there in the audience.

'If I understand it rightly,' said a woman whose clothes and make-up suggested she was attached to some television programme, 'you will be providing some kind of protec-tion to all the remaining members of this group. But, at the same time, one of them might be the murderer. Won't that be a pretty intricate task?'

'Not really,' said Van Veeteren. 'I can promise you that we shall cease to protect the murderer from himself the moment we know who he is.'

'Have you made a profile of the killer?' shouted some-body from the back.

'I can't say we have.'

'Will you be making one?'

'I always make a profile of the perpetrator,' said Van Veeteren, 'but I don't normally send it out into the ether.'

'Why not?' asked somebody.

The chief inspector shrugged.

'I don't really know,' he said. 'I suppose I hold the old-fashioned view that one ought to stick to the facts when it comes to the media. Theories are best suited to the inside of my head. At least, my theories are. Any more questions?'

'How long is it since you failed to solve a case?'

'About eight years.'

'The G file?'

'Yes. You seem to know about it . . . As you can all hear, the level of questioning has sunk. I think we'd better leave it at that.'

'What the hell!' exclaimed the red-haired reporter.

'As I said,' said Van Veeteren, rising to his feet.

'For Christ's sake, this is incredible!' said Reinhart when he, Münster and Van Veeteren gathered in the chief inspector's office ten minutes later. 'The murderer rings the doorbell, is let in, sits down on the sofa and drinks a cup of tea. Then takes out a gun and kills him. Incredible!'

'And then simply goes away,' Münster added.

'Conclusion?' demanded Van Veeteren.

'He knew him,' said Münster.

'Or her,' said Reinhart.

'You mean the bullet in the balls suggests a her?'

'Yes,' said Reinhart, 'I do.'

'But it's hardly any less incredible if it's a woman,' said Münster.

There was a knock on the door and Heinemann came in.

'What are you doing?' he asked as he perched cautiously on the window seat.

'These two are standing here saying it's incredible all the time,' muttered the chief inspector. 'I'm just sitting and thinking.'

'I see,' said Heinemann.

'What's everybody else doing?' asked Reinhart.

'Rooth and deBries have gone off to interview the neighbours in a bit more detail,' said Heinemann. 'Moreno and Jung were going to take his workplace, I think you said.'

'That's right,' said Van Veeteren. 'There doesn't seem to be much point in looking for a murderer among his relatives and friends in this case, but we have to hear what they have to say. Somebody might have noticed something. You can take this little lot, Münster . . .'

He handed a list to Münster, who read it as he walked slowly backwards through the door.

'Heinemann,' said the chief inspector, 'I suggest you continue searching for links . . . Now you've got an extra one to work on. Let's hope there's a lower common denominator than the whole group.'

Heinemann nodded.

'I think there will be,' he said. 'I'm thinking of asking Hiller for a bit of help in getting me permission to look at their bank details.'

'Bank details?' said Reinhart. 'What the hell for?'

'There's no harm in having a look,' said Heinemann. 'If these three have been up to something, the odds are it won't withstand all that much daylight. And such things usually leave traces in bank accounts. Is there anything else you want me to do, Chief Inspector?'

'No,' said Van Veeteren. 'You might as well keep on doing what you've been doing.'

Heinemann nodded. Put his hands in his trouser pockets and left Van Veeteren and Reinhart on their own.

'He's not so thick,' said Reinhart. 'It's mainly a question of tempo.'

Van Veeteren took out a toothpick and broke it in half.

'Reinhart,' he said after a while, 'will you be so kind as to explain something for me?'

'Shoot,' said Reinhart.

'If it's as Heinemann says and these three have had some kind of criminal past together, and that they know very well . . . er, knew very well . . . who the perpetrator is . . . why the hell did Innings let him in and serve him tea before allowing himself to be shot?'

Reinhart thought for a while, digging away with a matchstick at the bowl of his pipe.

'Well,' he said eventually, 'he – or she, I mean – must presumably have been in disguise, I assume. Or else . . .'

'Well?'

'Or else they know who it is, but don't know what the person looks like. There's a difference. And it was a long time ago, of course.'

Van Veeteren nodded.

'Have you any cigarettes?'

Reinhart shook his head.

'Afraid not.'

'Never mind. Just a few more questions, so that I know I'm not barking up the wrong tree. If it really is just a small group that the killer is after, Innings must have known that his turn would be coming. Or suspected it, at least. Isn't that right?'

'Yes,' said Reinhart. 'Especially if he was going to be the last one.'

Van Veeteren thought about that for a few seconds.

'And must have known who the killer is?'

'Who's behind it all, in any case. A slight difference again.'

'Is there any possibility, do you think, that Innings wouldn't recognize one of the group?'

Reinhart lit his pipe and thought that one over.

'They haven't seen one another for thirty years,' he said. 'We know what they all look like nowadays, but they don't. They may just have that old photograph to go on . . . And their memories, of course.'

'Go on,' said Van Veeteren.

'Even so, I think I'd recognize the blokes I did National Service with. Without any trouble at all, in fact.'

'Same here,' said the chief inspector. 'Especially if I'd been prepared for it. So, conclusion?'

Reinhart puffed away at his pipe.

'If we're talking about a small group,' he said, 'then the murderer is an outsider. It could be a contract killer, of course, but I think that's hardly likely.'

Van Veeteren nodded.

'Don't you think that's the way it is?'

'Yes,' said Reinhart. 'As I've said before, I'm inclined to think that the murderer is a woman, and as far as I know there isn't a woman in the group.'

'You're sometimes bloody brilliant at observing things,' said the chief inspector.

'Thank you. There's one thing we mustn't forget, though.'

'What's that?'

'There's nothing to stop it being a woman who intends to kill the whole lot of 'em.'

'There's nothing much to stop a woman doing anything at all,' sighed Van Veeteren. 'Apart from us. Shall we get this thing solved now, then?'

'Let's. It's about time,' said Reinhart.

26

The distance to Loewingen – the latest murder scene – was not much more than thirty kilometres, and as he settled down in the car he regretted that it wasn't a bit further. A few hours' driving wouldn't have done him any harm; even when he got up, he'd felt the unfulfilled need for a long and restful journey. Preferably through a grey, rain-sodden landscape, just like this one. Hours in which to think things over.

But in fact it was minutes instead – he managed to stretch it to half an hour by taking the alternative route via Borsens and Penderdixte, where he had spent a few summers as a seven- or eight-year-old.

There were two reasons why he had postponed his visit until Friday. In the first place Münster and Rooth had already spoken to Ulrike Fremdli and also the three teenagers on the Wednesday evening, and it might be a good idea not to give the impression that the police were hounding them every day. And in the second place, he'd had plenty to occupy himself with yesterday even so.

You could say that again. During the afternoon he and Reinhart had addressed the delicate business of organizing protection for the as yet not murdered (as Reinhart insisted on calling them).

The five living abroad were without doubt the easiest ones to sort out. After a brief discussion it was decided quite simply to leave them to their own devices. This was made clear in the letter circulated to everybody concerned, which urged them to turn to the nearest police authority in whatever country they were living in, if they felt threatened or insecure in any way.

There are limits after all, Reinhart had said.

As for those still in the country but outside the Maardam police district, something similar applied. Reinhart spent more than three hours telephoning colleagues in various places and simply instructing them to protect Mr So-and-so from all threats and dangers.

It was not a pleasant task, and afterwards Reinhart had gone to Van Veeteren's office and requested a job with the traffic police instead. The chief inspector had rejected this request, but told Reinhart that he was welcome to throw up in the waste-paper basket if he felt the need.

It was one of those days.

In the Maardam police district there were now thirteen

possible victims left, and to look after them Van Veeteren assembled – if one were to be honest – a ragbag of constables and probationers, and left it to the promising and enthusiastic Widmar Krause to instruct and organize them.

When he had done that and leant back for a moment, Van Veeteren tried to make a snap judgement of how effective this expensive protection would really be, and concluded that if it had been a condom he'd been assessing, to put it brutally, they might just as well have gone ahead without it.

But fictitious – or simulated – protection was nevertheless preferable to nothing at all, he tried to convince himself. With covering his own back in the forefront of his mind.

Then Van Veeteren, Reinhart and Münster spent the rest of the afternoon and evening discussing the murderer's character and identity, and working out a system for how the interviews with the as yet not murdered should be conducted (and in this context as well, they decided to leave those living abroad to their own devices – at least for the time being). Increasingly frequently they were interrupted by the duty officer or Miss Katz, rushing in with so-called hot tips from the general public, which had started flowing in despite the fact that the press conference was only a few hours old.

By about eight, Reinhart had had enough.

'Fuck this for a lark!' he exclaimed and threw away the sheet of paper he'd just read. 'It's impossible to think if we have to keep beavering away like this all the time.'

'You could buy us a beer,' said Van Veeteren.

'All right. I expect you'll want cigarettes as well?'

'Just a few at most,' said the chief inspector modestly.

This was in fact what occupied his thoughts for the first half of the drive to Loewingen.

I ought not to smoke, he thought.

I drink too much beer.

Neither habit is good for me, certainly not the cigarettes. In connection with an operation for bowel cancer almost a year ago, an innocent doctor had said that an occasional glass of beer wouldn't do him any harm – Van Veeteren had immediately committed this advice to memory, and he knew that he would never forget it, even if he lived to be a hundred and ten.

Incidentally, wasn't it the case that an occasional cigarette could stimulate the thought processes?

Whatever, I ought to play badminton with Münster more often, he thought. Go out jogging now and then. If only I could get rid of this damned cold!

It was only after he'd passed the farm in Penderdixte where he'd spent some of his childhood that he changed track and started thinking about the investigation. This accursed investigation.

Three murders.

Three men shot in cold blood.

In rather less than a month.

This last one was without doubt more than a bit rich. No matter how much he thought about it, changed the angle or reassessed it, he simply couldn't make it add up.

The questions were obvious.

Was there in fact a smaller group within the group? (I hope to God there is! Reinhart had let slip over a beer the previous evening. And of course that was significant: Reinhart was not in the habit of placing himself in the hands of the sacred.)

If not, and if the murderer was intending to kill all of them – well, they must be dealing with a lunatic. With an incomprehensible, irrational and presumably totally mad motive. Nobody can have an acceptable (in any sense of the word) reason for killing thirty-three people, one after the other.

Not according to Chief Inspector Van Veeteren's yard-stick, in any case.

A cold and calculating lunatic like that would be the opponent they feared more than any other, they had all been touchingly in agreement on that.

But if there really was a smaller group?

Van Veeteren fished up two toothpicks from his breast pocket, but after tasting them, he dropped them on the floor and lit a cigarette instead.

In that case, he thought after the first stimulating drag, Innings should (must?) have known that he belonged to that little group, and was in danger. Without doubt.

But nevertheless he had invited the murderer into his house, and allowed himself to be shot without raising an eyebrow. Why?

And that wasn't all – he knew he could extend the argument further without exploding it: there was another crux.

If it was implausible to believe that Innings would invite somebody in he knew was intending to kill him, he can't have suspected anything. But: if he knew he was in danger, it seemed beyond the bounds of possibility that he would invite a stranger into his house.

Ergo, the chief inspector thought as he slowed down behind a tractor: the person Innings invited to tea and allowed himself to be murdered by must be somebody he trusted.

'That must be right, OK?' he said aloud to nobody in particular as he overtook the enthusiastically gesticulating farmer. 'Somebody he knew, for Christ's sake!'

That was as far as he got.

He sighed. Inhaled deeply but was repulsed by the taste.

He felt like a poor idiot who had been released from the asylum but was now drooling over a three-piece puzzle that had been thrust into his hand as a test to pass before being allowed back into society.

It was not an attractive image, but the images that flitted through his mind rarely were.

Hell and damnation, Van Veeteren thought. I hope Reinhart can solve this one.

Loewingen was a sprawling little town with a few industries, even fewer blocks of flats, and masses of individual houses and villas. Despite an ancient town centre from the Middle Ages, this was one of those towns you simply lived in – one of all the late twentieth-century insufferable, monocultural wastelands, Van Veeteren thought as he finally found the housing estate he was looking for. Uniform, boring and safe.

Well, the extent to which it was safe might be arguable.

Ulrike Fremdli welcomed him, and ushered him to a seat on the same sofa the murderer must have sat on exactly two days earlier. She was a powerful-looking woman with neat brown hair and a face he reckoned must have been beautiful once upon a time. She seemed to be reticent and somewhat prim, and he wondered if she was taking sedatives – he thought he recognized the symptoms.

'Would you like anything?' she asked curtly.

He shook his head.

'How are you?' he asked.

She gave him a penetrating look.

'Bloody awful,' she said. 'I've sent the kids to my sister. I need to be alone.'

'You'll manage?'

'Yes,' she said. 'But please ask your questions and get it over with.'

'How long had you known each other?'

'Since '86,' she said. 'We moved in together eighteen months ago. We had a lot of trouble with his former wife before that.'

Van Veeteren thought for a moment. Decided to skip as much as possible and not beat about the bush.

'I'd like to make this as brief as possible,' he said. 'I take it you think the same way. I aim to catch whoever murdered your husband, and I'd like some answers to a few quite specific questions.'

She nodded.

'It's important that I get honest answers.'

'Fire away.'

'All right,' said Van Veeteren. 'Do you think he knew he was in danger?'

'I don't know,' she said after a tense pause. 'I honestly don't know.'

'Was he worried, these last few days?'

'Yes, but there were reasons why he should be, you might say.'

Her deep voice trembled slightly, but not much.

'I'll tell you what I think,' said Van Veeteren. 'I think Innings was one of a smaller group, and it's the members of that group the murderer is out to kill.'

'A group?'

'Yes, a few of the National Servicemen who got up to something thirty years ago . . . Possibly later as well. In any case, there must be a link between some of the thirty-five. What do you think?'

She shook her head.

'I've no idea.'

'Did he ever talk about his military service?'

'Never. Well, we spoke about it recently, of course, but not much.'

Van Veeteren nodded.

'If you think of anything that might suggest there could be a link of the kind I've mentioned, will you promise to get in touch with me?'

'Yes, of course.'

He gave her his business card.

'You can phone me direct, that's easier. Anyway, next question. Can you tell me if your husband was in touch with any new contacts during the week before it happened?

Did he meet anybody you didn't know, or people he didn't normally mix with?'

She thought it over.

'Not as far as I know.'

'Take your time. Think it through day by day, that usually helps.'

'He met people at work as well . . . We only meet in the evenings, really.'

'Let's concentrate on the evenings. Did he have any visitors these last few days?'

'No . . . No, I don't think so. Not that I noticed, at least.'

'Did he go out at all in the evening?'

'No. Hang on, yes: last Friday. He went out for a few hours last Friday.'

'Where?'

'Somewhere in town. Some restaurant or other, I think. I was asleep when he came back home.'

'Who was he out with?'

She shrugged.

'I don't know. Some friends from work, I expect. Burgner, perhaps.'

'He didn't say anything about it?'

'Not as far as I recall. We had visitors – my brother and his family – quite early on Saturday, so I don't think we ever got round to discussing it.'

'Did he often go out on his own?'

She shook her head.

'No. Once a month, at most. The same as me, in fact.'

'Hmm,' said Van Veeteren. 'Nothing more?'

'Do you mean, was he out any other evening?'

'Yes.'

'No, he was at home . . . let me think . . . yes, Sunday, Monday and Tuesday.'

Van Veeteren nodded.

'OK,' he said. 'Do you know anything about those telephone calls?'

'I've read about them,' she said. 'The officers who were here on Wednesday asked me about that as well.'

'And?'

'No, nothing.'

'Do you think he received any?'

'I don't know.'

'OK,' said Van Veeteren, leaning back on the sofa. 'Then I have only one more question. Do you suspect anybody?'

'What?' she exclaimed. 'What the hell do you mean?'

Van Veeteren cleared his throat.

'One of the things that confuses us,' he explained, 'is that he invited the murderer in without any more ado. That suggests he knew the person concerned. If he did, then you might do as well. I mean, you've been together for ten years after all.'

She said nothing. He could tell by looking at her that this hadn't occurred to her until now; but he could also see that she didn't have an answer.

'Will you promise me to think about it?'

She nodded.

'Please think as well about whether he might have felt under threat. That's an extremely important question – and it could be that the tiniest detail could give us a clue that could put us on the right track.'

'I understand that.'

He stood up.

'I know that you're going through sheer hell,' he said. 'I've been stomping around in tragedies like this for more than thirty years. You're welcome to contact me even if you only want to talk. Otherwise I'll be in touch again in a few days.'

'Our life together was so good,' she said. 'I suppose we ought to have realized that something that worked so well couldn't last for ever.'

'Yes,' said Van Veeteren. 'That's more or less the way I look at life as well.'

When he paused in the street outside and tried to imagine the route the murderer would have taken, it struck him that he rather liked her.

Quite a lot, if truth be told.

*

'Knowing what I know now,' said editor-in-chief Cannelli, 'quite a lot of things fall into place.'

'What, for example?' Jung wondered.

'That there was something bothering him.'

'How was that noticeable?'

Cannelli sighed and gazed out of the window.

'Well,' he said, 'I had a few longish chats with him . . . about headlines, pictures and suchlike. That was routine, several times a week. But there was something about his concentration that struck me. He seemed to be thinking about something else all the time . . .'

'How long had you known him?'

'Five years,' said Cannelli. 'Since I took charge of the newspaper after Windemeer. He was good – Innings, that is.'

Jung nodded.

'Do you know if he met anybody outside his usual circle of contacts lately? If somebody – or something – cropped up here at work that could possibly be connected with his unease?'

He realized that this was a pretty convoluted question, and Cannelli responded to his apologetic smile with a shrug of the shoulders.

'We produce a newspaper, Inspector. People are running in and out all day long . . . I'm sorry, but I don't think I can help you.'

Jung thought for a moment.

'OK,' he said eventually, closing his notebook. 'If you think of anything and all that . . .'

'Of course,' said Cannelli.

Moreno was sitting in the car, waiting for him.

'How did it go?' she asked.

'Pretty pointless.'

'Same here. How many did you talk to?'

'Three,' said Jung.

'Four for me,' said Moreno. 'But I think one thing is crystal clear.'

'What's that?'

'He knew he was in danger. He was behaving oddly, that's what everybody says.'

Jung nodded and started the car.

'At least, that's what they all say with hindsight,' he said. 'What a shame that people never react in time.'

'Yes indeed,' said Moreno. 'Mind you, if we were to take care of everybody who seems a bit worried, we probably wouldn't have much time left to devote to anything else.'

'Absolutely right,' said Jung. 'How about a coffee? It's good for the nerves.'

'OK,' said Moreno.

27

She dithered for a day and a half.

She had read about it for the first time on the Thursday evening – in one of the newspapers on the bus on the way home – but it wasn't until much later the same night that her suspicions were aroused. In the middle of a dream that vanished immediately into the shadows of the subconscious, she woke up and could picture it in her mind's eye.

The occupied telephone booth in the hall. The back pressed up against the grey-tinted glass. The tape recorder pressed against the receiver.

It had only happened once, and that was at least three weeks ago now. But the image persisted. That Tuesday evening. She had intended phoning a fellow student to ask about something, but seen immediately that it was occupied. It can't have lasted more than three or four seconds – she had simply opened her door, noted that the phone booth was occupied, and gone back into her room.

Five minutes later it was free and she'd been able to make her call.

It was remarkable that this brief, totally meaningless sequence should have stayed with her. Now when she had been woken up by it, she couldn't recall having thought about it before at all.

And of course, it was precisely that – these vague and slightly unlikely circumstances – that made her hesitate.

On the Friday afternoon she had bumped into her on the stairs. There was nothing unusual about that either – it was a banal, everyday occurrence – but when she woke up with a start early that Saturday morning, the two trivial images had somehow combined.

Melted into each other and roused a dreadful suspicion.

She ought really to have consulted Natalie first, but Natalie had gone home to her parents for the weekend, and her room was empty. However, after an early jog in the park (that was cut short because of the rain), a shower and breakfast, she had made up her mind.

Something prevented her from using the telephone in the hall (was it fear? she asked herself later) and instead she used a public phone box by the post office to ring the police.

It was 9.34, and the call and her information were registered by Constable Willock, who promised to pass it on to the senior officers on the case and report back to her eventually.

She returned to her room to study, and wait.

Her conscience was clearer, but she had a nagging feeling of unreality.

Reinhart sighed. He had spent the last ten minutes trying to perform the trick of half lying down on a standard office chair, but the only notable result was that he now had back ache. At the base of his spine and also between his shoulder blades. Van Veeteren was sitting opposite him, slumped over his desk, which was littered with paper, files, empty coffee mugs and broken toothpicks.

'Say something,' said Reinhart.

Van Veeteren muttered and started reading a new sheet of paper.

'Hot air, nothing else,' he said after another minute and crumpled it up. 'There's no substance in this either. Loewingen is a suburb for the middle classes, in case you didn't know. All the wives work, and all the kids attend nursery school. The nearest neighbour at home when the murder took place was six houses away, and she was asleep. This case is not exactly gliding smoothly along the rails.'

'Asleep?' said Reinhart, with a trace of longing in his voice. 'But it was one in the afternoon, for Christ's sake!'

'Night nurse at the Gemejnte hospital,' Van Veeteren explained.

'So there are no witnesses, is that what you're saying?'

'Exactly,' said the chief inspector, continuing to leaf through the papers. 'Not even a cat.'

'He certainly seems to have been worried,' Reinhart pointed out after a moment of silence. 'Everybody has commented on that. He must have known that he was in trouble.'

'Certainly,' said Van Veeteren. 'We can probably assume we're looking at a small group.'

Reinhart sighed again and abandoned the chair. Stood gazing out of the window instead.

'Bloody rain,' he said. 'I ought to be reborn as a swamp. Haven't you found anything at all to work on?'

There was a knock on the door and Münster came in. He nodded and sat down on the chair Reinhart had just vacated.

'He was out last Friday night,' said Van Veeteren.

'Innings?' wondered Münster.

'Yes. Maybe we should check up on what he was doing. He was probably having a beer with a few colleagues, but you never know.'

'How can we check up on that?' asked Reinhart.

Van Veeteren shrugged.

'Hmm,' he said. 'We'll put Moreno and Jung on it. They can ask a few questions at his workplace again. See if they can find somebody who was with him. And then, I wonder . . .'

'What do you wonder?' asked Reinhart.

'In town, I think she said . . . He was at a restaurant in town, his wife thought. Did she mean Loewingen or Maardam?'

'Loewingen's not a town, it's a dump,' said Reinhart.

'Could be,' said Münster. 'But there are a few restaurants there even so.'

'Yes, yes,' muttered Van Veeteren. 'That'll be Jung's and Moreno's headache. Where are they, by the way?'

'At home, I expect,' said Reinhart. 'I've heard it said that it's Saturday today.'

'Go back to your office and ring them and wake them up,' said Van Veeteren. 'Tell them I want to know where he was and with whom by Monday afternoon at the latest. How the hell they do that is up to them.'

'With pleasure,' said Reinhart, walking to the door. Just then Miss Katz appeared with two bundles of paper.

'Tip-offs from the detective known as the general public,' she explained. 'A hundred and twenty since yesterday afternoon. Constable Krause has sorted them out.'

'How?' asked Münster.

'The usual categories,' snorted Van Veeteren. 'Daft and slightly less daft. Can you run through them, Münster, and come back to me an hour from now?'

'Of course,' sighed Münster, picking up the papers.

Ah well, the chief inspector thought when he was alone again. The wheels are turning. What the hell was it I'd thought of doing myself?

Ah yes, an hour down in the sauna, that was it.

28

'I'm going away for a bit,' said Biedersen.

'Oh, are you?' said his wife. 'Why?'

'Business,' said Biedersen. 'I'll probably be away for a few weeks at least.'

His wife looked up from the cooker hotplates she was busy cleaning with the aid of a new product she'd found in the shop yesterday that was said to be more effective than any other make.

'Oh, will you?' she said. 'Where are you going?'

'Various places. Hamburg among others. There are quite a few contacts I need to follow up.'

'I understand,' said his wife, and started scrubbing again, thinking that she didn't at all. Understand, that is. But it didn't matter, of course. She had never interfered in her husband's affairs – running an import company (or was it two now?) was a complicated and not especially appealing business. Nothing for a woman like her. Ever since they married, they had been in agreement about one thing: they would each look after their own side of family life. He would look after the finances, and she would take care of the home and the children. All of whom had fled the nest now, and formed their own families on more or less similar lines.

Which in turn gave her time to devote herself to other things. Such as cooker hotplates.

'How's it going?' she asked.

'How's what going?'

'Well, your business. You seem to have been a bit stressed these last few days.'

'Nonsense.'

'Are you sure?'

'Yes, of course.'

'That's good to know. But you'll keep in touch, won't you?'

'Naturally.'

But when he'd left, she found herself still wondering if there hadn't been something wrong nevertheless. Ever since – she worked it out – Tuesday evening, when he'd come home rather late and in a bit of a nervous state, he had been unusually irritated and touchy.

And then they had found one of his old National Service mates murdered, and that had knocked the stuffing out of him, she could see that. Even if he hadn't wanted to admit as much, of course.

So perhaps it was a good thing for him to get away from it all for a while. Good for all concerned, as they say. There were things she also didn't want to admit as well, such as not objecting to having their large house to herself for a change. She had nothing against that at all, she decided, and put a little extra elbow grease into her scrubbing.

When the chief inspector came back from the sauna, Münster was already sitting there, waiting. It looked as if he'd been there for quite a while, in fact, as he'd had time to supply himself with a mug of coffee and the morning paper.

'So,' said the chief inspector as he sat down at his desk, 'let's hear it then.'

Münster folded up his newspaper and produced three pale yellow cards.

'I think it would be best if somebody else went through the material as well,' he said. 'It's a bit difficult to keep awake when you have to read so much rubbish. One bloke has evidently called three times and claimed that his mother is the murderer.'

'Really?' said Van Veeteren. 'And you're sure he isn't telling the truth?'

'Pretty sure,' said Münster. 'He's well into his seventies, and his mother died in 1955. And then there's somebody who claims to have been present at the time – in Innings's house, that is – and seen exactly what happened. The killer was a gigantic immigrant with a scimitar and a black patch over one eye.'

'Hmm,' said Van Veeteren. 'Do you have anything a bit more credible to tell me?'

'Yes, I certainly do,' said Münster. 'Several things we ought to follow up. These three are probably the most interesting ones.'

He handed over the cards, and the chief inspector read them while working a toothpick from one side of his mouth to the other.

'I'll take this one,' he said. 'You can check the other two. Give the rest of the interesting ones to Reinhart, and he can arrange follow-ups.'

Münster nodded. Drank up his coffee and left the room.

Van Veeteren waited until the door was closed, then looked at the card again and dialled the number.

'Katrine Kroeller?'

'Just a moment, please.'

There was a pause of half a minute or so, then he heard a girl's voice in the receiver. No more than nineteen or twenty at most, he thought.

'Hello, Katrine Kroeller here.'

'My name is Chief Inspector Van Veeteren. You've reported an observation in connection with an investigation we are busy with. Can I come and have a chat with you?'

'Yes . . . Yes, of course. When will you be coming?'

'Now,' said Van Veeteren, looking at the clock. 'Or at least, in twenty minutes or so. Your address is Parkvej 31, is that correct?'

'Yes.'

'OK, I'll see you shortly, Miss Kroeller.'

'Yes . . . You're welcome. I hope . . .'

'You hope what?'

'I hope you're not just wasting your time.'

'We shall see,' said Van Veeteren, and hung up.

If only she knew how much of our time is wasted, he thought. Then he wriggled into his jacket and set off.

She was waiting for him at the gate. As he thought, she was a bright-looking girl of about twenty – she looked very Nordic, with a ponytail and a long neck. She was carrying an umbrella, and she escorted him carefully along the paved path to the front door at the gable end of the large two-storey house, making sure he didn't need to step on the soaking wet lawn.

'It's not all that easy to find your way here,' she explained. 'There are four of us renting rooms. Mrs Klausner, our landlady, lives on the ground floor.'

Van Veeteren nodded. Both the house and the garden suggested well-heeled upper middle class; but of course there were always people hovering at the edge of their social class, he reminded himself. People who had to take in lodgers and resort to other similar ways of making ends meet.

'Let's hear it,' he said when he had sat down in her room with its sloping ceiling and blue wallpaper. 'If I understand the situation rightly, you saw a woman using a tape recorder in a phone booth.'

She nodded.

'Yes, outside here in the hall. It's there for the tenants to use. I saw her inside it, holding a tape recorder against the receiver . . . One of those little cassette things.'

'Who?'

'Miss Adler, the woman who lives next to me.'

'Adler?' said Van Veeteren.

'Yes. Maria Adler. There are four of us, but I don't know her at all. She keeps herself to herself.'

'When was this?'

'Three weeks ago, or thereabouts.'

'Just the once?'

'Yes.'

'How come that you remember it?'

She hesitated.

'I don't really know, to tell you the truth. I hadn't given

it a second thought. But then it came back to me when I read about those murders in the newspaper.'

Van Veeteren nodded, and thought for a moment. She seemed to be a reliable witness, that was obvious. Calm and sensible, not inclined to exaggerate or be hysterical.

And slowly, very slowly, the thought began to sprout in his case-hardened consciousness. That this could be it. If this pale girl knew what she was talking about – and there was no reason to think she didn't – it was not impossible that the murderer was right here. Ryszard Malik's and Rickard Maasleitner's and Karel Innings's murderer. In the very next room. He could feel his pulse beating in his temples.

In this respectable villa in the respectable district of Deijkstraa. Surrounded by doctors, lawyers, successful businessmen and God only knows who else.

A woman, then, just as Reinhart had predicted – yes indeed, there was a lot to support that thesis . . . Perhaps most of all this feeling he had, that he always seemed to have when something was happening. A little signal saying that now . . . now things were suddenly getting serious, after all those days of hard work and despair.

And it was winking at him at this very moment.

The signal. That red warning light.

Naturally, there were plenty of other reasons for using a tape recorder in a telephone booth; he was the first to admit that. It was simply that he didn't want to believe them, had no desire to do so. He wanted this to be the breakthrough, that was the bottom line.

'So she's in there?' he said, indicating with his head.

She nodded.

'Maria Adler?'

'Yes.'

'Do you know if she's there at the moment?'

Katrine Kroeller shook her head. Her ponytail waved back and forth.

'No. I haven't seen her today. But she's very quiet, so it's possible she's in.'

Van Veeteren stood up and tried to work things out. If he were to follow the police rule book, the correct procedure in this situation would naturally be to phone for reinforcements. There ought to be several officers involved. The woman in that room could very well be the person who had shot dead in cold blood three of her fellow human beings during the last month. She had a gun, presumably also ammunition, and she didn't normally miss.

He didn't even have his police weapon with him. As usual, it ought to be said.

So of course he ought to phone. It wouldn't take long for a few more officers to get here.

He looked round.

'May I borrow this?' he said, picking up an oblong-shaped wooden statuette standing on a bookshelf. Presumably African. Easy to handle. Three-quarters of a kilo, or thereabouts.

'Why?'

He didn't answer. Stood up and went out into the hall. Katrine Kroeller followed him hesitantly.

'The next door here?'

She nodded.

'Go back to your room.'

She reluctantly did as she was told.

With his left hand he slowly depressed the door handle. His right hand was clutching the statuette. He noticed that he was still sweating a little after the sauna.

The door opened. He burst in.

It took him less than two seconds to register that the room was empty.

More than empty.

Abandoned. The tenant who had been living here had left and had no intention of returning.

She had moved to somewhere else.

'Shit!' he exclaimed.

Stood motionless for a few more seconds, looking round the barren room.

No personal belongings. No clothes. No washing-up in the kitchenette alcove. The bed made in such a way that you could see there were no sheets. Just a pillow, a blanket and a quilt.

'Shit!' he muttered again, and went back out into the hall.

Miss Kroeller peeped out through her door.

'She's done a runner,' said Van Veeteren. 'Go and fetch . . . what's the name of your landlady?'

'Mrs Klausner.'

'Yes, that's the one. Tell her I want to speak to her in your room immediately. When did you last see Miss Adler, by the way?'

Katrine Kroeller thought for a moment.

'Er, yesterday, I think. Yes, yesterday afternoon.'

'Here?'

'Yes, on the staircase. We just happened to pass.'

Van Veeteren pondered that.

'OK, fetch Mrs Klausner. Is it possible for me to use this telephone?'

She opened the door of the booth and keyed in her personal code.

'It's all yours,' she said.

'Thank you,' said Van Veeteren, and dialled the number of the police station.

Two minutes later, he was talking to Reinhart.

'I think we've found her,' Van Veeteren said. 'But she's done a runner.'

'Oh, shit!' said Reinhart. 'Where?'

'Deijkstraa. Parkvej 31. Get yourself here with some of the forensic guys. Fingerprints, the lot. Münster as well. I'll be expecting you twenty seconds from now.'

'We'll be there in ten,' said Reinhart, and hung up.

29

'What time is it?' asked Van Veeteren.

'Half past five,' said Reinhart.

'All right. Let's have a summary, Münster. And those of you who've been lounging around at home, sit up and listen carefully.'

For the last half-hour the investigation team had been all present and correct – apart from Jung and Moreno who had succeeded in remaining incommunicado all afternoon. It was still Saturday, 17 February, and they had achieved a breakthrough.

Or a possible breakthrough, at least.

Münster leafed through his notepad.

'This woman,' he began, 'calling herself Maria Adler, moved into Mrs Klausner's house – into one of the four rooms she has to let – on Sunday, 14 January. Exactly five weeks ago, in other words. She said she had enrolled for a three-month economics course at the Elizabeth Institute. There is in fact such a course, starting on 15 January, but it only lasts for six weeks, and they've never heard of Maria Adler. When she moved in she paid the rent for half the occupation in advance, she never mixed with any of the other tenants, and she seems to have vacated her room once and for all yesterday afternoon, or possibly yesterday evening. The reason why we know about her is that Katrine Kroeller – one of the other tenants – had seen her with a tape recorder pressed up against the receiver in a phone booth, and she let us know about it after having read in the newspapers about that telephone music . . . Well, that's about it, more or less.'

'Is that all we have to go on?' asked deBries after a pause. 'It doesn't sound all that convincing . . .'

'That's all we have so far,' said Reinhart. 'But she's the one, I can feel it in my bones.'

'So far we've found four different Maria Adlers nation-wide,' said Münster, 'but she's not any of them. I expect we'll find another one or two, but I've no doubt we can assume that she has been using a false name.'

'Didn't this landlady check up on what kind of people she let rooms to?' asked Rooth.

'Mrs Klausner assumes the best in people,' Reinhart explained. 'She doesn't know how old she was, nor where she came from – nothing . . . She assumed the best because her prospective tenant paid half the rent in advance.'

'Our technicians have gone over the room with a

fine-tooth comb,' said Münster. 'So we can take it that we have her fingerprints, at least. So if she's on our database, we can identify her.'

'Are you saying she simply cleared off?' asked Heinemann, holding up his glasses against the ceiling light to check that his polishing had been effective.

'Yes,' said Van Veeteren. 'That's what's so damned frustrating. If only that girl had phoned us yesterday instead, we'd have had her by now.'

'Typical,' said Rooth. 'What does she look like?'

Reinhart sighed.

'That bloody artist is in my office with Mrs Klausner, the girl who rang us and another of the tenants. He's been sketching away for over an hour now, but he says he needs a bit more time . . .'

'A photofit picture?' said deBries. 'Don't we have an actual photo?'

'No,' said Münster. 'But it's not really what you would call a photofit picture. They've seen her every day, more or less, for over a month. It will be just as accurate as a photograph.'

'And it will be in every bloody red-top tomorrow morning,' Reinhart growled.

'Hmm,' said Heinemann. 'But what if it isn't her after all? It could just be somebody who's run away from her husband. Or something of the sort. As far as I understand it, there's nothing definite . . .'

Van Veeteren blew his nose, long and loud.

'Damned cold,' he said. 'Yes, you're right, of course. But we'll take the risk. I also have the distinct impression that she's the one.'

'If she's innocent, no doubt we'll be hearing from her,' Reinhart said.

'But the opposite also applies,' said deBries. 'If we hear nothing from anybody, we can assume that she's the one.'

'We can also assume that she'll change her appearance a bit,' said Münster.

'I'm sure you're right,' said Van Veeteren.

Nobody spoke for a while.

'I wonder where she's gone to,' said Rooth.

'And why,' said Reinhart. 'Dammit all, there are so many important questions. Why did she do a runner just now?'

'The day before we received the tip-off,' said Münster.

'Interesting,' said Rooth. 'But it could mean that she's finished what she set out to do, of course.'

'A possibility,' said Van Veeteren, contemplating a toothpick bitten away beyond recognition. 'Her task might have been to kill these three, and she's done just that.'

'Has anybody checked her alibi?' Rooth asked. 'Just in case. Might she have been away at precisely these times?'

'We've started,' said Van Veeteren. 'We'll let the artist

finish his drawings first, then we'll have another go at these ladies. But I don't really think they are going to be of much help. They don't seem to have any idea of what the rest of them in that same house are up to. The landlady reads two novels per day, and Maria Adler didn't mix with any of the others. If anybody were to bump into her at the relevant time, it would be pure coincidence. Or an unfortunate happening, one should perhaps say.'

'I get you,' said Rooth.

'How much longer does that artist need?' asked Reinhart. 'Surely he doesn't need half a day to create a face? Is there any more coffee?'

'Rooth,' said the chief inspector, 'for Christ's sake, go and find out what's happening. Tell him we have to have a picture soon if we're going to be able to place it in the newspapers.'

'OK,' said Rooth, rising to his feet. 'Wanted, dead or alive.'

'Preferably alive,' said the chief inspector.

'That was the last one,' said Jung, looking at the list. 'What do you think?'

'I suppose we'll have to hope it was Klumm's Cellar,' said Moreno. 'If not, he must have been in Maardam.'

'Good God,' said Jung. 'How many restaurants are there in Maardam? Two hundred?'

'If you include pubs and cafes, it's probably twice as many as that,' said Moreno. 'It's a great task, this one. It was such fun talking to all his workmates first as well. Why did you join the police?'

'People who are no good at anything become police officers,' said Jung. 'Anyway, shall we see if we can find this waiter? We might just get lucky. Then we'd better ring round and see if we can find somebody who was with him . . . Before we start on Maardam, that is. Or what do you think?'

Moreno nodded and consulted her notebook.

'Ibrahim Jebardahaddan,' she read. 'Erwinstraat 16 . . . That's just before you come to that sports field, I think.'

Fifteen minutes later Jung rang the doorbell of a flat on the first floor of a rather shabby three-storey block. Fifties, or early sixties. Crumbling plaster and mainly foreign names on the list in the entrance. A bronze-skinned woman on the far side of middle age opened the door.

'Hello . . . Who are you looking for?' she said with a timid smile and a pronounced foreign accent.

'Ibrahim Jebardahaddan,' said Jung, who had been practising both in the car and on the stairs.

'Please come in,' she said, ushering them into a large room containing about a dozen people of various ages, sitting on chairs and sofas. Some children were playing on the floor. Faint music in a minor key played by stringed instruments was coming from hidden loudspeakers. A low, square table was laden with bowls of exotic-looking food emitting warm, aromatic fragrances that seemed almost tangible.

'Smells good,' said Jung.

'Perhaps we ought to mention that we are police officers,' said Moreno.

'Police officers?' said the woman, but there was no trace of fear in her voice. Only surprise. 'Why?'

'Routine inquiries,' said Jung. 'We're trying to find out about a certain person who might have had a meal at the restaurant Ibrahim evidently works at . . .'

A young man had stood up and was listening.

'That's me,' he said. 'I work at Klumm's Cellar. What's it all about? Perhaps we should go to my room?'

His foreign accent was less pronounced than the woman's. He led them through the hall and into a small room containing not much more than a bed, a low chest of drawers and some large cushions. Jung showed him the photograph of Innings.

'Can you say if this person visited your restaurant last week, on Friday evening?'

The young man cast a quick glance at the photograph.

'Is that Innings?'

'Yes.'

'Yes, he did. He had a meal at our place last Friday. I saw on TV that he'd been killed. And in the newspapers. I recognize him.'

'Are you sure?' asked Moreno.

'A hundred per cent. I've already told my friends that I saw him there. I was the one who served him as well. A few days before he was shot. Yes, Friday it was.'

'Good,' said Moreno. 'Do you know who was with him as well?'

Jebardahaddan shook his head.

'No, I didn't see him so clearly. It was a man, but he had his back towards me, if you see what I mean . . . I don't know if I'd recognize him again.'

Jung nodded.

'It doesn't matter. Presumably it was one of his friends – we can check on that in other ways. Anyway, thank you very much.'

The woman who had let them in appeared in the doorway with the same timid smile.

'Have you finished? Then you must come and eat with us. This way, please.'

Moreno looked at the clock. Then at Jung.

'Why not?' she said. 'Thank you very much. We'd love to.'

'We certainly would,' said Jung.

*

Van Veeteren stared at the picture. Reinhart, Münster and deBries were crowded behind him.

'So this is what she looks like?' said the chief inspector.

It was a very well-drawn portrait, no question about it. A woman somewhere between thirty-five and forty, it seemed. Quite short, straight hair. Thin lips and a somewhat bitter expression around her mouth. Round glasses, a slightly introverted look. Straight nose. Quite a few wrinkles and marks on her skin.

'He says the eyes were the most difficult,' said Rooth. 'So much depends on the moment. Her hair is ash-blonde . . . Mousey, if you like.'

'She looks a bit haggard,' said Reinhart. 'With a bit of luck we might find her in police records.'

'Have they finished fingerprinting?' Heinemann asked.

'I think so,' said Münster. 'There must be masses of them; she's been living there for a month, after all. I suppose it'll be best if deBries takes care of that, as usual?'

DeBries nodded. Van Veeteren picked up the picture and scrutinized it from close quarters.

'I wonder . . .' he muttered. 'Manon's spring . . . Yes, why not?'

'What are you on about?' Reinhart wondered.

'Nothing,' said Van Veeteren. 'Just thinking aloud. Anyway, Münster: make sure this picture goes out to every damned newspaper in the land.'

He rummaged around among the papers on his desk.

'Together with this communiqué,' he added. 'Apart from that, I think the best thing we can do now is to go home and get some sleep. I want you all back here tomorrow morning at ten o'clock. We'll be swamped with tips and speculations. With a bit of luck, we'll get her tomorrow.'

'I wonder,' said Reinhart.

'So do I,' said the chief inspector. 'I'm just trying to spread a little optimism and a belief in the future. Goodnight, gentlemen.'

30

Sunday, 18 February, announced itself with warm breezes and a vague promise of spring. For anybody who had time to detect promises.

Van Veeteren got up at six, despite the fact that he had been listening to Sibelius and Kuryakin until late into the night. He fetched the *Allgemejne* from the letter box and established that the picture of Maria Adler was on the front page. Then he went to the bathroom and took a long shower, constantly adjusting the tap to make it increasingly cold, and tried to envisage the coming day.

That it would be long – another long day in succession – was beyond all doubt, of course; but he also knew there was a little chance. A possibility that it might be the last day of this investigation. Regarding the arrest, that is. Actually capturing the murderer. Then other things would kick in, other wheels would begin to turn – interrogation, charging, custody and all the other formal procedures of the legal process, but that was a different matter. The hunt would be over. It would mean that his own role had come to an end, somebody else would take over ultimate responsibility. Other officers, better equipped for such a role. Was that really what it was all about, he wondered. Was it really just those ingredients that drove him – getting his teeth into the prey and placing it at the feet of the red-jacketed/black-robed hunter/judge. The bloodhound instinct?

Nonsense! he decided, and had a final rinse in icy-cold water. These arbitrary analogies.

He left the shower and turned his attention to breakfast instead. Newly brewed coffee, yogurt and four slices of toast with butter and strong cheese. He had always found it difficult to feel really hungry in the morning, but today he forced himself. He knew he shouldn't begin today with coffee and a cigarette, as had been his custom for many years when forced to get to grips with the world and life at daybreak.

But on the other hand, he thought, as he studied the picture in the newspaper, this chance, this suspicion he had that today might be crowned with success was not particularly strong. Perhaps no more than a pious hope and a chimera, something he needed in order to raise the strength to go to work on a Sunday morning in February.

Who the hell wouldn't need such a stimulus?

In any case, the woman he so far only knew as Maria

Adler aroused his respect. If respect was the right word to use in the context.

There was something impressive about her. And frightening, of course. The feeling that she had full control over what she was doing was incontestable. Her way of striking and then withdrawing, over and over again, suggested both coldness and decisiveness. She had remained concealed in Mrs Klausner's house for a month, carried out her operations with unerring precision, and now she had disappeared. And as he stared at her everyday, slightly enigmatic face, he tried to analyse what this disappearance might imply.

Either – as somebody had pointed out – it simply meant that she had finished. Her intention had been to murder just these three persons, for some reason the police as yet had not the slightest idea of, and since the task was accomplished she had chosen simply to leave the stage.

Or – he thought, as he scattered a generous amount of muesli over his yogurt – she realized it would be too risky to stay in the house. She knew (how?) that it was time to leave her hiding place.

Or – a thought one couldn't dismiss out of hand – she had chosen to move a little closer to her next victim. To take up a better striking position, as it were. Malik and Maasleitner and Innings had all been within easy distance of Deijkstraa – the first two in Maardam itself, the third only a few miles away. If it was in fact the case that Miss Adler had several more people on her list, and they belonged to the group who lived in different parts of the country (or even abroad), well, there was naturally a good reason for finding a new base from which to operate.

Van Veeteren started on the toast. If there were any other possibilities in addition to those three, he hadn't been able to think of them. He realized that number two did not necessarily exclude numbers one and three, of course; none of them seemed to him any more probable than the others.

Perhaps she had finished murdering.

Perhaps she had sensed the closing in of her pursuers.

Perhaps she was on her way to victim number four.

By a quarter past eight he had finished both his breakfast and his newspaper. When he contemplated the pale and by no means especially threatening sky through the balcony door, he decided to walk to the police station for a change.

His cold seemed to have given up the ghost, and he thought he had good reason to extend the healthy start to this day of rest – especially as he was unlikely to get much of that.

Things turned out to be rather worse than he had feared.

By lunchtime the picture of the wanted woman calling

herself Maria Adler had reached every nook and cranny in the whole country, and the only people who had managed to avoid it would have to be either blind or sleeping off the effects of their Saturday-night boozing.

According to Inspector Reinhart's understanding of the situation, that is.

By as early as eleven o'clock, the number of calls had passed the five-hundred mark, and by not much more than an hour later, that figure had doubled. Four operators were at the switchboard receiving calls; a couple of officers made a preliminary assessment and sorted them into two (later three) groups according to urgency, whereupon the material was sent upstairs to the fourth floor where Van Veeteren and the others tried to make a final assessment and decide on what further action to take.

Another three women (to add to Münster's four) had called to say their name was Maria Adler. None of them had anything at all to do with the murders and could prove it, and none of them seemed to be too happy at being called Maria Adler at the present time. A poor woman up in Frigge, the wife of the mayor, was called something entirely different, but evidently looked exactly like the picture in the newspapers – she had been reported by four different people in her home town, and had phoned the police herself, in tears, both locally and at the headquarters in Maardam. The mayor himself was intending to sue.

However, the majority of the calls came from the Deijk-straa area. All of them claimed – no doubt correctly – that they had come across this Miss Adler in various places during the period she had been living in Mrs Klausner's house. In the supermarket. At the post office. In the street. At the bus stop on the esplanade . . . and so on. No doubt most of these sightings were also correct, but, needless to say, they were of very little value to the investigation.

What they were looking for were two types of infor-mation, as had been stressed in the press release and repeated in the newspapers and in broadcast news bulletins.

Firstly: information that could (directly or indirectly) link the wanted woman to any of the murder scenes.

Secondly: evidence to indicate where Miss Adler had gone to after leaving Mrs Klausner's house on Friday after-noon.

By noon only a regrettably small number of calls had been received in those categories. There may be indications suggesting that Maria Adler had taken a northbound train round about six o'clock on Friday evening. One witness claimed to have seen her at the station, another standing on a platform where he was waiting for a friend – a woman who didn't quite look like the picture of her in the mass media, but might well have been her even so.

If these two claims were correct, the train in question must have been the 18.03, and shortly after half past noon

Van Veeteren decided to send out a follow-up message to the mass media, urging anybody who had been travelling on that train and might have seen something to get in touch with the police.

A few hours later a handful of passengers had contacted the police, but what they had to say was hardly of significance. It sounded more like a collection of irrelevant details and guesses, and there were therefore grounds for believing that the train line (as Reinhart insisted on calling it) was not very promising.

By three o'clock the officers in charge of the investigation were beginning to show the strain. They had spent the day in two rooms, Van Veeteren's and Münster's offices, which were next to each other, and the piles of paper and empty coffee mugs had increased steadily for six hours.

'Hell's bells,' said Reinhart. 'Here's another call from the old witch who's seen our woman in Bossingen and Linzhuisen and Oosterbrügge. Now she's seen her in church at Loewingen as well.'

'We ought to have a better map,' said deBries. 'With flag pins or something. I think we've had several tip-offs from Aarlach, for instance. It would make things easier . . .'

'You and Rooth can fix one,' said Van Veeteren. 'Go to your office so that you don't disturb us.'

DeBries finished off his Danish pastry and went to fetch Rooth.

'This is a real bugger of a job, sheer drudgery,' said Reinhart.

'I know,' said Van Veeteren. 'No need to remind me.'

'I'm beginning to think she's the most observed woman in the whole country. They've seen her everywhere, for Christ's sake. In restaurants, at football matches, car parks, cemeteries . . . in taxi cabs, buses, shops, cinema queues . . .'

Van Veeteren looked up.

'Hang on,' he said. 'Say that again!'

'What?' asked Reinhart.

'All those places you chanted.'

'What the hell for?'

Van Veeteren made a dismissive gesture.

'Forget it. Cemeteries . . .'

He picked up the telephone and called the duty officer.

'Klempje? Get hold of Constable Klaarentoft without delay! Yes, I want him here in my office.'

'Now what are you on to?' asked Reinhart.

For once things went smoothly, and half an hour later Klaarentoft stuck his head round the door after knocking tentatively.

'You wanted to speak to me, Chief Inspector?'

'The photographs!' said Van Veeteren.

'Which photographs?' asked Klaarentoft, who took an average of a thousand a week.

'From the cemetery of course! Ryszard Malik's burial. I want to look at them.'

'All of them?'

'Yes. Every damned one.'

Klaarentoft was beginning to look bewildered.

'You've still got them, I hope?'

'Yes, but they've only been developed. I haven't printed them out yet.'

'Klaarentoft,' said Van Veeteren, pointing threateningly with a toothpick. 'Go down to the lab this minute and print them! I want them here within an hour.'

'Er, yes, of course, will do,' stammered Klaarentoft, and hurried out.

'If you can do it more quickly, so much the better!' yelled the chief inspector after him.

Reinhart stood up and lit his pipe.

'Impressive issuing of orders,' he said. 'Do you think she was there, or what are you after?'

Van Veeteren nodded.

'Just a feeling.'

'Feelings can be helpful at times,' said Reinhart, blowing out a cloud of smoke. 'How are Jung and Moreno doing, incidentally? With Innings and that Friday evening, I mean.'

'I don't know,' said Van Veeteren. 'They've found the right place, it seems, but not whoever was with him.'

'And what's Heinemann doing?'

'He's in his office nosing into bank account details, apparently,' said Van Veeteren. 'Just as well, this would be a bit much for him.'

'It's starting to be a bit much for me as well, to tell you the truth,' said Reinhart, flopping back down on his chair. 'I have to say I'd prefer her to come here in person and give herself up. Can't we put that request in the next press release?'

There was a knock on the door. Münster came in and perched on the edge of the desk.

'Something occurred to me,' he said. 'This woman can hardly be older than forty. That means she would have been ten at most when they were at the Staff College . . .'

'I know,' muttered Van Veeteren.

Reinhart scratched his face with the stem of his pipe.

'And what are you trying to say in view of that?'

'Well,' said Münster, 'I thought you'd be able to work that out for yourself.'

It took Klaarentoft less than forty minutes to produce the photographs, and when he had put them on Van Veeteren's desk he lingered in the doorway, as if waiting for a reward

of some kind. A coin, a sweet, a few grateful and compli-
mentary words at least. The chief inspector grabbed hold
of the pictures, but Reinhart had noticed the hesitant giant.

'Hmm,' he said.

Van Veeteren looked up.

'Well done, Klaarentoft,' he said. 'Very good. I don't
think we need you any more today.'

'Thank you, Chief Inspector,' said Klaarentoft, and left.

Van Veeteren leafed through the shiny photographs.

'Here!' he bellowed suddenly. 'And here! I'll be damned!'

He skimmed quickly through the rest.

'Come here, Reinhart! Just look at these! That's her all
right.'

Reinhart leant over the desk and studied the pictures
of a woman in a dark beret and light overcoat; one was
in profile, the other almost full face. They were evidently
taken with only a short interval between: the photographer
had simply changed his position. She was standing by the
same grave and seemed to be reading what it said on the
rough, partly moss-covered stone. Slightly bent, and one
hand holding back a plant.

'Yes,' said Reinhart. 'That's her, by God.'

Van Veeteren grabbed the telephone and called the duty
officer.

'Has Klaarentoft left yet?'

'No.'

'Stop him when he appears, and send him back up here,' he said, and hung up.

Two minutes later Klaarentoft appeared in the doorway again.

'Good,' said Van Veeteren. 'I need enlargements of these two. Can you do that?'

Klaarentoft took the pictures and looked at them.

'Of course,' he said. 'Is it . . .'

'Well?'

'Is it her? Maria Adler?'

'You can bet your life it is,' said Reinhart.

'I thought there was something odd about her.'

'He has a keen nose,' said Reinhart when Klaarentoft had left.

'Yes indeed,' said Van Veeteren. 'He took twelve pictures of the clergyman as well. We'd better arrest him right away.'

'At last,' said Reinhart when he snuggled down behind Winnifred Lynch in the bath. 'It's been a bastard of a day. What have you done?'

'Read a book,' said Winnifred.

'A book? What's that?' said Reinhart.

She laughed.

'How's it going? I take it you haven't caught her?'

'No,' said Reinhart. 'Over 1,300 tip-offs, but we don't know where she is nor who she is. It's a bugger. I thought we might even solve it today.'

'Hmm,' said Winnifred, leaning back against his chest. 'All she needs is a wig. No suspicions even?'

'She's probably gone northwards,' said Reinhart. 'She might have taken a train. We'll be talking to a bloke tomorrow who thinks he might have been in the same carriage as she was. He rang just before I left.'

'Any more?'

Reinhart shrugged.

'I don't know. We don't know about the motive either.'

She thought for a moment.

'You remember I said it would be a woman?'

'Yes, yes,' said Reinhart, with a trace of irritation.

'A wronged woman.'

'Yes.'

She stroked his thigh with her fingers.

'There are many ways of wronging a woman, but one is infallible.'

'Rape?'

'Yes.'

'She was ten years old at most when they left the Staff College,' said Reinhart. 'Can't be more than forty now, or what do you think?'

'No, hardly,' said Winnifred. 'Awful, but there's something of that sort in the background, believe you me.'

'Could well be,' said Reinhart. 'Can't you look a bit deeper into your crystal ball and tell me where she's hiding as well? No, let's forget this for a while. What was the book you read?'

'*La vie devant soi*,' said Winnifred.

'Emile Ajar?'

'Yes.'

'And?'

'I think I need a child.'

Reinhart leant his head against the tiles and closed his eyes. Sensed two completely irreconcilable images flashing through his brain, but it all happened so quickly that he never managed to grasp their significance.

Always assuming they had any.

'May I give you one?' he said.

'If you insist,' she said.

31

'She could well have taken that train,' said Münster. 'He seems pretty sure of what he's talking about.'

'Good,' said Van Veeteren. 'Where did she go to?'

Münster shook his head.

'Alas,' he said. 'He got off in Rheinau, but she didn't, so . . . Somewhere further north than Rheinau, it seems.'

'There must be more people who saw her?' said Reinhart.

'You'd have thought so. In any case, there was somebody else in the same carriage, according to Pfeffenholtz.'

'Pfeffenholtz?'

'Yes, that's his name. But there was somebody else there, all the way from Maardam. A skinhead. And it seems he was still there after Rheinau.'

'Wow,' said Reinhart.

'Dark glasses, Walkman and a comic,' said Münster. 'Between eighteen and twenty, about. Eating sweets all the time, and a cross tattooed over his right ear.'

'A swastika?' Reinhart asked.

'Evidently,' sighed Münster. 'What should we do? Send out a "wanted" notice?'

Van Veeteren grunted.

'A swastika and sweets?' he said. 'Good God no. Somebody else can go chasing after neo-Nazi puppies. But this Pfeffenberg—'

'—holtz,' said Münster.

'OK, OK, Pfeffenholtz. He seems to know what he's talking about?'

Münster nodded.

'OK,' said Van Veeteren. 'Go back to your office and pick out the ones from the Staff College who might fit in. The ones who live north of Rheinau, in other words. Fill me in when you've done that.'

Münster stood up and left the room.

'Have you thought about the motive?' Reinhart asked.

'I've spent the last month wondering about that,' muttered the chief inspector.

'Really? What do you reckon then? I'm starting to think in terms of rape.'

Van Veeteren looked up.

'Go on,' he said.

'It must be a woman looking for revenge for something or other,' Reinhart suggested.

'Could be.'

'And rape would fit the bill.'

'Could be,' repeated the chief inspector.

'Her age makes it a bit complicated though. She must have been very young at the time. Only a child.'

Van Veeteren snorted.

'Younger than you think, Reinhart.'

Reinhart said nothing and stared into thin air for a few seconds.

'My God,' he said eventually. 'That's a possibility, of course. Sorry to be so thick.'

'No problem,' said Van Veeteren, and reverted to leafing through papers.

DeBries arrived at the same time as Jung and Moreno.

'Can we take mine first?' said deBries. 'It won't take long.'

Van Veeteren nodded.

'She's not in criminal records.'

'A pity,' said Reinhart. 'Still, as things are now, it probably wouldn't help us if we knew who she was. But it could be interesting of course.'

'Innings?' said Van Veeteren when deBries had left the room.

'Well,' began Moreno. 'We've fixed the restaurant. He had a meal at Klumm's Cellar out at Loewingen, but we haven't managed to find out who he was with.'

'Good,' said Van Veeteren. 'That was no doubt the intention. How carefully have you checked?'

'Extremely carefully,' said Jung. 'We've spoken to all his colleagues and friends, and all his relatives up to seven times removed. None of them was out with Innings that Friday evening.'

The chief inspector broke a toothpick in half and looked pleased. As pleased as he was able to look, that is, which wasn't all that much. Nevertheless, Reinhart noticed his state.

'What's the matter with you?' he asked. 'Don't you feel well?'

'Hmm,' said Van Veeteren. 'But you have the witness from the restaurant, I gather?'

'Only a waiter,' said Moreno. 'And he didn't get to see much of the person Innings was with. A man aged between fifty and sixty, he thought. He had his back towards the waiter most of the time it seems.'

'You can bet your life he had,' said Van Veeteren. 'Anyway, take those photographs of the group who attended Staff College together. The new ones, of course. Ask him if he thinks he can point anybody out.'

Jung nodded.

'Do you think Innings was eating with one of them then?'

Van Veeteren looked inscrutable.

'Moreover,' he said, 'be a bit generous when you ask him if he can identify anybody. If he's not sure, get him to pick out the three or four most likely even so.'

Jung nodded again. Moreno looked at the clock.

'Today?' she asked hopefully. 'It's half past four.'

'Now, right away,' said Van Veeteren.

Shortly after Van Veeteren got home, Heinemann phoned.

'I've found a connection,' he said.

'Between what?'

'Between Malik, Maasleitner and Innings. Do you want me to tell you about it now, over the phone?'

'Fire away,' said Van Veeteren.

'OK,' said Heinemann. 'I've been going through their bank records, all three of them – it's more awkward than you might think. Some banks, Spaarkasse for instance, have routines that are highly peculiar, to say the least. It can't be much fun dealing with financial crimes, but I suppose that's the point . . .'

'What have you found?' asked Van Veeteren.

'Well, there's a similarity.'

'What, exactly?'

'June 1976,' explained Heinemann. 'On 8 June, Malik takes out ten thousand guilders from his savings account at the Cuyverbank. On the 9th, Maasleitner draws an identical amount from the Spaarkasse. The same day, Innings is granted a loan by the Landtbank for twelve thousand . . .'

Van Veeteren thought for a moment.

'Well done, Heinemann,' he said eventually. 'What do you think that implies?'

'You can never be sure, I suppose,' said Heinemann. 'But a spot of blackmail might not be out of the question.'

Van Veeteren thought again.

'You see where we need to go from there, I suppose?'

Heinemann sighed.

'Yes,' he said. 'I suppose I do.'

'You need to check and see if anybody else in the group made a similar transaction at the same time.'

'Exactly,' said Heinemann. 'I'll start on that tomorrow.'

'Don't sound so miserable,' said the chief inspector. 'You can start with the ones who live up north – with a bit of luck that might be enough. Have a word with Münster and he'll give you a list tomorrow morning.'

'All right,' said Heinemann. 'I have to go and look after the kiddies now.'

'Kiddies?' asked the chief inspector in surprise. 'Surely your children are grown-up?'

'Grandchildren,' said Heinemann, and sighed again.

Well, well, Van Veeteren thought as he replaced the receiver. We're getting there, the noose is tightening.

He fetched a beer from the fridge. Put on the Goldberg Variations and leant back in his armchair. Placed the photographs on his knee, and began to study them with a slight feeling of admiration.

Thirty-five young men.

Five dead.

Three of them thanks to this woman's efforts.

This woman in a dark beret and a light overcoat, with the trace of a smile on her face. Leaning over a gravestone. A birthmark on her left cheek – he couldn't recall seeing that on the picture the artist had drawn, but then it was no bigger than a little fingernail.

Klaarentoft had made an excellent enlargement in any case, and as Van Veeteren sat in his chair, studying her face, he suddenly had the impression that she had raised her gaze a little. Peered over the top of the gravestone and looked at him.

A bit cheeky, he thought. A little bit roguish even, but at the same time, serious.

WOMAN WITH A BIRTHMARK

And very . . . very determined.
How old are you in fact? he wondered.
And how many do you have on your list?

32

But then everything came to a dead halt.

The distinct feeling that the investigation, which was now entering its second month, had been on the right lines at the weekend – caused by such developments as the discovery of Maria Adler in the house in Deijkstraa and the visit to the restaurant by Innings – turned out to have been a little hasty. Instead of gathering pace and culminating in the capture of the man – or, rather, woman – behind the three murders, the sum of all the efforts being made gave the impression of something slowly but inevitably trickling out into the sand.

'We're drifting out to sea,' asserted Reinhart on Thursday morning. 'Land behind!'

And the chief inspector was forced to agree. The so-called train line – suggesting that Maria Adler had travelled on the 18.03 northbound train from Maardam Central Station – could be neither confirmed nor disproved. Pfeffenholtz's evidence, strong as it was, was uncorroborated. No sweet-eating skinhead had been in contact. Nor any other passenger. Perhaps Miss Adler had indeed travelled to somewhere north of Rheinau, or perhaps not.

But even if she had, as Reinhart pointed out, what the devil was there to say that she was still there? And that her move was because of the intentions imputed to her?

Nothing at all, he announced, answering his own rhetorical question.

On Tuesday afternoon, in accordance with Van Veeteren's instructions, Jung and Moreno had interviewed Ibrahim Jebardahaddan again in Loewingen. The young Iranian was at first very doubtful about his ability to pick out anybody, but when Moreno explained that it was especially important and serious, he picked out five people from the Staff College group that he thought might possibly have been sitting opposite Innings on the Friday in question.

When the chief inspector saw the list of names, he did not appear to be best pleased with the result; which is why Jebardahaddan was summoned to the police station on the Thursday for another session with the photographs.

This time the five photographs he had picked out were mixed with not only some of the others from the group, but also pictures of about thirty other people who had nothing to do with the case: and the witness managed to pick out only two of the five faces he had chosen previously. Both of them lived south of Maardam, one of them as far distant as South Africa.

When Ibrahim Jebardahaddan had left the police station on unsteady legs, Moreno remarked that this was the first time she had seen him wearing glasses. The general consensus was that the restaurant line was a dead end, at least for the present.

As for contact with the as yet not murdered (to use Reinhart's term), the group had now been reduced to twenty-five (excluding those living abroad), and on Wednesday the investigation team was due to hear the results of the latest interviews with them. The judgement that Karel Innings had been a person roughly halfway between Malik and Maasleitner was more or less universal. A generally liked, sociable and positive young man, most of them recalled. With no strong links to either Malik or Maasleitner.

As far as anybody could remember.

Some of the group had declined to make any comment at all – for some unknown reason, according to the local police authorities. Some had also declined the offer of some form of protection or guarding, and three had been impossible to contact because they were not at home.

The link between the three victims was thus restricted to the banking transactions in June 1976 unearthed by

Heinemann; but as yet he had been unable to find any similar transactions entered into at that time by any other members of the group.

'Much more awkward than you would think,' he explained when he reported to the Friday meeting reviewing the case. 'Generally speaking we have to get specific permission for every single account we want to investigate.'

'Ah well,' sighed the chief inspector. 'We know whose interests they are looking after. Where are we now then? What does Reinhart have to say?'

'We haven't moved from the same spot,' said Reinhart. 'It's nine days since Innings was murdered. And a week since Miss Adler did a runner from Deijkstraa. She's had plenty of time to hide herself away, that's for sure.'

'I think she's finished,' said Rooth.

'I don't,' said Reinhart.

'We could keep a special eye on those on Münster's list,' suggested deBries. 'The ones who live up north, that is.'

'Do you think it's worth the effort?' asked the chief inspector.

'Is it buggery,' said Reinhart. 'The only thing we ought to be concentrating on at the moment is a long, free weekend.'

'Is there anybody who objects to Inspector Reinhart's

proposal?' asked Van Veeteren wearily, whereupon a grave-like silence descended on the senior investigative team.

'OK,' said Van Veeteren. 'Unless anything special turns up, we'll assemble again here on Monday morning at nine o'clock. Don't forget that we have over two thousand more tip-offs to work through.'

A few hours later, when the chief inspector was about to enter the Club in Styckargränd, he was met in the lobby by the manager, Urwitz, carrying in his arms a hopelessly drunk consultant from one of the local hospitals, a specialist in infectious diseases.

'We have to send him packing,' he explained. 'We can't stop him singing and weeping and upsetting the ladies.'

Van Veeteren nodded and helped the manager to lug the doctor up the stairs to the waiting taxi. These things happen, he thought. They dumped their burden in the back seat.

'Where to?' asked the driver, looking sceptical.

Urwitz turned to Van Veeteren.

'Do you know him?'

'Only in passing,' said Van Veeteren with a shrug.

'He maintains that his wife is entertaining her lover, so he can't go home. Can that be true?'

'No idea,' said the chief inspector. 'But if he has a wife,

it's probably as well not to send him home in this state no matter what.'

The manager nodded, and the driver looked even more thoughtful.

'Make up your minds, or take him out again,' he said.

'Take him to the police station at Zwille,' said Van Veeteren. 'Pass on greetings from V.V. and tell them to be nice to him and let him sleep it off.'

'V.V.?' asked the driver.

'Yes, that's right,' said Van Veeteren, and the taxi moved off.

'*O tempora, o mores*,' sighed Urwitz, and escorted Van Veeteren down into the basement.

'You look a bit miserable,' remarked Mahler as the chief inspector sat down at the table. 'Are you fasting for Lent already?'

'I lead an ascetic life all year round,' said Van Veeteren. 'A match?'

'Of course,' said Mahler, starting to set up the pieces. 'The elusive lady continues to be elusive, according to what I've heard?'

Van Veeteren made no reply but drank half a glass of beer instead.

'And that incident we spoke about,' said Mahler. 'Have you found it?'

The chief inspector nodded and adjusted his pieces.

'I think so,' he said. 'But until I can fix the date, all I can do is be miserable and mark time.'

'I understand,' said Mahler. 'Or rather, I don't,' he added after a while.

'It doesn't matter,' said Van Veeteren. 'I've decided to lie low and wait for a few days in any case. Let her make a move . . .'

'Shoot another one?'

'I hope not,' sighed Van Veeteren. 'Speaking of moves . . .'

'All right,' said Mahler, leaning forward over the board and starting his concentration routine.

When Van Veeteren left the Club shortly after half past midnight, he had two draws and a win under his belt; and, since it wasn't raining, he was inclined to think – despite all the setbacks in the current investigation – that life was just about managing to keep its head above water.

When he came to Kongers Plejn, however, he had it brought home to him that this was a somewhat too hasty judgement. He had just turned the corner and found himself in the midst of a gang of bellowing young men who had evidently been lying in wait for a suitable victim.

'Gottcha, you fucking ancient old bastard!' growled a broad-shouldered youth with close-cropped red hair as he forced Van Veeteren up against the wall. 'Your money or your prick?'

My prick, Van Veeteren had time to think, before another youth slapped his face with the back of his hand. The chief inspector could taste the blood on his tongue.

'I'm a police officer,' he said.

This information was greeted with roars of laughter.

'Police officers are our favourites,' said the youth, pressing him up against the wall, and the others sniggered in delight.

The one who had hit him tried again, but this time Van Veeteren parried, at the same time thrusting his knee up between the close-cropped red-head's legs. The youth doubled up and groaned.

Van Veeteren delivered a right hook and succeeded in hitting somebody in the nasal region. He heard clearly how something gristly was rendered even more gristly, and, as far as he could judge, the damaged area was not in his own hand.

The injured youth retired, but that was naturally the end of Van Veeteren's successes. The three remaining – and uninjured – youths forced the chief inspector down on all fours and began beating him up.

Van Veeteren curled up like a hedgehog, and all the time

the punches and kicks were landing on him, all he could think of was:

Silly little brats! Where are your daddies now, damn them?

After a while – it probably was no more than ten or fifteen seconds – they went away and left him. Ran off shouting and yelling.

'Hell and damnation . . .' muttered Van Veeteren as he slowly got to his feet. He could feel he was bleeding from his lips and from a wound over his eyebrow; but when he started moving his arms and legs he was able to establish that he was relatively unharmed.

He scanned the empty square.

Where the hell are all the witnesses? he thought, then resumed his walk home.

A little later, when he examined himself in the bathroom mirror, it occurred to him that it had been absolutely right to put the investigation on ice over the weekend.

An officer in charge looking like this could hardly be a source of inspiration for his team.

Then, in his capacity as a private citizen, he phoned the police and reported the assault. He also insisted, in his capacity as a detective chief inspector, that he should be the one to interrogate any of the young delinquents the police managed to find.

'Were they immigrants?' asked the duty constable.

'No,' said Van Veeteren. 'Bodybuilders, I'd say. Why should they be immigrants?'

He received no answer.

When he had washed and gone to bed, he was surprised to note, on reflection, that he hadn't felt in the least bit scared during the whole of the incident.

Indignant and annoyed, but not scared.

I suppose I'm too old for that, he thought.

Or perhaps it needs something worse than that to put the wind up me.

Or then again – it occurred to him just as he was about to fall asleep – perhaps I'm no longer scared of anything on my own account.

Only for others.

For society. For future developments.

For life?

Then he recalled a silly riddle Rooth had come up with the other day.

Question: How do you make a random number generator nowadays?

Answer: You pour two beers into a bodybuilder.

Then he fell asleep.

EIGHT

16 FEBRUARY TO 9 MARCH

33

The Pawlewski Hotel had seen better days, but then so had Mr Pawlewski.

And better guests.

More specifically, he had seen them fifty years ago and more, when he had to stand on a blue-painted and scratched stool in order to be able to see over the edge of the reception desk. When it was still Pawlewski senior and Pawlewski grandsenior running the show. And his mother and grandmother ruled the roost in the restaurant and linen store, and kept the cooks and pomaded bellboys in good order. While the century was yet young.

A lot of water had flowed under the bridge since then. An awful lot of water. Nowadays the stool stood under a tired palm tree in his own den, the former so-called bridal suite on the fifth floor of the hotel.

Everything has its day.

Biedersen spent the first three evenings in the bar in the company of numerous whiskies and the assortment of doubtful characters that comprised the clientele, roughly half of them one-night guests and the rest introverted regulars. All of them were men. All had thinning hair and almost all had drooping shoulders, some kind of beard or moustache, and vacant expressions. He didn't waste a minute on any of them, and from Monday night onwards he drank from the bottle he had in his room instead.

This made the days monotonous and indistinguishable. He got up round about noon. Left his room an hour later and spent the afternoon wandering around the town, so that the chambermaid had an opportunity to come in and mark the commencement of a new day. He would drink black coffee in some cafe or other, preferably Günther's near the town centre; try to read a newspaper or perhaps several, go for a long walk and buy some cigarettes plus the evening's bottle, which he would choose with a degree of care that struck him as unjustified but nevertheless essential. As if it were one of the basic rules in a game – he was not sure if he was playing it or if he was one of the pieces, but for the moment it was the only thing taking place. There was nothing else at all.

He returned by devious routes to the Pawlewski the moment he noticed that the dirt-grey dusk was beginning to fall. It happened early in a town like this, accompanied by the acid rain and the smog from coal fires.

Stretched out on his newly made bed, with sick-looking pigeons cooing outside on the roof, he drank his first whisky of the day before taking a bath, with number two within easy reach on the floor. Went down to the restaurant for dinner, usually as one of the first diners, occasionally completely alone in the over-sized, mouse-brown room with uninspiring crystal chandeliers and tablecloths that had once been white. Drank beer with the food, coffee and cognac afterwards; and each night he remained sitting there a little longer.

He tried to last out for a few extra minutes; to shrink and cut back as much as possible the accursed boredom of what remained of the waking day. And it was as he returned from these meals – on his way to the bar or up to his room – that Mr Pawlewski saw him. Pawlewski usually spent virtually all his waking hours more or less invisible behind the reception desk; from there he could observe and pass judgement and as usual ascertain that most things had seen better days.

Who this particular guest was, and what the hell he was doing in this lugubrious town in a month like February, were the kind of questions that, in his capacity of observer and man of the world, he had ceased to ask forty or more years ago.

★

At first the intoxication and numbing of the senses was an aim in itself. Simply to get away, to run away and put distance between himself and what was happening had been the primary, not to say the only, reason he had when he left home. The idea that eventually he would have to adopt a different strategy, would have to work out practical new tactics and courses of action, was as yet merely a thought dormant in the back of his mind; or at least was not something hanging over him, demanding that he should do something. Even so, these days were filled with the complicated actions and routines necessary to enable him to enjoy the blessing of sleeping in a state of unconscious intoxication.

Dreamless sleep for eight hours. Dead to the world. Beyond reach of everything and everyone. In the morning he would wake up sweating profusely, and with a headache strong enough to keep all other sensations miles away. Then, simply by taking a couple of tablets and yet again preparing himself for the afternoon hours spent on the streets and in cafes, he had set the warped wheels of time turning once more. Gained another day.

By the seventh night it was all over, this purifying and cauterizing alcohol bath. The desired distance had been achieved, his fear was in check, and he needed to apply himself to the strategies once more.

Scrutinized and filtered through a week of turbid,

soothing whisky, the proportions of his opponent had become possible to assess accurately. He could envisage her again. His faux pas and the fiasco in Berenhaam, followed by the shocking murder of Innings, had elevated her from the real world – the murderer was a phantom that couldn't be stopped, a superwoman; the only thing he could possibly do was go into hiding and wait. Vanish. Go underground, and hope.

That is why he had run away. Made himself invisible. Not just stuck his head in the sand, but dug down and concealed all of him. Away from everything and everyone. Away from her.

But on the ninth day he had weighed his gun in his hand, and begun to look ahead again.

First of all it was necessary to reject two possibilities.

The first was the police. To abandon his self-defence. Give himself up and tell them the whole story. Allow the bitch to win.

It took him two drams to dismiss that thought.

The other was to remain in hiding. For as long as was necessary.

That took him a bit longer. Four drams, maybe six. But he managed it.

So what should he do?

He drank more. A lot more.

Days. All the rest of the days he stayed at the Pawlewski Hotel, to be precise. Needless to say, this had been his original thought, the one that had been lying dormant in the back of his mind – to find a place like this, and to stay there. To stay in this damned, filthy, bad-smelling hotel until he was ready and knew what he was going to do next.

Stay here and wait for the strength, the determination, and the ideas.

There must be a way.

A way of killing this damned bitch. And the more he thought about it, the clearer it became that this wasn't just about himself. Not just his own skin. That strengthened his resolve. All the others . . . the friends she had murdered, the widows and children, and the lives she had destroyed in the course of her blood-stained campaign, just in order to . . .

All the people who had suffered. Just in order to . . .

His duty. His duty, for God's sake, was to kill her. Challenge her on her own terms, then outwit her and obliterate her from the surface of the earth once and for all.

Eliminate this accursed bitch.

The anger inside him grew into hatred. Powerful, incandescent hatred coupled with the feeling of having a mission to accomplish, a duty to perform – he was filled with the strength he needed to carry it out.

Courage. Strength. Determination.

And the method?

Was there more than one?

Two drams. Let it circulate in the mouth, as if it were cognac. The same question over and over again. One evening after the other. More whisky? The method? Was there more than one?

No. Only one.

Lower his guard. Leave himself open.

Give her the chance to strike first.

Then parry and kill her.

That was the way.

Yes, the Pawlewski Hotel had seen better guests.

How and where?

Where? That was the most important thing. Where the hell could he find a corner into which he could entice her without giving her too much of an advantage? He still didn't know what she really looked like – naturally, he had studied pictures of her printed in the newspapers, but the only sure thing was of course that with a facial expression like the one she had there . . . she was never going to approach him with a remarkably peaceful expression like that.

Another woman this time. No matter what she looked like. Unexpected and completely unknown. But where? Where the hell would he be able to set the trap?

And how?

It took a whole night to sketch out the plan, and when he eventually fell asleep in the grey light of dawn, he didn't believe it would still hold water in the cold light of day.

But it did. On the Tuesday, he had lunch in the restaurant for the first time, and when he checked through the plan with the aid of two cups of extra-strong black coffee, he found the occasional crack, but nothing that couldn't be papered over, and nothing wide enough for him to fall through.

It was watertight.

Biedersen left the Pawlewski Hotel at about two in the afternoon of Wednesday, 28 February. His gaze only met that of Mr Pawlewski behind the reception desk for a fraction of a second, but that was enough for him to be sure that those remarkably all-seeing yet nothing-seeing eyes would never recall a certain Jürg Kummerle who had spent twelve nights in room 313.

In view of this, for the twelve days and nights that had

never existed, he gave Mr Pawlewski an extra 100-guilder note.

If she had found him during this dreadful period, she would have won – he knew that. But she hadn't, and now he was ready again.

34

'The first of March today,' announced the chief of police, snapping off a withered leaf from a hibiscus. 'Take a seat. As I said, I'd like to hear some kind of summary, at the very least. This case is gobbling up a lot of resources.'

Van Veeteren muttered and flopped down into the shiny leather armchair.

'Well?'

'What do you want to know? If I had anything significant to tell you, I'd have done so without your needing to ask me.'

'Is that something I can rely on?'

The chief inspector made no reply.

'We've been guarding and protecting twenty people for two weeks now. Would you like me to tell you how much that costs?'

'No thank you,' said Van Veeteren. 'You can call them off if you like.'

'Call them off!' exclaimed Hiller, sitting down at his

desk. 'Can you imagine the headlines if we cancel the protection and she then clobbers another one? We're in a big enough mess as it is.'

'The headlines won't be any better if we leave things as they are and she picks one off even so.'

Hiller snorted and started rotating his gold watch round his wrist.

'What do you mean by that? Are you suggesting that the guards are of no significance? They could be the very thing that's holding her back.'

'I don't think so,' said Van Veeteren.

'What do you think, then? For Christ's sake tell me what you do think!'

The chief inspector took out a toothpick and examined it critically before inserting it into his lower row of teeth. Turned his head round and tried to peer through the window through the dense expanse of greenery.

'I think it's raining. For instance.'

Hiller opened his mouth. Then closed it again.

'It's not possible to say,' Van Veeteren continued, after a pause for effect. 'Either she's finished, or she's intending to kill more. Whatever, just at the moment she's lying low. Perhaps she's waiting for us to lower our guard . . . and for the next victim to do the same. Clever. That's what I'd do.'

Hiller made a noise that the chief inspector was inclined to associate with a randy but unhappy seal.

'But what are you doing?' he managed to say eventually. 'For God's sake tell me what you are doing about it!'

Van Veeteren shrugged.

'We're working through tip-offs from the general public,' he said. 'Quite a few are still coming in, despite the fact that the newspapers have lost interest.'

Hiller breathed deeply and tried to look optimistic.

'And?'

'Not much there. I'm wondering whether we ought to go out on a limb, although that would involve a bit of a risk, of course. We could concentrate on a few possible candidates and leave the rest to their fate. That might give results.'

Hiller thought about that.

'Are there any? Ones who are more likely than the others, that is?'

'Could be,' said Van Veeteren. 'I'm looking into that now.'

The chief of police stood up and went over to his plants again. Swayed back and forth with his back to the chief inspector, using his thumbs and index fingers to remove some specks of dust from some leaves.

'Do that then,' he said, turning round. 'Use that blasted intuition of yours and make something happen!'

Van Veeteren heaved himself up from the armchair.

'Is that all?' he asked.

'For now,' said the chief of police, gritting his teeth.

'What did he have to say?' asked Reinhart.

'He's nervous,' said the chief inspector, pouring some coffee into a plastic mug. Raised it to his mouth, then paused.

'When was this brewed?' he asked.

Reinhart shrugged.

'February, I should think. This year, in any case.'

There was a knock on the door and Münster came in.

'What did he have to say?'

'He wondered why we hadn't arrested her yet.'

'You don't say,' said Münster.

Van Veeteren leant back, tasted the coffee and pulled a face.

'January,' he said. 'Typical January coffee. Münster, how many have we failed to get in touch with yet? Of the as yet unmurdered, that is.'

'Just a moment,' said Münster, and left the room. Returned a minute later with a piece of paper in his hand.

'Three,' he said.

'Why?' asked the chief inspector.

'They're away,' said Münster. 'Two of them on business, one on holiday, visiting his daughter in Argentina.'

'But surely we can get in touch with her?'

'We've sent her a message, but they haven't replied yet. We haven't been pressing all that hard, to be fair . . .'

Van Veeteren produced the well-thumbed photograph.

'Which of them is it?'

'His name's Delherbes. He lives here in Maardam. It was deBries who talked to him last time.'

Van Veeteren nodded.

'And the other two?'

'Biedersen and Moussner,' said Münster. 'Moussner is in South East Asia somewhere. Thailand and Singapore and so on. He'll be back home before long. Sunday, I think. Biedersen is probably a bit closer to home.'

'Probably?' said Reinhart.

'His wife wasn't very sure. He often goes off on business trips, maintaining contacts now and then, it seems. He runs an import company. England or Scandinavia, she thought.'

'Scandinavia?' said Reinhart. 'What the hell does anybody import from Scandinavia? Amber and wolf skins?'

'Of course,' said Van Veeteren. 'Has anybody seen Heinemann today?'

'I spent three minutes with him in the canteen this morning,' said Münster. 'He seemed pretty worn out.'

Van Veeteren nodded.

'Could be the grandchildren,' he said. 'How many tips have we left to go through?'

'A few hundred, I'd say,' said Reinhart.

The chief inspector forced the remainder of the coffee down, with obvious reluctance.

'All right,' he said. 'We'd better make sure we've finished ploughing through that shit by Friday. Something had better happen soon.'

'That would be helpful,' said Reinhart. 'As long as it's not another one.'

Dagmar Biedersen switched off the vacuum cleaner and listened.

Yes, it was the telephone again. She sighed, went to the hall and answered.

'Mrs Biedersen?'

'Yes, that's me.'

'My name is Pauline Hansen. I'm a business acquaintance of your husband's, but I don't think we've met?'

'No . . . no, I don't think so. My husband's not at home at the moment.'

'No, I know that. I'm calling from Copenhagen. I've tried to get him at the office, but they say he's away on business.'

'That's right,' said Dagmar Biedersen, rubbing a mark off the mirror. 'I'm not sure when he's coming home.'

'You don't know where he is?'

'No.'

'That's a pity. I have a piece of business I'd like to discuss with him. I'm sure he'd be interested. It's a very advantageous deal, with rather a lot of money involved; but if I can't get hold of him, well . . .'

'Well what?' wondered Dagmar Biedersen.

'Well, I suppose I'll have to turn to somebody else. You've no idea where I might be able to contact him?'

'No, I'm afraid not.'

'If you should hear from him in the next few days, please tell him I've called. I'm certain he'd be interested, as I said . . .'

'Just a moment,' said Dagmar Biedersen.

'Yes?'

'He phoned the other day and said he'd probably be spending a few days in the cottage as well.'

'The cottage?'

'Yes. We have a little holiday place up in Wahrhejm. It's his childhood home, in fact, although we've done it up a bit, of course. You might be able to catch him there, if you're lucky.'

'Is there a telephone?'

'No, but you can phone the village inn and leave a

message for him. But I can't swear that he'll be there at the moment. It was just a thought.'

'Wahrhejm, did you say?'

'Yes, between Ulming and Oostwerdingen. Just a little village. The number is 161621.'

'Thank you very much. I'll give it a try – but even so, if you hear from him, I'd be grateful if you mentioned that I've called.'

'Of course,' said Dagmar Biedersen.

Verbal diarrhoea, she thought as she replaced the receiver; and when she started the vacuum cleaner again, she'd already forgotten the woman's name.

But the call was from Copenhagen, she did remember that.

35

Dusk was beginning to set in as he drove into Wahrhejm. He turned right at the village's only crossroads, passed the inn, where they had already lit the red lanterns in the windows – the same lanterns, he thought, as had been hanging there ever since he was a child.

He continued past the chapel, Heine's house, the pond, whose still water looked blacker than ever in the failing light. Passed Van Klauster's house, Kotke's dilapidated old mansion, and then turned left into the little road between the post-boxes and the tall pine trees.

He drove in through the opening in the stone wall and parked at the back, as usual. Hid the car from the gaze of the street – an expression his mother used to use and that he had never been able to shake off. But today, of course, it was appropriate. The kitchen door was at the back as well, but he didn't unload his food supplies yet. He got out of the car and examined the house first. Outside and inside. The kitchen and the three rooms. The loft. The outhouse. The cellar.

No sign. She was not here, and hadn't been here. Yet. He applied the safety catch on the pistol and put it into his jacket pocket.

But she would come. He started unloading the provisions. Switched on the electricity. Started the pump. Allowed the taps to run for a while and flushed the lavatory. Nobody had set foot in the place since October, when he had invited a business acquaintance to spend the weekend there; but everything seemed to be in order. Nothing had given up the ghost during the winter. The refrigerator was humming away. The radiators soon felt warm. The television and radio were working.

For a second or two the pleasure he felt at returning home succeeded in ousting the reason for his visit from his mind. Most of the furniture – and also the pictures and tapestries and all the hundreds of other little things – was still there and in the same state as when he had been a young boy, and the moment of arrival, the first sight of the place again, always brought with it a feeling of leaping back in time. Instantly, vertigo-inspiring. And it happened again now. But then the circumstances caught up with him, needless to say.

The circumstances?

He switched off the lights. He felt at home in the

darkness inside the house, and he knew that no matter what happened he would not need a torch in order to find his way around. Neither indoors or out of doors. He knew every nook and cranny. Every door and creaking stair. Every path, every bush and every root. Every stone. Everything was in its place and had always been there, and that gave him a feeling of confidence and security – something he might have hoped during the planning stage, but hardly dared to count on.

Anyway, the outhouse.

He unhasped the door. Dragged the mattress up the stairs as best he could. Placed it carefully by the window. Not much headroom up there. He had to crawl, or crouch down. He went back to collect pillows and blankets. It was colder in the outhouse, there was no source of heat at all, and it was clear that he would have to wrap himself up well.

He adjusted the mattress until it was in the optimal position under the sloping roof. Lay down and checked that everything was as he had foreseen.

Perfect, more or less. He could look out through the slightly rippled, old-fashioned glass pane and see the gable end of the house, with both the front door and the kitchen door in his field of view. The distance was no more than six to eight metres.

He opened the window slightly. Took out the gun and

stuck it out through the opening. Moved it back and forth, testing. Took aim.

Would he hit her at this distance?

He thought so. Perhaps not accurately enough to kill her outright, but he would probably have time for three or four shots.

That should be sufficient. He was sure it would be enough. He was not a bad marksman, even though it was several years since he'd been out with the hunting club up here.

He returned to the house. Ferried over a few more blankets and some of the provisions. The idea was that he would spend his time lying here. Spend as much time as possible in the correct position in the outhouse loft.

He would be lying here when she came.

He would ambush her and give her the *coup de grâce*.

He would finish off the mad bitch once and for all through this open window.

Pure luck, he would tell the police afterwards. It could just as easily have been she who got me instead . . . Lucky I was on my guard!

Self-defence. Of course it was self-defence, for God's sake – he didn't even need to lie.

But he would not reveal the real reason. The root of the evil. The reason why he knew he was next on the list.

He had done all he could. Went back to the house and listened.

It's strange how quiet it is, he thought, and remembered that this was what he always felt here. The silence that came rolling in from the forest and obliterated every slight sound. Wiped out everything with its enormous, silent soughing.

The armies of silence, he thought. The Day of Judgement . . .

He checked his watch and decided to pay a visit to the inn. A short walk there and back, along the familiar road.

Just for a beer. And perhaps also the answer to a question.

Any strangers around lately?

Any new faces?

When he got back, the darkness lay thick over the house and its environs. The buildings and the scraggy fruit trees could just about be made out against the background of the forest – rather better here and there against the somewhat lighter sky over the treetops. He had drunk two beers and a whisky. Spoken to Lippmann and Korhonen, who had charge of the bar nowadays. Not a lot of customers, of course: a normal weekday at the beginning of March. And not many strangers, not recently either. The occasional one who had passed through and called in, but nobody who had been there more than once. Women? No, no, not as far as they could remember. Neither Lippmann nor Korhonen. Why was he asking? Oh, business reasons. Nudge, nudge. Did he really think they would swallow that? Pull the other one. Teehee. And cheers! Good to see you back here in the village.

Homecoming.

He tiptoed over the wet grass. It hadn't rained at all this evening, but damp mists had drifted in from the coast and settled down over the open countryside bordering the forests like an unseen presence. He kept stopping and listening, but all he could hear was the same impenetrable silence as before. Nothing else. He withdrew behind the outhouse in order to rid his body of the remnants of the beer. Carefully opened the door, which usually squeaked a bit but didn't on this occasion. He would oil it tomorrow, just in case.

Crouched down in order to negotiate the cramped staircase again, and crawled over to his bed. Fiddled around with the blankets. Wriggled in and snuggled down. Turned over on his side and peered out. The house was dark and inert down below. Not a sound. Not a movement. He slid the pistol under his pillow, and placed his hand over it. He would have to sleep lightly, of course – but he usually did.

Always woke up at the slightest sound or movement. So would no doubt do that now as well.

Blankets wrapped round his body. Face close to the window pane. Hand over the gun.

So. Bring her on.

36

'I don't know,' said the chief inspector. 'It's just an opinion – but if these three were up to no good together, you'd think that at least some of the others ought to have known about it. So it's more likely that something of this sort would happen towards the end of the course. But then, that's only speculation, pure and simple.'

'Sounds reasonable though,' said Münster.

'Anyway, rapes in 1965. How many have you found?'

'Two,' said Münster.

'Two?'

'Yes. Two cases of rape reported, both of them in April. The first girl was attacked in a park, it seems. The other in a flat in Pampas.'

Van Veeteren nodded.

'How many rapists?'

'One in the park. Two in the flat. The pair in the flat were sentenced, the one in the park got away with it. He was never found.'

Van Veeteren leafed through his papers.

'Do you know how many rapes have been reported so far this year?'

Münster shook his head.

'Fifty-six. Can you explain to me how the hell the number of rapes could shoot up so drastically?'

'Not rapes,' said Münster. 'Reported rapes.'

'Precisely,' said the chief inspector. 'How do you rate the chances of tracking down a thirty-year-old unreported rape?'

'Poor,' said Münster. 'How do we know it's a matter of rape anyway?'

The chief inspector sighed.

'We don't know,' he said. 'But we can't just sit here twiddling our thumbs. You can have another job instead. If it gets us somewhere I'll invite you to dinner at Kraus.'

Mission impossible, Münster thought, and so did the chief inspector it seemed, as he cleared his throat somewhat apologetically.

'I want to know about all births registered by the mother with the father given as unknown. December '65 to March '66 or thereabouts. In Maardam and the surrounding district. The names of the mothers, and the children.'

'Especially girls?' Münster asked.

'Only girls.'

★

That evening he went to the cinema. Saw Tarkovsky's *Nostalgia* for the fourth, or possibly the fifth, time. With the same feelings of admiration and gratitude as usual. The masterpiece of masterpieces, he thought as he sat there in the half-empty cinema and allowed himself to be gobbled up by the pictures; and he suddenly thought of what the vicar had said at his Confirmation service – a gentle preacher with a long white beard, and there were doubtless many in the congregation who considered him a very close relation of God the Father himself.

There is evil in this world, he had declared, but never and nowhere so much that there is no room left over for good deeds.

Not a particularly remarkable claim in itself, but it had stuck in Van Veeteren's mind and occasionally rose up to the surface.

Such as now. Good deeds? Van Veeteren thought as he walked home after the showing. How many people are there living the sort of lives which don't even have room for nostalgia?

Is that why she's murdering these men? Because she never had a chance?

And room for good deeds? Was that really always available? Who exactly decided on the proportions? And who started off the relentless hunt for a meaning in everything? In every deed and every happening?

Things occur, Van Veeteren thought. Things happen, and perhaps they have to happen. But they don't need to be good or evil.

And they don't need to mean anything.

And his gloom deepened.

I'm an old sod, an old, tired detective who's seen too much and doesn't want to see much more, he thought.

I don't want to see the end of this case that's been occupying me for the past six weeks now. I want to get off the train before we get to the terminus.

What were all those vile thoughts about flushing out and hunting that were so noble and meaningful at the start?

I don't want to get to the point where I'm staring at the bleak and grubby causes of all this, he thought. I know the background is just as ugly as the crimes. Or suspect that, at least, and I would like to be spared everything.

A futile prayer, he knew that – but isn't futility the home ground of prayer? What else could it be?

He turned into Klagenburg and wondered briefly if he ought to call in at the cafe. He failed to reach a conclusion, but his feet passed by the brightly lit doorway of their own accord, and he continued his walk home.

Things happen, he thought. I might just as well have gone in.

And as he lay in bed, there were two thoughts that overwhelmed him and kept him awake.

Something is going to happen in this case as well. Just happen. Soon.

I must think about whether I have the strength to last out for much longer.

And then the image of Ulrike Fremdli – Karel Innings's wife – popped up in his mind's eye. Hovered there in the dark mist between dream and reality, between slumber and consciousness, and was gradually interleaved by and combined with Tarkovsky's ruined church and Gorchakov's wading through the water with the flaming torch.

Something's bound to happen.

37

'Hello?'

Jelena Walgens's hearing was not what it had once been. She found it especially difficult to understand what people said on the telephone – and, needless to say, she would have preferred to discuss whatever the topic was over a cup of coffee. With something freshly baked on the side. A little chat about this and that. But the young man was persistent, sounded pleasant, and of course it would be possible to settle matters over the phone even so.

'How long did you say? A month only? I would prefer to have a tenant for a bit longer than that . . .'

'I could pay you a bit extra,' argued the young man. 'I'm a writer. Alois Mühren. I don't know if you've heard of me . . . ?'

'I don't think so.'

'What I'm looking for is a nice quiet hideaway where I can write the final chapter of my new book. I certainly don't need more than a month. All the people and the hustle and bustle of a city make things so difficult for a writer, if you see what I mean.'

'I certainly do,' said Jelena Walgens as she searched through her memory.

But she couldn't think of anybody by that name. She read quite a lot, and had always done so; but he was a young man, and maybe she hadn't quite heard the name right. Alois Mühren? Was that what he'd said?

'One month,' she said. 'Until the first of April, that is. Is that what you want?'

'If possible. But perhaps you have other prospective tenants?'

'A few,' she lied. 'But nobody who's committed themselves yet.'

In fact this was the third week in succession she'd placed the advert in the newspaper, and apart from an off-putting German who seemed to have misunderstood everything it was possible to misunderstand, and no doubt stank of sauerkraut and sausages, he was the only one who'd called. What was the point of hesitating? A month was a month after all.

'Would you be happy with five hundred guilders?' she asked. 'It's a bit of a nuisance having to advertise again when you move out.'

'Five hundred guilders would be fine,' he said without hesitation, and the deal was done.

*

After lunch she drew a map and wrote instructions. One kilometre after the church in Wahrhejm, turn left when you come to the hand-painted sign. Two hundred metres through the trees towards the lake, no more. Three cottages. The one nearest the lake on the right was hers.

Keys and an explanation of how to make the awkward water pump work. The cooker, and the electric mains. The boat and the oars.

She had only just finished when he arrived. Rather a pale young man. Not very tall, and with polished manners, she thought. She offered him coffee, of course – it was already brewed. But he declined. He couldn't wait to get out there and start writing. She understood perfectly.

He wasn't the least bit impolite or cocky. On the contrary. He was courteous, as she would explain later to Beatrix Hoelder and Marcela Augenbach. Courteous and polite.

And a writer. When he'd left, she tasted the word several times. Writer. There was something sweet about it, that had to be admitted. She liked the idea of having somebody sitting and writing in her little cottage by the lake, and perhaps she even entertained the hope that at some point in the future he would remember her and send her a copy of the book. When it was finished, of course. That would take time, she imagined. What with publishers and all the rest of it. Perhaps he would dedicate the book to her, even?

She made up her mind to go to the library before long and see if he was represented on the shelves.

Mühlen, was that his name? Yes, that's what it said on the contract they had both signed. Alfons Mühlen, if she had read it correctly. He seemed a bit effeminate, she had to say, and she wondered if he might be homosexual. A lot of writers were, even if they pretended not to be, according to what Beatrix had claimed once. But then again, she claimed all kinds of things.

She'd never heard of him, that was for sure. Neither had Beatrix nor Marcela; but he was a young man, after all.

Still, he'd paid in cash, without quibbling. Five hundred guilders. She would have been satisfied with three.

So, it was an excellent deal, all things considered.

Alfons Müller?

Ah, maybe she had heard the name after all.

38

He felt cold.

For the fifth morning in succession, he was woken up by feeling freezing cold.

For the fifth morning in succession, it took him less than one second to remember where he was.

For the fifth morning in succession, he felt for his pistol and looked out of the window.

The house was still there in the hesitant light of dawn. Just as untouched, just as unvisited and unaware as when he had fallen asleep at some point during the night.

Unmolested. She wasn't coming. She hadn't come last night either. The cold made his body ache all over. It was inconceivable that it was impossible to keep warm up here, despite the abundance of quilts and blankets. Every morning he had woken up in the early stages of dawn, feeling frozen stiff. Checked the state of everything by looking out of the window, then gone downstairs and into the house and the warmth created by the stove. He always made a big fire in the evenings when he came back from the inn. A really roaring fire in the iron stove in the kitchen, making sure that it would retain its heat until well into the following morning.

He followed the same routine this morning. Carefully scrutinized the whole area, outside in the raw morning air and inside the house. Gun in hand. With the safety catch off.

Then he sat down at the kitchen table for coffee. Took a couple of drams of whisky as well, to drive the cold out of his body. Listened to the seven o'clock news on the radio while he made plans for the coming day. Pistol close at hand on the worn, fifty-year-old waxed tablecloth. Back against the wall. Invisible from the window.

Getting through the day was becoming harder and harder. He couldn't endure more than three or four hours at a time in the forest, and when he came back in the early afternoon, on the alert as ever, he generally sat down on the sofa again. Or lay down in the loft for an hour or two, waiting.

He would sit or lie there and glance through something from his father's library, which was not exactly voluminous and not particularly varied. Adventure stories. Brash, cheap literature bought by the yard at auctions or at sales time. He would quite like to read the occasional one, to be honest, but found it hard to concentrate.

Other things nagged and disturbed him. Other things.

Then he would go out for another walk, for an hour or so. As dusk drew in. Would come back home in the dark. It felt like something he was waiting for, this darkness: a confidant and an ally. He knew that he had the upper hand as soon as night fell. If they were to confront each other while it was dark, he was at an advantage. He might need it.

Then he would have dinner in the dark kitchen. He never switched on a light – the worst-case scenario would be if she came across him in a lit-up window.

He had only been into the village once, to do some shopping. He tried to avoid it, at any rate during daylight hours. Nor did he go there during the evenings those first few days, but he soon realized that the isolation would be intolerable if he couldn't at least spend an hour at the inn with a beer.

He went there on the third evening. He made a risk assessment before setting out, and realized that the dangerous part would be returning home. On the way in, he could make sure he was walking behind hedges, through private gardens or along the village street that had no lighting. Inside the inn, lots of the drinkers had a clear view of the door. That fact would hardly present her with an opportunity, even if she found out where he was.

But walking back home was a different matter. Dangerous. If she knew he'd been in the inn, she had every opportunity of setting up an ambush: and so he took every possible precaution on his walk back to the house. Avoided the road. Dashed out of the inn and round the corner of the building, staying in the shadows there for quite a while. Then he would head for home cross-country, terrain he had known in detail since he was a boy – changing direction, zig-zagging irrationally, and approaching the house from a different direction every night. Extremely carefully, and gun in hand. Every sense on red alert.

But nothing happened.

Night after night, and absolutely nothing happened.

Not a single dodgy happening. Not the slightest indication. Nothing suspicious at all.

Two things nagged at him when he went to bed.

The first was a headache, caused by a whole day of tension and strain. To cope with that, every night he would take two tablets, washed down with a swig of whisky in the dark kitchen.

That helped to some extent, but it didn't cure it.

The other thing was a thought. The thought that she might not come at all. The possibility that while he was spending these days in isolation and on red alert, she was actually somewhere else. Somewhere a long way away.

In an apartment in Maardam. In a house in Hamburg. Anywhere at all.

The possibility that this was the punishment she had decided to give him. Simply to let him wait. Wait for the murderer who never came. Wait for death, whose visit had been postponed.

And as one evening followed another, both these accompaniments grew in stature. The headache and the thought. A little bit bigger every evening, it seemed.

And neither tablets nor whisky could do anything to help.

She pulled up beside an elderly man walking along the side of the road. Leant over the empty passenger seat, wound down the window and attracted his attention.

'I'm looking for Mr Biedersen. Do you know where his house is?'

This was the second time she'd driven through the village. Dark outside. Quite dark inside the car as well, hat pulled down over her eyes, and a minimum of eye contact. A calculated risk, that's all. As they say.

'Yes, of course.'

He pointed the house out and explained where it was. It wasn't far away. Nothing in the village was far away. She memorized what he had said, thanked him and continued on her way.

It's all so easy, she thought. Still just as easy.

She knew that the car gave her all the camouflage she needed; and it was indeed from the car – the hired Fiat that had been another expense but also a necessity – that she discovered him. That same evening. Parked in the darkness and drizzle opposite the inn. It was still a calculated risk; but there wasn't much of an alternative. In a place like this a stranger couldn't turn up many times before questions started to be asked. Who? Why?

Unnecessary, and dangerous. There was no point in driving around, looking for him. But it was important to find him even so. Before he found her.

This time she had an opponent, not merely a prey. There was a certain difference.

She watched him go in. Didn't see him come out.

The next evening, the same thing. While he was in there, she paid a visit to the house. Scrutinized it from the road for several minutes before driving back.

Thought about how to go about it.

He must know.

He had gone out of his way to entice her here, she had realized that from the start.

The third evening she went a step further. Drove into the village and parked the car behind the church. Walked down to the inn. Went in without hesitation and bought some cigarettes at the bar. She could see him sitting right at the back, out of the corner of her eye. A beer and a whisky. He seemed alert and tense, but paid her no attention. There were more people in there than she'd expected, in fact. Twenty or so, half of them in the bar, the rest in the restaurant.

Three evenings out of three, she thought.

That meant that in all probability, it would be the same on day four and day five.

It was obvious what to do next. She had the upper hand again.

It was about time. All the waiting and the passage of time had been to her advantage, that was clear. But now things were coming to a head. The money she had left was committed, down to almost the last guilder. Every day cost money, and she no longer had the option of holding back, for the sake of it.

Just one opportunity. She wouldn't get another. The option of making a mistake was no longer a possibility either. It was clear that she would have no second chance of putting things right, if she made a mess of it.

So what she must do was to arrange things in the best possible way. In line with the others, and making this a worthy conclusion.

It was quite a long time since she had started out on this mission. There was only one of them left. Just one of them still alive, she thought as she returned to the little cottage by the lake.

And in the flickering light of the paraffin lamp she arranged his death.

Later, at first light, she woke up and was unable to fall asleep again. So she got up and dressed. Went down to the lake and walked out onto the jetty. Stood there for quite a while, gazing out over the dark water and the mists, and tried to recall the almost ecstatic rapture she had felt in the beginning. Tried to weigh that up against the calm she felt now.

The superior feeling of perfection and control.

She could find no real balance – but nor could she find any objections. Everything was falling into place. Soon it would be over. Everything.

Two more days, she decided. In two more days. That might be a good time, bearing in mind the date as well.

Then she went back indoors, and sat down at the table. Started writing.

At my mother's interment . . .

39

Melgarves? Something about this Melgarves rang a bell . . .

Jung fished around among the papers cluttering up his desk.

'Did you serve Maureen breakfast in bed today, then?'

Jung looked up.

'Eh? Why on earth should I do that?'

'You mean you don't know what day it is today?' said Moreno, glaring at him.

'No.'

'International Women's Day. March the eighth.'

'Good God,' said Jung. 'I'd better buy her something. Thank you for letting me know. Did you get breakfast in bed?'

'Of course,' said Moreno with a smile. 'And a bit more besides.'

Jung wondered for a moment what that might imply, then returned to his lists of incoming tip-offs.

'This Melgarves character,' he said. 'I don't understand why he's ended up on this list.'

'André Melgarves?'

'Yes indeed. He's one of the group. He's phoned in and passed on some information or other, but he's been bracketed with all the others . . . Krause must have missed his significance.'

'That's not like him,' said Moreno.

She crossed over the room and read the brief notes over Jung's shoulder. Frowned, and started chewing the pencil she had in her hand . . . Anyway, a certain Mr André Melgarves had phoned from Kinsale in Ireland and announced that he had information that could be of interest to the ongoing investigation. They were welcome to give him a call. His address and telephone number were duly recorded.

'When did this come in?' Moreno asked.

Jung looked at the back of the card.

'The day before yesterday,' he said. 'I think it's probably as well for the chief inspector to take this himself – what do you reckon?'

'I think so,' said Moreno. 'Go and show him it now – but don't mention that it came in two days ago. He seemed a bit grumpy this morning, I thought.'

'You don't say?' said Jung, getting to his feet.

★

The young man was dressed in jeans and a T-shirt with BIG IS BEAUTIFUL printed on it. He was very suntanned, and his short-cropped hair looked like a field of ripe wheat. He was chewing away at something, and staring at the floor.

'Name?' said Van Veeteren.

'Pieter Fuss.'

'Age?'

'Twenty-one.'

'Occupation?'

'Messenger.'

'Messenger?'

'For a security company.'

I see, thought Van Veeteren. Almost a colleague. He swallowed a feeling of impotence.

'Anyway, I'm not the officer in charge of your case,' he explained, 'but I have a few things to say about it and I'd like to have an answer to a question. Just one.'

Pieter Fuss looked up, but as soon as he caught the chief inspector's eye he reverted immediately to examining his trainers.

'On Friday, 23 February,' said Van Veeteren, 'at half past midnight, I was walking towards Rejmer Plejn. I was on my way home after an evening with some good friends of mine. I suddenly found my way blocked by you and four other young men. One of your friends pushed me up against a wall. You punched me in the face. You eventually forced me down onto the pavement. You hit me and kicked me. You had never seen me before. My question is: why?'

Pieter Fuss's expression did not change.

'Have you understood my question?'

No reply.

'Why did you attack an unknown person? Punch him and kick him? There must be a reason, surely?'

'I don't know.'

'Can you speak a little louder? I'm recording this.'

'I don't know.'

'I don't understand. Are you saying you don't know why you do things?'

No answer.

'You were five against one. Do you think that was the right thing to do?'

'No.'

'So you do things that you think are wrong?'

'I don't know.'

'If you don't know, who does?'

No answer.

'What do you think your punishment ought to be?'

Pieter Fuss mumbled something.

'Louder!'

'I don't know.'

'All right,' said Van Veeteren. 'Listen to me. If you can't give me a sensible answer to the question why, I shall see to it that you get at least six months for this.'

'Six months?'

'At least,' said Van Veeteren. 'We can't have people running around who don't know why they do what they do to their fellow human beings. You can have two days to think about this in peace and quiet . . .'

He paused. For a moment it looked as if Fuss was about to say something, but then there was a knock on the door and Jung poked his head inside.

'Are you busy, Chief Inspector?'

'No, not at all.'

'I think we've had a tip that could be of interest.'

'What exactly?'

'One of the group has rung from Ireland. We thought you might like to follow it up yourself?'

He handed over the card.

'OK,' said the chief inspector. 'Can you escort this promising young man down to the duty officer. Be a bit careful – he's not all that sure what he's doing.'

Fuss stood up and slunk away with Jung. Van Veeteren read what it said on the card.

André Melgarves? he thought with a frown.

Then he contacted the switchboard and asked them to

phone the number. Ten minutes later he had Melgarves on
the line.

'My name is Van Veeteren. I'm in charge of this case.
You've said that you have information to give us.'

'I don't really know if it's significant,' Melgarves said,
and his doubt seemed more obvious on the crackly line
than the words themselves.

'Let's hear it,' said Van Veeteren. 'It would help if you
could speak a bit louder. I think we have a bad line.'

'Ireland,' explained Melgarves. 'The tax is advantageous, but everything else is rubbish.'

'I see,' said Van Veeteren, pulling a face.

'Anyway, something occurred to me. I've received your
letters and instructions. And I spoke on the phone to somebody. I've got some idea of what's been going on, despite
being miles away. My sister has sent me some newspapers
and cuttings. And, well, if I can be of any help, then obviously I'm at your disposal. It's an awful business.'

'It certainly is,' said Van Veeteren.

'What struck me,' said Melgarves, 'is only a minor
detail, but it's something that Malik, Maasleitner and
Innings were mixed up in. It might be irrelevant, but if
I understand the situation aright, you've had trouble in
finding a link between them.'

'We have had certain problems,' admitted Van Veeteren.

'Well, it was in connection with our demob party,' said Melgarves.

'Demob party?'

'Yes, we had a big farewell do in Maardam. Arno's Cellar – I don't think it exists any longer . . .'

'No, it's closed down,' said Van Veeteren.

'Just two days before we were released. Yes, it was a party that everybody attended – and some of the officers and lecturers as well. No women, men only. We'd rented the whole place and . . . well, there was quite a lot of drinking going on, obviously.'

'The link?' wondered the chief inspector.

Melgarves cleared his throat.

'I'm coming to that. We kept going until rather late – two, half past two I'd say; and quite a few were pretty drunk. Some passed out, to be honest. I wasn't completely sober myself, but it was one of those evenings, you might say. And it was allowed – we didn't have any duties until the following afternoon, and . . . Well, only two more days before demob, and all that . . .'

'I understand,' said Van Veeteren with a trace of irritation in his voice. 'Perhaps you'd like to come to the point, Mr Melgarves?'

'Well, afterwards,' said Melgarves. 'That's when I saw them. Those of us who'd stayed on to the very end staggered out of Arno's. We were in groups, and kicking up a bit of a row, I'm sorry to say. Making our way back to Löhr – and that's when I happened to see them. I'd slunk into an alley to, er, relieve myself, and when I'd finished I ran into them. They were in a doorway, and they had a girl with them – no more than seventeen or eighteen, I'd say. And they were giving her a rough time.'

'Giving her a rough time? What do you mean by that?'

'Well, trying to talk her into it, I suppose.'

'Talk her into what?'

'Oh, come on, you know.'

'I suppose so. And?'

'Anyway, they were standing round her. They were pretty pissed, and I don't suppose she was all that interested, or however you might put it. In any case, they were going on at her, and laughing, and wouldn't let her go.'

'Did she want to go?'

Melgarves hesitated.

'I don't know. I think so, but I don't really remember. I've thought about it, of course, but I only stayed there a few seconds, and then I ran to catch up with the others. Not that they would have been what you might call desirable company.'

Van Veeteren thought it over.

'And she wasn't a prostitute?' he asked.

'Could be, but maybe not,' said Melgarves.

'How come that you remember all this after thirty years?'

'I can understand why you ask me that. I suppose it's because of what happened the next day.'

'The next day? What happened then?'

'Well, it was as if something had happened. Innings was really the only one I was acquainted with, just a bit, and he didn't seem to be himself for a couple of days afterwards. He just wasn't himself, somehow . . . He seemed to be evasive. I recall asking him what had happened to the girl, but he didn't answer.'

'What do you think happened?'

'I don't know,' said Melgarves. 'I mean, we were demobbed the following day, and we had other things to think about.'

'Of course you had,' said Van Veeteren. 'When exactly was this party, can you remember that?'

'It must have been 29 May,' said Melgarves. 'We were demobbed at the end of the month.'

'29 May 1965,' said the chief inspector, and suddenly felt his temples pounding as he prepared to ask his next question.

And anticipated the answer. He cleared his throat.

'So, Malik, Maasleitner and Innings,' he said. 'Was there anybody else?'

'Yes,' said Melgarves. 'There were four of them. That Biedersen was with them as well.'

'Biedersen?'

'Yes. He and Maasleitner were probably the ones behind it all. Biedersen rented a room in town as well.'

'A room in town?'

'Yes. For the last few months we were allowed permanent night leave, as they called it. In other words, we didn't need to be in our billets at night. Biedersen had a student room. He threw a few parties there, I gather, but I didn't go to any of them.'

The line started crackling terribly, and the chief inspector was forced to bellow out his final questions in order to overcome the noise.

'These three, plus Werner Biedersen. Is that right?'

'Yes.'

'With a young woman?'

'Yes.'

'Did anybody else see this?'

'Could be. I don't know.'

'Have you spoken to anybody else about it? Then or now?'

'No,' said Melgarves. 'Not as far as I recall, at least.'

Van Veeteren thought for a few more seconds.

'Many thanks,' he said eventually. 'Thank you for some extremely useful information, Mr Melgarves. I'll get back to you.'

He hung up.

Now, he thought. We're almost there.

'What the hell do you mean?' he roared ten minutes later. 'Do we still not know where he is?'

Münster shook his head.

'Hell and damnation!' bellowed the chief inspector. 'What about his wife?'

'Not at home,' Münster explained. 'DeBries keeps on phoning all the time.'

'Where do they live?'

'Saaren.'

'Saaren?' said Van Veeteren. 'Up north . . . It all fits in. How far is it to there? A hundred and fifty kilometres? Two hundred?'

'Something like that,' said Münster.

Van Veeteren took out four toothpicks. Broke them in two and threw the bits on the floor. Reinhart appeared in the doorway.

'Have we got him?' he asked.

'Got him?' roared Van Veeteren. 'Have we hell! He's been off the map for several weeks, and his missus is out shopping!'

'But it is Biedersen?' said Reinhart.

'Biedersen,' said Münster. 'Who's next, that is. Yes.'

'Have you got a cigarette?' asked Van Veeteren.

Reinhart shook his head.

'Afraid not. Just my old briar. What do we do now, then?'

The chief inspector clenched his hands and closed his eyes for two seconds.

'OK,' he said, opening his eyes again. 'This is what we do. Reinhart and I drive up to Saaren. You lot keep on chasing after his wife from here. If you find her, tell her to stay at home until we come, or she'll be jailed for life. Then we shall have to see what happens next.'

Reinhart nodded.

'Ask her if she knows where he is,' he added. 'And keep us informed. We'll try to find her as well, of course.'

Münster made a note.

'So, we're off now,' said Van Veeteren, gesturing towards Reinhart. 'Go down to the pool and collect a car. I'll be at the entrance five minutes from now. I just need to collect a few things first.'

'Are you sure that it's so bloody urgent?' asked Reinhart when Van Veeteren had settled into the passenger seat.

'No,' said Van Veeteren, lighting a cigarette. 'But when you've been in a straitjacket for seven weeks, I'll be damned if it isn't time to stretch your legs a bit.'

40

He woke up with a start and fumbled for his pistol. Took hold of it and looked out of the window. Noted that everything looked the same as before – except that the sun was shining.

He realized that it must be the sun that had warmed up the loft. He was lying just underneath the ceiling, but it wasn't at all the same all-pervading chill as he'd experienced so far. On the contrary, it was nice and warm – and it was a few minutes to ten.

Ten! It dawned on him that he had slept for over nine hours on end. He had snuggled down in bed shortly after half past twelve the previous night, and he didn't recall having lain awake for very long. No sleepless periods during the night either.

So he'd been lying here for nine hours. And what had been the point? He'd have been much more of a helpless victim than a guard dog, that was for sure. Would he have even woken up if she had come creeping up the stairs.

He rolled over onto his side and opened the window wide. The sunshine was very bright out there. Small birds were fluttering around in the shrubbery outside the kitchen door. The sky was blue, dotted here and there with tufts of scudding cloud.

Spring? he thought. What the hell am I doing here?

He recalled the previous evening. He'd stayed at the inn until eleven o'clock, and then thrown caution to the wind on the way back home. He'd simply stood up and left. Taken the main street – the chapel, Heine's, Van Klauster's – and then the narrow lane home to his cottage.

He'd had his pistol in his hand all the time, to be sure – with the safety catch off. But still . . .

He'd even entertained the thought of using the real bed, but something had held him back.

It was a week now. Eight days, to be precise, and as he brewed some coffee and buttered some bread in the kitchen, he decided that this would have to do. Today would have to be the last day. He would have to face up to the facts and acknowledge that he was wasting his time. It wouldn't bear fruit. He would have bugger all to show for it, so that was that.

He might just as well have left right away, before lunch; but Korhonen had promised to show him some pictures of his new Thai fancy woman, and so he'd said he would be there tonight as well.

But after that, he'd draw the line. The realization that it had been a mistake to come here had been growing inside him for some time now – the realization that it was pointless, and that these weren't the circumstances in which she intended to confront him.

His telephone call to his wife four days ago – and her mention of the woman from Copenhagen who had been trying to contact him – had naturally been an indication and a confirmation. But not that she intended turning up here. Merely that she knew where he was.

It must have been her – he'd realized that right away: he didn't have any female business contacts in Copenhagen. Nor any male ones, come to that. But this delay . . . These days that passed by without anything happening. The only way he could interpret it was that she had declined his invitation. Refused to meet him on his terms.

The cowardly bitch, he thought. You murdering whore, I'll get the better of you, no matter what!

Nevertheless, he didn't relax his safety procedures this final day. Despite his recognition of the fact that his calculations had failed, he spent his accustomed hours out in the forest. Ate his meals as usual, did a bit of packing after dark, and was aware of the fact that he mustn't be reckless.

On his guard, as usual. His gun was always within reach. And he kept himself hidden.

Only one more night. Just one.

He didn't bother to consider how he would go about things in future. He didn't have the strength, after all those efforts that had led to nowhere.

He would leave here tomorrow.

He would make some new decisions tomorrow.

He listened to the eight o'clock news, then sneaked out into the darkness. Paused as usual outside the front door, pistol in hand, eyes skinned and ears cocked; then he set off for the village, and the inn. The air was still warm, and it seemed to him that the spring he'd woken up to that morning had decided to stay on. At least for a few more days.

'Shouldn't we contact the police in Saaren?' said Reinhart when they'd been driving for forty kilometres and the chief inspector hadn't said a word.

'Have you forgotten who's chief of police there?' asked Van Veeteren.

'Oh my God! Yes, of course. Mergens. No, it would be best to keep him out of this.'

Van Veeteren nodded and lit his third cigarette within twenty minutes.

'What the hell would we say to him, anyway?' he said after a while. 'Ask him to come down like a ton of bricks on Mrs Biedersen, and lock her up until we get there?'

Reinhart shrugged

'He'd like that,' he said. 'No, you're right. We'll deal with this ourselves.'

'Can't you go a bit faster?' Van Veeteren wondered.

It was a quarter to eight before deBries managed to get through to Dagmar Biedersen. She had just got back from a shopping spree and a last-minute visit to the hairdresser, and she sounded washed out. When contact was made with Van Veeteren and Reinhart, it transpired that they were only about ten minutes away from Saaren; and so it was decided that it wasn't necessary to involve other police districts at this stage.

'Good timing,' said Reinhart. 'We'll go straight to her place. Tell her we'd like a couple of beers.'

'But what exactly are you implying?' asked Mrs Biedersen, placing two protective hands over her new hairdo.

'Can't we sit down somewhere and discuss the whole business quietly and calmly?' Van Veeteren suggested.

Reinhart led the way into the living room and sat down on a red plush sofa. The chief inspector invited Mrs Biedersen to sit down in one of the armchairs, while he remained standing.

'We have reason to believe that your husband is in danger,' he began.

'In danger?'

'Yes. It's connected with those earlier deaths. Can you tell us where he is at the moment?'

'What? No . . . Well, perhaps, but surely it can't be . . .'

'I'm afraid it can,' said Reinhart. 'Where is he?'

Without warning, Dagmar Biedersen burst into tears. Something had given way inside her, and her meagre chest was convulsed by sobbing. Tears came flooding forth.

Oh, hell! Van Veeteren thought.

'My dear Mrs Biedersen,' he said, 'all we want to know is where he is, so that we can sort everything out.'

She took out a handkerchief and blew her nose.

'Excuse me,' she said. 'I'm being silly.'

You certainly are, Van Veeteren thought. But answer the question, for Christ's sake.

'He's probably . . . up in the cottage, I assume. That's where he called me from a few days ago, at least.'

'The cottage?' Reinhart repeated.

'Yes, we have a holiday cottage, or whatever you'd like to call it – it's where he grew up, in fact. We go there some-times. He often spends time there on his own, as well . . .'

'Where?' asked Van Veeteren.

'Oh, excuse me. In Wahrhejm, of course.'

'Wahrhejm? And where is Wahrhejm?'

'Excuse me,' she said again. 'It's between Ulming and Oostwerdingen. Just a little village. It's about a hundred kilometres from here.'

Van Veeteren thought for a moment.

'Are you sure he's there?'

'No, as I said . . . But I think so.'

'Is there a telephone in the cottage?'

'No, I'm afraid not. He usually phones from the inn. He likes to be undisturbed when he's up there.'

Van Veeteren sighed.

'Just our bloody luck,' he said. 'Would you mind leaving us alone for a couple of minutes, Mrs Biedersen. The inspector and I need to exchange a few words.'

'Of course,' she said, and vanished into the kitchen.

'Now what?' asked Reinhart when she was out of earshot.

'I don't really know,' said Van Veeteren. 'I have the feeling that it's urgent – but of course there's nothing to say that it really is.'

'No,' said Reinhart. 'I have the same feeling. But you're the boss.'

'Yes, I know that,' said Van Veeteren. 'And you're the one who does whatever I say. Go and phone the police in Ulming – they must be the nearest – and tell them to get out there and nab him.'

'Nab him?'

'Yes, arrest him.'

'On what grounds?'

'I couldn't care less. Make something up, whatever you like.'

'With pleasure,' said Reinhart.

While Reinhart was doing what he'd been told to do in Biedersen's study, the chief inspector turned his attention to the worried wife, in the hope of extracting further information.

'To be absolutely honest with you,' he said, 'it's probable that this woman is aiming to kill your husband, Mrs Biedersen. Naturally, we hope to stop her.'

'Oh my God,' said Dagmar Biedersen.

'When did you last see him?'

She thought for a moment.

'A couple of weeks ago – almost three weeks, in fact.'

'Does anybody else know that he's there?'

'Er, I don't know.'

'Is there any possibility that this woman has found out that he's there? Somehow or other?'

'No – but . . .'

He could see how the realization suddenly dawned on her. The colour drained from her face, and she opened and closed her mouth several times. Her hands wandered back and forth over the buttons of her rust-red blouse without finding a possible resting place.

'That . . . er . . . that woman,' she said.

'Well?'

'She phoned.'

Van Veeteren nodded.

'Go on!'

'A woman phoned from Copenhagen. She claimed to be a business acquaintance of my husband's, and then . . .'

'And then?'

'And then she asked if I knew where he was. Where she could get in touch with him.'

'And so you told her?' asked Van Veeteren.

'Yes,' said Dagmar Biedersen, slumping back in the armchair. 'I told her. Do you think . . . ?'

Reinhart returned.

'Done,' he said.

'All right,' said Van Veeteren. 'Let's go. We'll be in touch, Mrs Biedersen. You'll be staying at home tonight, we hope?'

She nodded, and was breathing heavily, her mouth open wide. Van Veeteren gathered that she would be barely capable of getting up from the sofa, never mind anything else.

★

'The place is full of women,' said Biedersen, looking round the bar.

'Don't you know what day it is today?'

'No.'

'International Women's Day,' said Korhonen. 'This is what usually happens every year. Every damned woman in the village turns up.'

'A bloody silly invention,' said Biedersen.

'Of course, but it's good for business. Anyway, you can sit here in the corner as usual, and avoid having to get too close to them. A beer and a whisky chaser, as usual?'

'Yes please,' said Biedersen. 'Have you got the photos of your Thai fancy woman?'

'I'll come and show you them in just a minute or two,' said Korhonen. 'I just have to serve the ladies first.'

'OK,' said Biedersen. Took both his glasses and sat down at the empty table in the corner between the bar counter and the kitchen door.

Hell and damnation, he thought. This is an opportunity for camouflage if ever I saw one. I'd better play safe tonight.

And he felt in his jacket pocket.

41

'What the hell's going on?' wondered Ackermann.

'I don't know,' said Päude, starting the car. 'In the middle of the match as well.'

'The match?' said Ackermann. 'Bollocks to the match. I was just about to start pulling her knickers down when he phoned. That delicious little Nancy Fischer, you know.'

Päude sighed and switched on the radio to hear the end of the football report, instead of having to listen to an account of his colleague's love life – he was treated to enough of that on a regular basis.

'Halfway in, you might say,' said Ackermann.

'What do you think of this Biedersen character?' asked Päude in an attempt to change the subject.

'Cunning,' said Ackermann. 'Do you reckon we should just arrest him for vagrancy and wait for further orders? You don't think he's dangerous, do you?'

'Munckel said he wasn't.'

'Munckel can't tell the difference between a hand grenade and a beetroot.'

'OK, we'd better be a bit careful then. How far is it to Wahrhejm?'

'Eighteen kilometres. We'll be there in ten minutes. Shall we put the siren on, or the light at least?'

'Good God no! Discretion he said, Munckel said. But I don't suppose you know what the word means?'

'Of course I do,' said Ackermann. 'Discretion is the better part of valour.'

'Another one?' said Korhonen.

'Yes, of course,' said Biedersen. 'Must just go and take a leak first. But that's a good-looking piece of skirt you've got there. A hell of a good-looking piece of skirt.'

'Easy to maintain as well,' said Korhonen, smirking.

Biedersen stood up and noticed that he was a bit tipsy. Perhaps it'll be as well to cut out the whisky and stick to good old beer, he thought as he worked his way round the contingent of women sitting at two long tables and disturbing the peace. Laughing and singing. Apart from himself there were only two male customers in the whole of the bar. The old school caretaker who was sitting at his usual table with a newspaper and a carafe of red wine. And an unaccompanied man in a dark suit who had arrived a quarter of an hour ago.

All the rest were women, and he held onto the gun in his jacket pocket as he passed them, with his back to the wall.

Women's Day, he thought as he stood and allowed the beer to take the natural way out. What a bloody silly idea!

The door opened and the man in the dark suit came in. He nodded at Biedersen.

'At least we can get a bit of peace in here,' said Biedersen, gesturing with his head at all the commotion outside. 'I've nothing against women, but . . .'

He broke off and reached for his jacket pocket, but before he had a chance to grab his pistol he heard the same plopping sound twice, and knew it was too late. A dark red flood washed over his eyes, and the last thing he felt, the very last thing of all, was a terrible pain below the belt.

Päude pulled up outside the inn.

'Go in and ask the way,' he said. 'I'll wait here.'

'OK,' said Ackermann with a sigh. 'His name's Biedersen, right?'

'Yes,' said Päude. 'Werner Biedersen. They're bound to know where he lives.'

Ackermann got out of the car and Päude lit a cigarette. It's a relief to be rid of him for a few minutes, he thought.

But Ackermann was back after ninety seconds.

'Stroke of luck,' he said. 'I bumped into a bloke on his way out who knew where he lives. Keep going straight ahead, a hundred and fifty metres or so.'

'All right,' said Päude.

'Then turn left,' added Ackermann.

Päude followed the instructions and came to a low stone wall with an opening in it.

'Looks dark in there,' said Ackermann.

'But there's a house there in any case. Take the torch and have a look. I'll wait here. I have the window open so you only need to shout if you need me.'

'Wouldn't it be better if you went?' Ackermann asked.

'No,' said Päude. 'Get going.'

'OK,' said Ackermann.

I'm seven years older after all, thought Päude, as Ackermann got out of the car. With a wife and children, and all that.

The radio suddenly crackled into life.

'Hello. Päude here.'

'Munckel! Where the hell are you?'

'In Wahrhejm, of course. We've just got to his house. Ackermann's just gone in and . . .'

'Get him out again! Biedersen's been shot dead in the

Gents at the inn. Get your arses there and cordon the place off!'

'Oh, shit!' said Päude.

'Make sure that not a soul leaves the premises! I'll be there in fifteen minutes.'

'Roger,' said Päude.

More crackling, then Munckel vanished. Päude shook his head.

Oh, shit, he thought again. Then he got out of the car and shouted for Ackermann.

42

It can't be true, I'm dreaming, was the thought that Van Veeteren had sat wrestling with for the last twenty-five minutes. Ever since he heard the report on the radio.

This kind of thing simply doesn't happen. It must be a hoax, or a misunderstanding.

'I swear to God I thought I was dreaming!' said Reinhart as he pulled up. 'But we're there now. It looks as if what they said was right.'

Two police cars were already in place. Nose to nose diagonally across the road, with their blue lights flashing. Presumably to inform everybody in the village who had the good fortune to miss the news broadcast, Van Veeteren thought as they hurried into the inn. A uniformed officer was guarding the door, and several others were inside the premises, where the mood of fear and anxiety seemed to be tangible. The customers – almost exclusively women, he was surprised to see – had been herded together behind two tables, and their whispers and low-voiced discussions reached Van Veeteren's ears in the form of an unarticulated but long-suffering lament. A fleeting image of cattle about to be slaughtered flashed before his eyes. Or prisoners in concentration camps on their way to the showers. He shuddered, and tried to shake off any such thoughts.

Stop it! he commanded his own thoughts. It's bad enough without you making it any worse.

A man with thinning hair about the same age as Van Veeteren came up to him.

'Chief Inspector Van Veeteren?'

He nodded and introduced Reinhart.

'Munckel. Well, this is a cartload of shit if ever I saw one. He's in there. We haven't touched anything.'

Van Veeteren and Reinhart went to the Gents, where one of the constables was stationed.

'Ackermann,' said Munckel, 'let these gentlemen in.'

Van Veeteren peered inside. Studied the lifeless corpse for a few seconds before turning to Reinhart.

'Ah well,' he said. 'Exactly the same as usual. We might as well leave him lying there until the forensic team gets here. We can't do anything for him.'

'The silly bugger,' muttered Reinhart.

'When did it happen?' asked the chief inspector.

Munckel looked at the clock.

'Shortly after nine,' he said. 'We were alerted at a

quarter past – it was Mr Korhonen who phoned. He's the barman.'

A dark-haired man in his fifties stepped forward and introduced himself.

'It happened less than an hour ago,' said Van Veeteren. 'How many people have left the premises since then?'

'I don't really know,' said Korhonen hesitantly.

'Who found him?'

'I did,' said an elderly man with a loud voice and a checked shirt. 'I just went to the Gents for a pee, and there he was. Shot in the balls as well. A cartload of shit . . .'

A shudder seemed to pass through the group of women.

Oh yes, dammit! It had eventually dawned on Van Veeteren. International Women's Day, 8 March. That was why they were all here. Macabre – she couldn't have hit upon a better day.

'So when did Biedersen go in there?' Reinhart asked.

Korhonen cleared his throat nervously.

'Excuse me,' he said. 'I think I know who did it. It must have been that other guy.'

'Who are you referring to?' said Munckel. 'Why haven't you said anything before now?'

'That other guy,' he said again. 'The one sitting over there . . .'

He pointed.

'He went to the Gents immediately after Biedersen – I remember now.'

'A man?' said Van Veeteren.

'Yes, of course.'

'Where is he?' said Reinhart.

Korhonen looked around. The man in the checked shirt looked around. All the women looked around.

'He's left, of course,' said Munckel.

'He's gone!' shouted one of the women. 'I saw him leave.'

'You can bet your life he didn't hang around,' muttered Reinhart.

'Is one of you called Van Veeteren?' asked a dark-haired woman in her mid thirties.

'Yes, why?'

'This was lying on his table. I noticed it just now.'

She came up and handed over a white envelope. Van Veeteren took it and stared at it in bewilderment.

I'm dreaming, he thought again, and closed his eyes for a moment.

'Open it!' said Reinhart.

Van Veeteren opened it.

'Read it!' said Reinhart.

Van Veeteren read it.

'Where is there a telephone?' he asked, and was directed to the lobby by barman Korhonen. Reinhart went with him, signalling to Munckel that he should keep everybody where they were in the restaurant.

'What the hell's going on?' he whispered as the chief inspector dialled the number. 'Give me the letter!'

Van Veeteren handed it over, and Reinhart read it.

> *I'm waiting for you. Jelena Walgens*
> *can tell you where I am.*

Two lines. No signature.

What the hell? thought Reinhart. And then he said it out loud.

43

They parked at what seemed to be a safe distance, and got out of the car. It wasn't completely dark yet, and it was easy to distinguish the outlines of the houses at the edge of the lake. The wind was now no more than a distant whisper in the forest to the north-east, and the air felt almost warm, Van Veeteren noticed.

Spring? he thought, somewhat surprised. Reinhart cleared his throat.

'It must be that cottage furthest away,' he said. 'There doesn't seem to be anybody at home in any of them.'

'Some people occasionally manage to sleep at night,' said Van Veeteren.

They continued walking along the narrow track.

'Do you think she's in there?'

'I don't dare to think anything about this case any more,' said Van Veeteren, sounding somewhat subdued. 'But no matter what, we need to get in there and take a look. Or do you think we should summon Ryman's heavy tank brigade?'

'Good God no,' said Reinhart. 'It takes four days to mobilize them. Let's go in. I'll lead the way if you like.'

'The hell you will,' said Van Veeteren. 'I'm oldest. You can keep in the background.'

'Your word is my command,' said Reinhart. 'For what it's worth, I don't think she's at home.'

Crouching down, and with quite a long distance between them, they approached the ramshackle grey house with the sagging roof. Slunk slowly but deliberately over the damp grass, and when there were only another ten metres or so still to go, Van Veeteren launched the attack by rushing forward and pressing himself up against the wall, right next to the door. Reinhart followed him and doubled up under one of the windows.

This is ridiculous, Van Veeteren thought as he tried to get his breath back, keeping tight hold of his standard-issue pistol. What the hell are we doing?

Or is it serious business?

He forced the door open with a bang and charged in. Ran around for a few seconds, kicking in doors: but he soon established that the cottage was just as empty as Reinhart had anticipated.

If she was going to shoot us, she'd have done so long ago, he thought, putting his pistol away in his pocket.

He went into the biggest of the three rooms, found a switch and turned on the light. Reinhart came in and looked around.

'There's a letter here, addressed to you,' he said, pointing to the table.

The chief inspector came forward to pick it up. Weighed it in his hand.

The same sort of envelope.

The same handwriting.

Addressed to the same person.

Detective Chief Inspector Van Veeteren, Maardam.

And the feeling that he was dreaming simply refused to go away.

The precision, Van Veeteren thought. It's this damned precision that makes it all so unreal. There's no such thing as coincidence, Reinhart had said; but in fact the reverse was true. He understood that now. When the feeling of coincidence suddenly disappears completely, that's when we find it difficult to rely on our senses. To have faith in what they tell us about happenings and connections.

Yes, that must be how things work, more or less.

There were two basket chairs in the room. Reinhart had already sat down on one of them and lit his pipe. The chief inspector sat on the other one and started to read.

It only took him a couple of minutes, and when he had finished, he read it once again. Then he looked at the clock and handed the letter to Reinhart without a word.

At my mother's interment there was only a single mourner. Me.

Time is short, and I shall express myself briefly. I don't need your understanding, but I want you to know who these men were, the men I have killed. My mother told me – two weeks before she died – about how I was conceived.

My father was four men. It was the night of 29–30 May 1965. She was seventeen years old, and a virgin. They raped her repeatedly for two hours in a student room in Maardam, and in order to stop her screaming she had the underpants of one of the men stuffed into her mouth. The tie of one of the other men knotted round her mouth and the back of her neck. They also played music while I was being made. The same record, over and over again – afterwards she found out what the tune was called, and bought it. I still have it.

Once they had finished impregnating my mother, they carried her out and dumped her in some bushes in a nearby park. One of my fathers said that she was a whore, and that he'd kill her if she told anybody what had happened.

My mother duly kept silent about what had happened, but after two months she began to suspect that she was pregnant. After three, she was certain. She was still at school. She tried to kill me, using various tricks and methods she had heard about, but failed. I just wish she had managed it better.

She spoke to her mother, who didn't believe her.

She spoke to her father, who didn't believe her and gave her a good hiding.

She spoke to her clever elder sisters, who didn't believe her either, but advised her to have an abortion.

But it was too late. I wish it hadn't been.

My grandfather gave her a small sum of money in order to get rid of us, and I was born a long way away in Groenstadt. That's also where I grew up. My mother had found out my fathers' names, and was given some money by them when she threatened to expose them. When I was ten, she threatened them again, and received some more money, but that was all. They paid. They could afford it.

I knew from an early age that my mother was a whore, and I knew that I would become one as well. And the same applied to drinking, and drug-taking.

But I didn't know why things were as they were, not until she told me about my fathers shortly before she died.

My mother was forty-seven when she died. I am only thirty, but I've been whoring and drug-taking for so long that I look at least ten years older. I received my first clients before my fifteenth birthday.

In addition, I have the urge to kill inside me. I was told

the facts in November, and when I got to know my fathers a
bit later on, I made up my mind.

It was a good decision.

My mother's life was a torment. Torment and indignity.

So was my own. But it was good to understand, to
understand at last. I could see the logic. What else could
possibly be the outcome of a night of lovemaking like the
one when my fathers brought me to life?

What life?

I am the ripe fruit that grew out of a gang bang. It is
that same fruit that is now killing its fathers.

That is completing the circle.

To be sure, that sounds like a sort of dark poetry. In a
different life I could have become a poet instead. I could have
written and read. I had the ability inside me, but never had
the opportunity.

When I have finished, nothing living involved in that
night will have survived. We shall all be dead. That is the
logical outcome.

My mother – who had my father's underpants stuffed
into her mouth while the act of love took place – gave me
the task, and in her name I have murdered them all. Doing
so has given me great joy, more joy than anything else in my
life. At no point have I felt any guilt or regret, and nobody
will ever come and call me to account.

I am also pleased that my mother saved the money she

extracted from my fathers. It has been a great help to me, and I like the thought that in this way they have paid for their own deaths.

I say again: it has given me great satisfaction to kill my own fathers. Very great satisfaction.

I have been very precise all the time, and want to continue in that way to the very end. I am writing for two reasons. In the first place, I want the real reasons to be known. In the second place, I need to gain time – that is also why I left a note at the inn as well. If you are reading this letter at the time I intended and am hoping for, I have achieved my aims.

At 10 p.m. I shall be on the ferry that leaves Oostwerdingen and heads for the islands; but I shall not be on board when it calls at its first port.

I shall be carrying substantial weights that will drag me down to the bottom of the sea, where I hope the fish will soon have chewed away my tainted flesh.

I never want to come to the surface again. Not one single part of me.

Reinhart folded the sheets of paper and put them back into the envelope. Then sat for a while without speaking while he lit his pipe, which had gone out.

'What is there to say?' he said eventually.

The chief inspector was leaning back in the chair and had closed his eyes.

'Nothing,' he said. 'You don't need to say anything at all.'

'No signature.'

'No.'

'It's a quarter to one.'

Van Veeteren nodded. Sat up and lit a cigarette. Inhaled a few times. Stood up, walked across the room and switched off the light.

'What's the first port of call?' he asked when he had sat down again.

'Arnholt, I think,' said Reinhart. 'At around one.'

'Yes,' said Van Veeteren. 'That sounds about right. Go out to the car and try to make contact with the ferry. They can search the ship when it docks. She might have changed her mind.'

'Do you think so?' asked Reinhart.

'No,' said Van Veeteren. 'But we must continue playing our roles to the very end.'

'Yes, I suppose so,' said Reinhart. 'The show must go on.'

Then he went out and left the chief inspector alone in the darkness.

44

She locked the door, and almost immediately the ferry set off. Through the oval, convex port hole she could watch the harbour lights glide past before disappearing. This was her final extravagance: a single cabin up on B-deck. It had cost her more or less everything she had left; but this was no mere whim. This too was a necessity, and a logical requirement. She needed to be alone in order to make the final preparations, and there was no other way of ensuring that.

She checked her watch: seven minutes past ten. She sat down on the bed and felt the newly laundered sheet and the warm, red blanket with the shipping line's logo. She unscrewed the bottle and threw the cap into the waste bin, then drank direct from the bottle. Half a litre of cognac. Four-star. An inferior sort would have served the same purpose, of course, but there had been just enough money. Four-star cognac. Single cabin with a wine-red blanket and wall-to-wall carpet. The final extravagance, as mentioned.

She had two hours to spare; that was in accordance with

her timetable. Calculated from the moment she had seen the police car on the road outside the inn. No matter how efficiently they worked – and hitherto they hadn't exactly displayed much in the way of proficiency in this respect – it would be impossible for them to trace her here before midnight. First of all there was the crime scene, and the chaos at the inn; then they would have to find Jelena Walgens, conduct a confusing conversation with her and then drive back to Wahrhejm – she was convinced that this chief inspector wouldn't delegate anything of this nature to his subordinates. Then the telephone call to the ferry . . . No, anything less than two hours was out of the question.

Half past eleven, to be on the safe side. Ninety minutes in her own cabin on B-deck, that would have to be enough. It felt remarkably satisfying to be able to plan her own demise at last, not only that of others. She tipped the contents of her bag onto the floor. It would be as well to prepare things right away, in case anything went wrong. She found the end of the steel chain, and pulled up her sweater in order to expose her torso. Took another swig of cognac. Lit a cigarette before starting to wind the pliable steel round her waist. Slowly and methodically, round and round, exactly how she'd done it when practising.

Heavy, but easy to handle. She had chosen the chain carefully. Seven metres long and eighteen kilos. Steel links. Cold and heavy. When she had finished winding she tightened it a little bit more, then fixed it in place with the padlock. Stood up and checked the weight and her ability to move.

Yes, everything was in order.

Heavy enough to make her sink. But not too heavy. She needed to be able to walk. And clamber over the rail.

Another cigarette.

A drop more cognac.

A warm and conclusive wave of intoxication had started to flow through her body. She leaned her head against the wall and closed her eyes. Listened to, or rather felt, the vibrations of the heavy engines that were transmitted through her skull like a distant and pointless attempt at communicating. Nothing else. The drink and the smoke, nothing more. And the vibrations.

One more hour, she thought. It will all be over in another hour.

Just one more hour.

The wind took hold of her and threatened to throw her backwards. For a moment she was afraid that she might have miscalculated, but then she caught hold of the stair rail and recovered her balance. Stood up straight and closed the door.

The darkness was compact and the wind roared. She slowly worked her way into the wind, down the narrow, soaking wet passageway along the length of the ship.

Further and further forward. The rail was no more than chest high, and there were crossbars to climb up on. More or less ideal, for whatever reason. All that remained was to choose the right place. She continued a bit further. Came to a staircase with a chain across it; a notice swaying and clanking in the wind indicated that passengers were forbidden to venture up the stairs.

She looked round. No sign of a soul. The sky was dark and motionless, with occasional patches of light. The sea was black; no reflections. When she leant out and looked down, she could barely make it out.

Darkness. Darkness everywhere.

The muffled vibrations of the ship's engines. Gusts of wind and salt spray. Waves whipped up by the rotating propellers.

All alone. Cold, despite the cognac.

No other passengers had been bold enough to venture out on deck at this time of night. Not in this weather. They were all inside. In the bars. In the wine-red restaurant. At the disco or in their warm cabins.

Inside.

She clambered up. Sat on the rail for a second before kicking off with all the strength she could muster and flinging herself outwards.

She entered the water curled up in the foetal position, and the slight fear she had had of being sucked in by the propellers faded away as she was rapidly – much more rapidly than she had been able to imagine – dragged down into the depths.

45

While they were waiting for the expected call, two others came.

The first was from the duty officer in Maardam and concerned information from Inspector Heinemann about another possible link on the basis of bank account information. It was by no means certain, but there was evidence to suggest that a certain Werner Biedersen had made an unmotivated transaction transferring money from his firm to a private account (with subsequent withdrawals) at the beginning of June 1976; however, Heinemann had not yet been able to find a withdrawal corresponding to the amount in question.

Mind you – it was admitted – it could well be a question of a gambling debt or a few fur coats for his wife or some mistress, or God only knows what: in any case, the inspector would be in touch again within the next few days.

'Good timing,' said Reinhart for the second time that evening; but the chief inspector didn't even sigh.

'Say something sensible,' he said instead after a few minutes of silence in the darkness.

Reinhart struck a match and went to considerable lengths to light his pipe before answering.

'I think we're going to make a child,' he said.

'A child?' said the chief inspector.

'Yes.'

'Who?'

'Me,' said Reinhart. 'And a woman I know.'

'How old are you?' asked the chief inspector.

'What the hell does that have to do with it?' said Reinhart. 'But she'll soon be forty, so it's about time.'

'Yes, I suppose it is,' said the chief inspector.

Another minute passed.

'Well, I suppose I ought to congratulate you,' said the chief inspector eventually. 'I didn't even know you had a woman.'

'Thank you,' said Reinhart.

The other call was from Munckel, who reported the result of the preliminary medical examination. Werner Biedersen had been killed by a Berenger-75; three bullets in the chest, fired from a distance of about one metre. Two further bullets under the belt from about ten centimetres. Death had been more or less instantaneous, and had taken place at about ten minutes past nine.

Van Veeteren thanked the caller and hung up.

'There was something about that scene,' he said after a while.

Reinhart's chair creaked in the darkness.

'I know,' he said. 'I've been thinking about it.'

The chief inspector sat in silence for some time, searching for words. The clock on the wall between the two rectangular windows seemed to make an effort, but didn't have the strength to strike. He looked at his watch.

Half past one. The ferry must have been moored in Arnholt for at least half an hour by now. They ought to hear from there any minute now.

'That scene,' he said again.

Reinhart lit his pipe for the twentieth time.

'All the women in there . . . International Women's Day . . .' Van Veeteren went on. 'A man shot under the belt in the toilets . . . By his daughter, dressed as a man . . . a thirty-year-old rape . . . International Women's Day . . .'

'That's enough,' interrupted Reinhart. 'Let's talk about something else.'

'All right,' said Van Veeteren. 'Probably just as well. But it was stage-managed, that's obvious.'

Reinhart inhaled deeply several times.

'It always is,' he said.

'Eh?' said the chief inspector. 'What do you mean?'

'I don't know,' said Reinhart.

Van Veeteren suddenly seemed to be annoyed.

'Of course you do, stop pretending! What the hell do you know, in fact? You and I are sitting here in this god-forsaken ramshackle house out in the sticks, in the middle of the night, God only knows where, waiting for . . . Well, would you kindly tell me what exactly we are waiting for?'

'For dotting the "i"s and crossing the "t"s,' said Reinhart.

The telephone rang and Van Veeteren answered.

'Yes?'

'Chief Inspector Van Veeteren?'

'Yes.'

'Schmidt. Harbour police in Arnholt. We've been through the ship now and . . .'

'And?'

'. . . and what you say seems to be right. There is a passenger missing.'

'Are you sure?'

'As sure as it's possible to be. Obviously, she might have managed to hide away somewhere on board, but we don't think so. We've been pretty thorough. In any case, we'll continue searching when the ferry sets sail again: if she is on board, we'll find her before we get to the next port of call.'

He paused, but the chief inspector didn't say anything.

'Anyway, it's a woman,' said Schmidt. 'She had a first-class ticket, single cabin. She embarked, collected her key from Information and evidently spent an hour in her cabin.'

'Do you have her name?'

'Yes, of course. The ticket and the cabin were booked in the name of Biedersen.'

'Biedersen?'

'Yes. But they never ask for ID proof when the passenger pays cash, which she did: so it could be a false name.'

Van Veeteren sighed deeply.

'Hello? Are you still there?'

'Yes.'

'Is there anything else, or can we allow them to set sail? They are over an hour late now.'

'Of course,' said Van Veeteren. 'Cast off and get under-way.'

The call was terminated. Reinhart took off the ear-phones. Crossed his hands behind his head and leant back, making the chair creak.

Van Veeteren put his hands on his knees and got to his feet with difficulty. Walked back and forth over the creaking floorboards before pausing in front of one of the windows. Rubbed the pane with the sleeve of his jacket and peered out into the darkness. Dug his hands down into his trouser pockets.

'What do you think she was called?' asked Reinhart.

'It's started raining again,' said Van Veeteren.

If you enjoyed **Woman With A Birthmark** *you'll love*

THE INSPECTOR AND SILENCE

the next Inspector Van Veeteren mystery

In the heart of summer, the country swelters in a fug of heat. In the beautiful forested lake-town of Sorbinowo, Sergeant Merwin Kluuge's tranquil existence is shattered when he receives a phone call from an anonymous woman. She tells him that a girl has gone missing from the summer camp of the mysterious Pure Life, a religious sect buried deep in the woods. Chief Inspector Van Veeteren is recruited to help solve the mystery.

But Van Veeteren's investigations at the Pure Life go nowhere fast. The strange priest-like figure who leads the sect – Oscar Yellineck – refuses even to admit anyone is missing. Things soon take a sinister turn, however, when a young girl's body is discovered in the woods, raped and strangled; and Yellineck himself disappears. Yet even in the face of these new horrors, the remaining members of the sect refuse to co-operate with Van Veeteren, remaining largely silent.

As the body count rises, a media frenzy descends upon

the town and the pressure to find the monster behind the murders weighs heavily on the investigative team. Finally Van Veeteren realizes that to solve this disturbing case, faced with silence and with few clues to follow, he has only his intuition to rely on . . .

'The atmosphere of the small town, the mysterious fringes of the forest full of aspens and blueberries, are evocatively drawn . . . The clarity of Nesser's vision, the inner problems of good and evil with which Van Veeteren struggles, recall the films of Bergman'

Independent

Chosen for the *Metro* Crime Books of the Year feature

An excerpt follows here . . .

From a purely physical point of view, the morning of 18 July was perfect.

The sky was cloudless, the air clear and still cool; the dark water of the lake was mirror-like, and Sergeant Merwin Kluuge completed his run round the alder-lined shore, nearly seven kilometres, in a new record time: 26 minutes and 55 seconds.

He paused to get his breath back down by the marina, did a few stretching exercises then jogged gently up to the terraced house, where he took a shower, and woke up his blonde-haired wife by carefully and lovingly caressing her stomach, inside which she had been carrying the fruit and aspirations of his life for the past six months.

The terraced house was even more recent. Barely eight weeks had passed since they had moved in – with the kind assistance of his parents-in-law's savings; and he was still overcome by feelings of innocent wonder when he woke up in the mornings. When he put his feet on the wine-red wall-to-wall carpet in the bedroom. When he tiptoed from room to room and stroked the embossed wallpaper and pine panelling, which still exuded a whiff of newly sawn timber hinting at unimaginable possibilities and well-deserved success. And whenever he watered the flower beds or mowed the little lawn flanked by the trees, he could not help but feel warm and genuine gratitude to life itself.

Without warning, everything had suddenly fallen into place. They had been shunted onto a bright and sun-soaked new track, with himself and Deborah as the only carriages of any significance in a solidly built and smooth-running train heading into the future. All loose ends had been tied together when it became clear that Deborah was pregnant – or rather when that fact became public knowledge. They had married two weeks later, and now, on this lovely summer morning, when Merwin Kluuge toyed gently with the soft – and to the naked eye almost invisible – hairs on his wife's rounded stomach, he was filled with a sensation bordering on the religious.

'Tea or coffee?' he asked softly.

'Tea,' she replied without opening her eyes. 'You know I haven't touched a drop of coffee for three months now. Why do you ask?'

Oh yes, of course, Kluuge thought, and went into the kitchen to prepare the breakfast tray.

They had breakfast together in bed, watching the early

morning programme on their new 27-inch television set, and once again Kluuge ran his fingers gently over the tense skin, feeling for kicks and any other sign of life from Merwin junior. At precisely 07.45 he left his home and his married bliss.

He wheeled his twelve-gear bicycle out of the garage, clipped back his trousers, fixed his briefcase on the luggage carrier, and set off.

Exactly eleven minutes later he came to a halt in Kleinmarckt. The square was still more or less deserted; three or four market traders were busy opening up their stalls next to the town hall, arranging displays of fruit and vegetables. A few fat pigeons were strutting around the fountain, for want of anything else to do. Kluuge parked his bicycle in the stand outside the police station, secured it with a couple of stout locks, and wiped a drop of sweat from his brow. Then he walked through the semi-transparent glass doors, greeted Miss Miller in reception, and took possession of the chief of police's office.

He sat down behind the impressively large desk, removed his bicycle clips and turned to the first page of the notepad beside the telephone.

Missing girl??? it said.

He looked out of the window, which Miss Miller had opened slightly, and gazed at the blossoming elder. The chief of police had informed him that it was an elder, but anybody could see that it was blossoming.

From a purely physical point of view it was still a perfect morning; but as far as Merwin Kluuge's duties as acting chief of police were concerned, there was beyond doubt a cloud on the horizon.

At least one.

Precisely one.

'Holiday,' Chief of Police Malijsen had said, tapping him on the collarbone with two fingers. 'I hope to God you're fully aware of what the word holiday means. Peace and quiet. Being alone and left to yourself. Coniferous forests, mountain air and new waters to fish in. I've invested my hard-earned wages in hiring this damned cottage, and I have every intention of staying there for three weeks, provided the Japs don't attack us. Is that clear, Sergeant Kluuge?'

For the last thirty years Chief of Police Malijsen's credo had been that sooner or later the Japanese would inflict upon the world a new – but much better executed – Pearl Harbor, and he rarely missed an opportunity to mention it.

'You'll be in charge of the shop. It's time for you to stand on your own two feet and become more than a mere paper shuffler and a thorn in the side of Edward Marckx.'

Gathering together and sending off the monthly reports

from the Sorbinowo police district really did comprise the major part of Kluuge's regular duties; that had been the case ever since he first took up his post just over three years ago, and would no doubt continue to be until the day – still ten years or more away – when Malijsen reached an age enabling him to resign his job and devote all his time to pleasure, sitting in front of the television. Or tying fishing flies. Or building defences to foil the increasingly inevitable attack from the slant-eyed yellow hordes from the east.

According to Kluuge's view of the world and its inhabitants, Chief of Police Malijsen had a screw loose, an opinion probably shared by a few other Sorbinowo residents, but by no means all. Despite being a bit of a one-off character, Malijsen had the reputation of being the right man for his job, and for keeping the gap between right and wrong, between upright local citizens and crooks, open and wide. Even such a dodgy character as Edward Marckx – arsonist, jailbird, hot-tempered drug addict and violent brawler – had once, presumably in connection with one of his many brushes with the law, expressed his grudging admiration of the chief of police:

'A particularly obnoxious bastard, but with a heart in his body and a hole in his arse!'

Perhaps Kluuge could sign up to the second part of that assessment.

On his way out of the door, Malijsen had paused and

been serious for a few moments. Checked the torrent of words and raised an eyebrow.

'Are you sure you can cope with this?'

Kluuge had snorted quietly. Not rudely. Not nervously. 'Yes, of course.'

Nevertheless Malijsen had looked a bit doubtful and taken a card out of his wallet.

'For Christ's sake don't disturb me unless you really have to! There's a public telephone in the village, of course, but I need these weeks to get over Lilian.'

Lilian was Malijsen's wife, stricken by cancer; after many years of more or less unbearable suffering she had finally given up the ghost and departed from this world. Drugged up to the eyeballs, and a shadow of a shadow . . . That was in the middle of March. Kluuge had attended the funeral with Deborah, who had noted that the chief of police had shed the occasional tear, but not excessively.

'If the shit hits the fan, you can always get in touch with VV instead,' Malijsen explained. 'He's an old colleague of mine, and he owes me a favour.'

He handed over the card and Kluuge put it in his breast pocket without so much as glancing at it. A quarter of an hour later, he sat down behind the imposingly large desk, leaned back and looked forward to three weeks of calm and prestigious professional activity.

That was six days ago. Last Friday. Today was Thursday. The first call had come last Tuesday.

The second one yesterday.

Oh hell, Kluuge thought and stared at the card with the very familiar name. He drummed on it with his finger, thinking back to what happened two days ago.

'There's a woman who'd like to speak to you.'

He noted that Miss Miller avoided addressing him as 'Chief of Police'. She'd been doing that right from the start; at first it had annoyed him somewhat, but now he just ignored it.

'A telephone call?'

'Yes.'

'Okay, put her through.'

He lifted the receiver and pressed the white button.

'Is that the police?'

'Yes.'

'A little girl has disappeared.'

The voice was so faint that he had to strain his ears to catch what she was saying.

'A little girl? Who am I speaking to?'

'I can't tell you that. But a little girl has disappeared from Waldingen.'

'Waldingen? Can you speak a bit louder?'

'The Pure Life Camp at Waldingen.'

'You mean that sect?'

'Yes. A little girl has disappeared from their confirmation camp in Waldingen. I can't say any more. You must look into it.'

'Hang on a minute. Who are you? Where are you calling from?'

'I must stop now.'

'Just a minute . . .'

She had hung up. Kluuge had thought the matter over for twenty minutes. Then he asked Miss Miller to look up the number for Waldingen – after all, there was nothing there apart from an old building used as a centre for summer camps. After a while he had given them a call.

A soft female voice answered the phone. He explained that he'd been informed that one of the confirmands had disappeared. The woman at the other end of the line sounded genuinely surprised, and said that nobody had been missing at lunch two hours previously.

Kluuge thanked her, and hung up.

The second call had come yesterday. Half an hour before the end of office hours. Miss Miller had already gone home, and the phone had been switched through to the chief of police's office.

'Hello. Chief of Police Kluuge here.'

'You haven't done anything.'

The voice sounded a little louder this time. But it was the same woman, no doubt about it. The same tense, forced composure. Somewhere between forty and fifty, although Kluuge acknowledged that he was bad when it came to guessing age.

'Who am I speaking to?'

'I rang yesterday and reported that a little girl had disappeared. You've done nothing about it. I assume she's been murdered. If you don't do something, I'll be forced to turn to the newspapers.'

That was the point at which Kluuge felt the first pang of panic. He gulped, and his mind was racing.

'How do you know that a girl has disappeared? I've investigated the matter. Nobody is missing from the camp at Waldingen.'

'You mean you've called them and asked? Of course they'll deny it.'

'We've carried out certain checks.'

He thought that was quite a good line, but the woman wouldn't be fobbed off.

'If you don't do something, they'll kill some more.'

There was a click as she hung up. Kluuge sat there for a while with the receiver in his hand, before replacing it and diverting his attention to the portrait of Lilian Malijsen in her bridal gown, in a gilded frame at the far end of the desk.

My God, he thought. What if she's telling the truth?

He had heard quite a bit about the Pure Life. And read a lot. As he understood it, they got up to all kinds of things.

Speaking in tongues.

Exorcizing devils.

Sexual rituals.

Mind you, the latter was probably just a malevolent rumour. Wagging tongues and the usual upright envy. Rubbish! Kluuge thought, and returned to contemplating the blossoming elders. But somewhere deep down – perhaps at the very core of his emotions, to borrow one of Deborah's latest pet expressions – he recognized that this was serious.

Serious. There was something about that woman's voice. There was also something about the situation in itself: his own disgracefully well-organized existence – Deborah, the terraced house, his stand-in duties as chief of police, the perfect mornings . . . It was only fair and just that something like this should crop up.

There has to be a balance, as his father used to say. Between plus and minus. Between successes and failures. Otherwise, you're not alive.

He stuck a pencil in his mouth. Began chewing it as he tried to imagine Malijsen's reactions if it turned out that a little girl had been found murdered on his patch, and the police had been tipped off but ignored it. Then he imagined the consequences of disturbing the divine peace that ruled over the heavenly fishing grounds. Neither of these options produced especially cheerful visions in Merwin Kluuge's mind's eye. Nor especially useful ones with regard to his possible future career prospects.

The Pure Life? he thought. A little girl missing?

It wouldn't surprise him.

Not at all, dammit.

He'd made up his mind. Picked up the telephone and dialled the number of the police station in Maardam.

'A hand grenade?' said the chief of police.

'No doubt about it,' said Reinhart. 'A seven-forty-five. He chucked it in through an open window, it rolled along the floor and exploded under the stage. Incredibly lucky, only eight injured and they'll all pull through. If it had gone off on the dance floor we'd have had a dozen corpses.'

'At least,' said deBries, adjusting his wine-red silken cravat that had become slightly awry.

'Do you need any help with your scarf?' Rooth wondered.

'And then what happened?' Münster was quick to intervene.

'He peppered some parked cars with an automatic weapon,' Reinhart continued. 'A nice chap, no inhibitions to speak of.'

'My God,' said Ewa Moreno. 'And he's still on the loose?'

'Getting ready for this evening, no doubt,' suggested Rooth. 'We ought to go after him.'

'Professional soldier?' wondered Jung.

'Very possibly,' said Reinhart.

'Excuse me,' said Heinemann, who had arrived late. 'Could we start from the beginning again? I've only heard about it on the radio.'

Chief of Police Hiller cleared his throat and wiped his temples with a tissue.

'Yes, that's probably best,' he said. 'Reinhart, you've been there, so I think you ought to give us the full story. Then we'll have to decide how to allocate available resources.'

Reinhart nodded.

'Kirwan Disco,' he began. 'Down at Zwille, alongside Grote Square. Full of people. Shortly after half past two this morning – they close at three – an unknown person threw a hand grenade in through an open window. The explosion was audible all over the centre of town, but as I said, the damage was limited because it went off under the stage. The band that had been playing there ten minutes previously were still there, but they're not feeling too good.'

The door opened and Van Veeteren came in.

'Carry on,' he said, flopping down onto a chair. The chief of police looked at the clock. Reinhart raised an eyebrow before continuing.

'Eight people injured, but none of the injuries

427

life-threatening. Twenty or so with minor wounds were admitted to the Rumford and Gemejnte hospitals, but most of them will be allowed home today. There are a few witnesses who saw a man running away from the scene.'

'Not a lot to go on,' said Jung. 'It was dark, and they only saw him from quite a long way off. But all were sure that it was a male person though.'

'Women don't behave like that,' said Rooth. 'Not the ones I know, at least.'

'Typical male behaviour,' said Moreno. 'I agree.'

Chief of Police Hiller tapped his desk with his Ballograf in irritation.

'And then what?' asked Münster. 'You mentioned cars.'

Reinhart sighed.

'About half an hour later, somebody – let's hope it was the same idiot, or we're dealing with two of them – started shooting at parked cars outside the Keymer church. Probably from somewhere in Weivers Park. That could be heard all over town as well. It only lasted for about fifteen to twenty seconds, and nobody saw a damned thing. An automatic weapon. Two to three salvoes. About thirty shots, at a guess.'

'Klempje, Stauff and Joensuu are busy crawling around among the cars,' Jung explained. 'And Krause is taking care of the car owners.'

'A fun job,' said deBries.

'No doubt,' said Reinhart. 'Krause could probably do with some help. There are twelve owners concerned, including two German families in transit.'

'White Mercs,' elaborated Jung.

Van Veeteren stood up.

'Excuse me,' he said. 'I've forgotten my toothpicks downstairs in my office. I won't be long.'

He left the room, and silence reigned.

'Ah well,' said Hiller after a while. 'This is most annoying. What with it being the holiday period and all that.'

Nobody present reacted at all. Jung held his breath.

'Ah well,' repeated Hiller. 'We obviously need to set a few officers to work on this. All available resources. It's clearly a lunatic who could well strike again. At any moment. Well? Who's available?'

Reinhart closed his eyes and Münster studied his fingernails. DeBries left for the lavatory.

'Satan's shit,' said Rooth.

'Okay,' said Reinhart twenty minutes later, stirring his coffee gloomily. 'I'll take care of it. I'll have Jung and Rooth to help me in any case. And Münster, to start with at least.'

'Good,' said Van Veeteren. 'You'll soon sort it all out.'

Reinhart snorted.

'What did the gardener have for you? I heard a rumour.'

Van Veeteren shrugged.

'Dunno.'

'Dunno?'

'No. I thought I'd have lunch before confronting him.'

'Lunch?' said Reinhart. 'What's that?'

Van Veeteren examined a chewed-up toothpick and dropped it into the empty plastic mug.

'Do you know Major Greubner?'

Reinhart thought that one over.

'No. Should I?'

'I play him at chess occasionally. Sensible fellow. It might be an idea to pick his brains.'

'About this madman, you mean?'

Van Veeteren nodded.

'There's only one regiment based in this town, after all. I don't think they've started selling hand grenades in the supermarkets yet.'

Reinhart stared at the dregs in his coffee mug for a while.

'But perhaps I've got that wrong?'

'You never know,' said Reinhart. 'Do you have his number?'

Van Veeteren looked it up and wrote it down on a scrap of paper.

'Thank you,' said Reinhart. 'Anyway, duty calls. Do have a pleasant lunch.'

'Thank you,' said Van Veeteren.

'Come in,' said Hiller.

'I'm in already,' said Van Veeteren, sitting down.

'Please take a seat. I take it it's generally agreed that Reinhart looks after this lunatic?'

'Yes, of course.'

'Hmm. You're going on holiday at the end of this month, aren't you?'

Van Veeteren nodded. Hiller fanned himself with a memorandum from the Interior Ministry.

'And then what? You can't really be serious?'

Van Veeteren said nothing.

'You've had your doubts before. Why should I believe you'll actually do it this time?'

'We shall see,' said Van Veeteren. 'You'll get my final decision in August, but it looks like coming off this time. I just thought I'd better inform you. You like being informed, after all.'

'Hmm,' said the chief of police.

'What did you want me for?' asked Van Veeteren.

'Ah yes, there was something.'

'That's what Reinhart said.'

'A chief of police called from Sorbinowo.'

'Sorbinowo?'

'Yes.'

'Malijsen?'

'No, I think it's his stand-in while he's on holiday . . .'
Hiller took a sheet of paper from a folder.

'. . . Kluuge. He sounded a bit inexperienced, and he's
evidently been saddled with a disappearance.'

'A disappearance?'

'Yes.'

'But surely there must be help available closer to home?'
Hiller leaned over his desk and tried to frown.

'No doubt. But this Kluuge chappie has evidently been
instructed to turn to us if anything should crop up. By the
real chief of police, that is. Before he went on holiday. A
Wilfred Malijsen. Is he somebody you know?'

Van Veeteren hesitated.

'I have come across him, yes.'

'I thought as much,' said Hiller, leaning back in his chair.
'Because he mentioned you specifically as the man he
wants to go there and help out. To be honest . . . to tell you
the truth, I have the feeling there's something fishy behind
this, but as you've evidently talked Reinhart into taking on
the other business, you might just as well go there.'

Van Veeteren said nothing. Snapped a toothpick in two
and stared at his superior.

'Just to find out what's going on, of course,' said Hiller. 'One day, or two at most.'

'A disappearance?' muttered the chief inspector.

'Yes,' said Hiller. 'A little girl, if I've understood it rightly. Come on now, what more can you ask for, dammit all? There can't be a more idyllic place to be in than Sorbinowo at this time of year . . .'

'What did you mean by something fishy behind this?'

For a brief moment it looked as if the chief of police blushed.

But it's probably just his daily cerebral haemorrhage, Van Veeteren thought, then realized that was an expression he'd borrowed from Reinhart. He stood up.

'All right,' he said. 'I suppose I'd better go there and see what's happening.'

Hiller handed over the sheet of paper with the details. Van Veeteren glanced at it for two seconds, then put it in his pocket.

'That hortensia's looking a bit miserable,' he said.

The chief of police sighed.

'It's not a hortensia,' he explained. 'It's an aspidistra. It ought to be coping well with the heat, but it obviously isn't.'

'Then there must be something else it can't cope with,' said Van Veeteren, turning his back on the chief of police.